KELLY

Coming Home for Christmas: Three Holiday Stories
Enduring Light
Marriage of Mercy
My Loving Vigil Keeping
Her Hesitant Heart

NONFICTION

On the Upper Missouri: The Journal of Rudolph Friedrich Kurz
Fort Buford: Sentinel at the Confluence
Stop Me If You've Read This One

Miss Grimsley's
OXFORD
CAREER

CARLA KELLY

SWEETWATER BOOKS
AN IMPRINT OF CEDAR FORT, INC.
SPRINGVILLE, UTAH

ISBN 13: 978-1-4621-1210-4

Published by Sweetwater Books, an imprint of Cedar Fort, Inc.
2373 W. 700 S., Springville, UT, 84663
Distributed by Cedar Fort, Inc., www.cedarfort.com

LIBRARY OF CONGRESS CATALOGING-IN-PUBLICATION DATA

    Kelly, Carla.
    Miss Grimsley's Oxford career / Carla Kelly.
        pages cm
    ISBN 978-1-4621-1210-4 (acid-free paper)
    1. Women--England--Intellectual life--Fiction. 2. Women college students--Fiction. 3. Oxford (England)--Fiction. 4. Regency fiction. 5. Love stories. I. Title.
    PS3561.E3928M57 2013
    813'.54--dc23
                                                  2013001998

Previously published by Signet/New American Library in 1992

Cover design by Angela D. Olsen
Cover design © 2013 by Lyle Mortimer
Edited and typeset by Melissa J. Caldwell

Printed in the United States of America

10   9   8   7   6   5   4   3   2   1

In memory of Jean Dugat,
my dear teacher, who taught me and challenged me

Ay me! For aught that ever I could read,
Could ever hear by tale or history,
The course of true love never did run smooth.

—William Shakespeare
A Midsummer Night's Dream

Prologue

"**I**T PAINS ME TO THE QUICK TO MAKE this observation about my only son, but James, for a Gatewood, you are queer stirrups, indeed," said Lady Chesney.

This startling pronouncement was followed by a deep quaff of ratafia and a look of deeper concern at the offspring who sat, legs crossed, eyes on a book.

James Gatewood looked up and smiled at his mother. It was a sweet smile, one full of lazy Gatewood charm that only served to irritate his parent and send her back to the ratafia for further fortification.

"Why you could not bring yourself to smile like that at Lady Susan Hinchcliffe, or Augusta Farnsworth, I will never understand! Son, you would tax the patience of a martyr!"

The smile deepened. After one more glance at his book, Lord Chesney laid aside the volume. "Dearest mother, that would be impossible. Martyrs are dead. That is why they are martyrs."

This observation served only to rouse Lady Chesney to greater heights. "And there you go again! You know very well that I meant saint!"

Her son laughed and picked up his book again, settling back into the chair.

Lady Chesney was not about to let a good topic wither for lack of nourishment. "How you can expect to find a wife in the Bodleian Library, I cannot fathom. James, wasn't once at Oxford enough? You're the only Gatewood in recent memory to . . . to immolate himself there, and look at the results!"

"Mother, do you perhaps mean, 'to immerse myself'?" he teased. "And I do not expect to unearth a wife in the Bodleian. Indeed, it would be impossible, considering England's unenlightened state of national indifference to the education of females. I go there for scholarship."

Lady Chesney could only moan and reach for her handkerchief. "Other young men your age—your friends, I might add—are busy at their tailors, or bargaining for bloodstock at Tattersalls, or sitting in White's bow window like normal men!" She buried her face in her handkerchief and blew her nose. "I wish you would reconsider this off notion of yours. It is not too late!"

Lord Chesney only stood up, stretched, and reached over to ruffle her hair. He kissed her cheek and perched himself on the arm of her chair, his hand on her shoulder. He gave her a mild shake. "Mama, it isn't forever! I could not possibly turn down an appointment to All Souls. It is an honor I had not dreamed of, and I will read history there this year," he concluded, his voice firm.

The seriousness lasted no more time than it took to speak his intentions. Gatewood rested his cheek against his mother's hair. "Mama, look at it this way and take some consolation: at least I am not pursuing my fellowship in Shakespeare too. I could, you know."

Lady Chesney shuddered. "You *will* remind me of your dratted double first!" She dabbed at her eyes. "When my set gathers for loo and we discuss the exploits of our sons, I have to endure Lady Whittington's bragging about that oafish lump she claims is Lord Whittington's and his exploits in Spain. Christine Dysart proses on and on about her dear Little Darnley's latest win at Newmarket. All I have to brag about is some pesky book you wrote about fairies and donkey's heads! Lud, it's enough to set me off my meals."

"*Midsummer Night's Dream*, Mama," Lord Chesney said patiently. "It's a rather good play, even if it is Shakespeare. And I only wrote a small commentary."

"Stuff!" Lady Chesney exclaimed. "You are a disgrace to all the Gatewoods who ever turned a card or made a wager. While we are having such fun, here you are, your nose eternally in a book."

Gatewood abandoned his station at his parent's elbow and took up a more defensive stance in front of the fireplace. "We made a bargain, Mama—you and Papa and I, remember? Papa is gone now, but I am holding you to the bargain. I will study this year at All

Souls, and when the year is up, I promise to set up my nursery, and start riding to hounds, and gambling, and making my tailor's life miserable. Agreed?"

Lady Chesney sighed and nodded. "That ought to redeem the family honor, although I've a mind to tell people, when they inquire where you are this year, that you are taking the Grand Tour on the Continent."

"Mama! No one is taking the Grand Tour these days! Remember the Blockade?" He regarded her with tender affection. "Mama, when did you last look at a newspaper?"

Lady Chesney brushed aside world events with a wave of her handkerchief. "Too much small print, my dear. Very well, I will not complain," she said, and complained, "But you know that I do not approve. You are the head of the family now!"

"I know, Mama, I know," he soothed.

"You will remember to send out your collars every now and then to be starched?"

"Of course, Mama."

"I do not understand why you cannot take your father's valet with you to Oxford!"

"He would perish with boredom and kill me in my sleep, Mama," Gatewood said, the amusement creeping into his voice again. "Besides that, Lord Winnfield has made him a wonderful offer of employment."

"I suppose. At least promise me that you will not wear that beastly student's gown all the time. You are rumpled enough."

"Certainly, Mama."

Her tone softened. "And write to me occasionally."

"Yes, dearest. Oxford is not situated in the polar reaches."

"It is dreadful unmodish, and you know it!"

"Dreadful slow," he agreed with a twinkle in his eyes as he began a slow edge toward the door.

As his mother cast about for another argument, he reached the door, pausing with his hand poised above the handle, ready to bolt.

"I have hit upon it, Mama!" Gatewood exclaimed as he turned the handle. "You can tell your set that I have killed someone in a duel and must spend the year rusticating with relatives in Virginia. That ought to be sufficiently worthy of a true Gatewood!"

Lady Chesney puffed up for a resounding reply. Before it could leave her lips, her son was gone, laughing his way down the hall. "Oh, if you were only of an age for me to stop your quarterly allowance," she muttered.

She sprang to her feet, surprisingly agile for one of her bulk, and hurtled herself after him. All she saw was a pair of heels vanishing up the staircase. She shook her fist after him.

"It is my fervent wish that you meet your match at Oxford, you wicked, wicked, unnatural son!" she shouted, quite forgetting herself.

Her unnatural son's voice floated down from the second floor landing. "My dear, what could be safer than All Souls College?"

Chapter 1

*M*ASTER RALPH GRIMSLEY TUGGED at his collar, sighed, and looked up at his sister. "Do you know, El, I do not think this interview will go well for either of us. That bagwig Snead don't much like to be corrected, especially by you."

"'Doesn't,'" Ellen Grimsley corrected, her eyes on the saddled horse pawing the ground directly under the window where they sat. "And Papa hates above all things to be trapped by that prosing windpipe, especially when the fox has already been loosed."

As if to emphasize her words, the mellow tones of the hunting horn sounded through the open window. The wavering notes stretched out and then drifted away on the October breeze. Ellen shivered and pulled the window shut.

Ralph scrambled to his knees and pressed his nose against the windowpane. "Poor old fox," he said softly.

He glanced at Ellen again. "There is a certain injustice to this system," he said.

Ellen smiled for the first time since Vicar Snead's arrival, charmed by the thought that her little brother, who was but twelve, sounded full grown. She thought of Gordon, incarcerated at Oxford, who had never sounded that mature at twelve, and likely never would. *A certain injustice*, she thought, her eyes on the closed door to the book room.

Ralph remained kneeling in the window seat, his nose pressed to the glass. In another moment, he was blowing on the glass and then writing his Latin vocabulary on the pane. "El, if I write it backwards, then people outside can read it forwards."

"You could," she agreed as she tucked in his shirttail and then tickled him. "But as the only animate object outside is Papa's horse, I think it would be a waste of good breath."

Ralph laughed, turned around, and sat next to her again, resting his head against her arm. He closed his eyes in satisfaction. "I'm glad it's Horry getting married and not you, El. Promise me that you will never marry."

"I promise," she said promptly and then amended, a twinkle in her eyes. "But suppose I get a good offer? Mama is sure that if Horatia can bag the son of a baronet, then I ought at least to snare a vicar!"

Ralph frowned. "Well, as long as it's not Vicar Snead, that old priss." He brightened. "I think someone as fine as you could trip up a viscount at least."

"Silly!"

They were still smiling when the book room door opened, and the vicar minced out. He smiled his gallows smile at the Grimsley progeny, his thin lips disappearing somewhere inside his mouth. Carefully he smoothed a finger across each eyebrow—his only good feature—and stood aside for the squire.

Ellen's heart sank lower into her boots. Triumph was etched all over the vicar's rather spongy features. *Ellen, why do you not keep your mouth shut?* she thought. *Why aren't you a more dutiful daughter?*

The hunting horn sounded again, barely audible through the closed window. The squire lumbered to the window and pressed his nose against the glass in unknowing imitation of his younger son. The sigh that escaped him was plainly audible.

The vicar coughed and cleared his throat, recalling the squire to the proceedings at hand. "Squire Grimsley, I believe you have something to say to your daughter."

"My daughter?" the squire repeated absently. He opened the window and looked down at his horse.

Ellen bit her lip to keep back the laughter. Poor Vicar Snead! He hadn't been in the neighborhood long enough to know that one only asked easy questions of Squire Grimsley when the pack was loosed and the fox running fast. He would be hard put to remember any of his children, especially his daughters.

"Sir, your daughter!" the vicar repeated when the squire stayed where he was, his hands resting on the glass as if he wanted to push through it, leap on the waiting horse, and gallop toward the sound of the horn.

"My daughter?" the squire said, as though the

concept of parenthood were a new idea requiring further consideration.

"Ellen," Ralph added helpfully. "She's short for a Grimsley, and blonde, Papa. I think she's pretty," he concluded, unable to resist, even as his sister kicked his foot.

"And you are impertinent," the vicar snapped. He cleared his throat again. "Your daughter, Miss Grimsley."

The squire waved his hand in the direction of the clergyman.

"You have my permission, sir. Take her, she's yours."

The vicar gasped and turned the color of salmon. Ralph dissolved into helpless mirth.

The laughter recalled the squire to the distasteful business at hand. He turned away from the window with a reluctance that was almost palpable. Ralph stopped laughing and scooted closer to his sister, who put her arm around him.

"Ellen, you will apologize to the vicar for your rudeness this morning during Ralph's lesson."

Ellen rose, wishing for the millionth time that she was tall like the other Grimsleys. She turned the full force of her cobalt blue eyes upon the vicar, who went even redder and seemed to have trouble with his collar suddenly. He tugged on it and made strangling noises that made Ralph shake.

"Mr. Snead," she began softly, "I do apologize for correcting you this morning when you said that Boston was the capital of the United States."

"And?" asked the vicar, running his finger around the offending collar as Ellen continued to regard him, a slight smile on her face.

"And?" she repeated.

"And you will not interfere again," the vicar concluded.

"I can't promise that," she said. "Best that you brush up on your geography, sir, before you lead any more young boys astray."

"Daughter!" roared the squire.

Ellen winced, but she stood her ground. "Papa, Boston is not the capital of the United States."

"No?" The squire rubbed his chin, his eyes on the vicar. "Well, of course it is not! What do you say to this, sir?"

The vicar dabbed at the perspiration gathering on his upper lip. "She could have told me in private, sir."

Ralph sprang to his sister's defense. "Sir, as to that, I am sure she could not," he insisted. "Papa would never permit a *tête-à-tête* with a single gentleman such as yourself."

"Bother and nonsense," the vicar exclaimed. "I am her spiritual counselor, as long as she resides within the boundaries of my parish!" He turned to the squire and all but plucked at his pink coat. "Squire, I protest! Miss Grimsley corrects me in front of my other pupils. How does it look, sir?"

The squire forced his attention from the window to the domestic scene. "It looks to me, sir, as though you ought to take a good look at a map. Everyone knows that New York City is the capital of the United States.

Good day, vicar. Do come again when you can stay longer."

The vicar sniffed and patted his eyebrows again. "Very well, sir. I will withdraw now. Perhaps I shall compose a sermon from St. Paul about women not speaking in public!" He turned and strode majestically to the front door. The effect was marred when he closed the door upon his coattails and had to open it again to free himself.

The squire watched him go. "Our vicar is good evidence for the theory that all younger sons should be drowned at birth," he murmured, and then glanced at Ralph. "Present company excluded, of course."

Ralph grinned, pleased by his father's unexpected attention. Ellen sat down in the window seat again. "Papa, the capital of the United States is Washington, DC!"

The squire, his family duties attended to, was at the window again. "That's not my fault," he said and eyed his daughter. "What am I going to do with you, Ellen?" he asked.

"You could send me away to school, Papa," she said. The squire roared with laughter and pinched her cheek.

"You're the funny one," he said. "Lord, what use does a chit have for school? You had a governess for two years, my dear. That's enough. I have never heard that reading books will get you a husband." He looked about for his hat.

"But, Papa, isn't there more to life than the getting of a husband?" she persisted.

He took his hat from Ralph and settled it on his head. He turned to her with a puzzled expression. "What else is there for chits?" he asked.

"But, Papa—" she began and was cut off with a wag of the squire's finger in her face.

"None of that!" The squire took one last look out the window and hurried to the door. "From now on, you will stay out of the vicar's lessons. If you must walk into the village with Ralph, then visit your Aunt Shreve while your brother is at the vicarage." He frowned and took a few swings at imaginary enemies with his riding crop. "She's a dratted woman and a nuisance, but I can't have you hounding the vicar." He patted her cheek. "Even if he is a sorry excuse."

He had almost reached the door before other Grimsleys converged upon him like driverless coaches hurtling toward the same crossing. The squire looked about for a quick escape, but all routes were cut off.

Martha, towed along by one hand, cried the loudest and hiccupped as her mother pulled her toward the squire. She appeared strangely splotchy about the face and neck.

"Spots, Mr. Grimsley!" Mama shrieked. "Spots!"

Squire Grimsley sighed and looked about for an escape while Ellen watched in amusement. "'In sooth you 'scape not so,'" she murmured to Ralph, who nodded and smiled.

"*Taming of the Shrew*?" he asked, and she nodded, her hands on his shoulders, as they watched the rest of the Grimsleys unravel before their eyes. Even as she looked on, Horatia, her face pale, staggered toward the squire and sank into a chair, her hands covering her eyes.

"Sarah Siddons is warming up," Ralph whispered.

"She must wait her turn," Ellen whispered back. "Mama will win out."

"Spots!" Mama cried again. She tugged on her husband's arm. "Mr. Grimsley, this is serious business!"

The squire peered closer at his youngest child and then leaped back. "'Pon my word, if it persists, won't she be a sight when she skips down the aisle in front of Horry, strewing around them little posies that I am supposed to pay a king's ransom for in December!"

Mrs. Grimsley glared at her husband until he stepped back again. Her eyes narrowed. "We are having a wedding in less than two months' time, Mr. Grimsley. This is no joking matter!" She followed up her words by bursting into tears, noisy tears that cast Martha's efforts into the shade. The child ceased her wailing and stared up at her mother. Then her red-dotted face darkened again, and she added her miseries to her mother's woe.

Ralph put his hands over his ears and then nudged his sister, who still sat in the window seat, transfixed by the spectacle before her. "It is Horry's turn," he whispered. "This will be good."

"Hush, Ralph," Ellen whispered as Horatia, her lovely face filled with misery, staggered to her feet and latched onto the lapels of her father's riding coat.

Like others of the Grimsley race, she was tall and possessed a headful of guinea-gold curls that tickled Papa's nose and made him sneeze.

Wide-eyed, Ralph watched the tableau before him, then turned away. "Dear me," he managed, his shoulders shaking.

Ellen put her finger to her lips. *Was ever womankind plagued with such a helpless family?* she thought as she hurried to Martha and knelt in front of her little sister. Expertly, she ran her hands over the bumps on Martha's face, then stood up.

"Mama, do take it down a peg."

Mama only sobbed harder. "You and your dreadful slang! You are not faced with a crisis of monumental proportions!" Mama wept into her handkerchief. "Spots!"

"It is worse and worse, Mama!" Horatia burst out. "Chevering says . . ."

"Nonsense!" Ellen said, cutting off her sister in midsentence and resting her hand upon Martha's head. "Mama, let us begin with Martha. Did you take a good look at her? A really good look?"

Mama wiped her eyes and squinted down at her littlest daughter. "I think I know my own children, Ellen," she said, biting off her words.

Ellen knelt in front of her sister again, her hands firm on Martha's shoulders. "Tell me truly, Martha. Have you been in Mama's chocolates again?"

Martha, a finger in her mouth, looked from one parent to the other and back to Ellen again. She scratched her stomach and nodded.

"There you have it, Mama. It is merely a rash and will likely be gone before noon." She gave her little sister a shake. "And you stay out of Mama's

14

chocolates, miss! You know they are her 'ever-present help in trouble.'"

Mama wiped her streaming eyes. "Don't be sacrilegious, daughter! And speaking of that, wasn't that the vicar I saw leaving here in such a snit?"

Ellen nodded. Mama dabbed at her eyes again.

"And I had such hopes of him." Turned loose, Martha darted away. Mama sighed again. "My nerves, Ellen, my nerves!"

Ellen put her arms around her mother. "They are your closest companions, my dear," she soothed. "Mama, lie down now and think about this: you could invite Cousin Henrietta Colesnatch to stay with us for the duration of the wedding. You know how she loves to batten herself on relatives. She can watch Martha for you."

Mama opened her mouth to utter a protest, but she closed it instead and then regarded her daughter for a long moment. "I could do that, couldn't I?"

"You could, Mama," Ellen replied. "You could even go do it now. Cousin Henrietta could be here by tomorrow evening. She would spare no expense—as long as you paid the post chaise."

A thoughtful expression on her face, Mama followed her daughter Martha down the hall. Ellen turned her attention to Horatia, who still sobbed upon the squire's coat.

"My dear, what *is* the matter?" she asked. "Is Napoleon at the gates and no one told us?"

Horry cast her a watery glance. "It is worse than that." She clutched her father's lapels in both fists.

"Papa, did you really promise Edwin's father that you would toast us with Fortaleza sherry?"

Papa stared at his eldest daughter. "I may have, Horry. What is the problem with that? You know we save the best for special occasions."

Horatia's eyes filled with tears again. "I have come from belowstairs," she announced dramatically. "Chevering tells me that there is no Fortaleza left. Furthermore, he says that with the Blockade, there is no way to get any more. Papa, I shall die!"

The squire blinked and removed his daughter's hands from his rumpled, sodden lapels. He took one last, longing look out the window. "Surely we can find some good Madeira."

Horatia threw herself onto the window seat, sobbing and drumming her feet on the cushions. "Papa, you promised!" she sobbed between fresh gusts of tears. "You promised Edwin's father that we would be toasted with Fortaleza. And now I have this note from Edwin informing me that his papa is so looking forward to a sip of the world's finest sherry! Papa, I am undone."

The squire blinked again. "You cannot suppose that Edwin would cry off over a dusty bottle of sherry, my dear! That is a particle of nonsense not worthy of even you!"

Horatia took no comfort from his bracing words. "You know very well that Sir Reginald fancies himself a specialist in wines."

She struggled into a sitting position and pressed her hand to her heart. "This will cast such a cloud upon my nuptials that I do not see how I can possibly face Sir

Reginald." She returned to her tears and the handkerchief that Ralph handed her without a word.

Ralph watched in fascination. "'I wouldn't have thought the old girl to have had so many tears in her,'" he whispered to his sister.

Ellen regarded him in amusement mingled with exasperation. "This is no time for *Macbeth*, you silly chub," she whispered back. She looked at her sister, pale and miserable in the window seat, and then glanced at Papa, who hovered over her with miserable solicitation.

A year ago, she would have been jealous of the attention Papa expended on Horry. *I must have been growing up when I wasn't even aware of it*, she thought. *Someone in this family has to.* She thought another moment and then made up her mind.

"Papa, doesn't Aunt Shreve have a bottle or two of that sherry? I seem to recall that Grandfather Grimsley divided that case in the will."

The squire made a face. "As he divided everything!" he exclaimed, his voice loud, his face red. "Do you think I would ask my sister for anything?" He pulled Horatia to her feet, his arm about her. "Horry, I think your precious Edwin can drink Madeira. And so can his father! Paltry little baronet," he concluded.

Ellen winced as Horatia increased the volume of her misery. *Lord help us, in another minute she will be in strong hysterics, and Papa will storm and stamp, and Mama will come running in with hartshorn and burning feathers.* Ellen took a deep breath.

"Papa, I can ask Aunt Shreve for a bottle of Fortaleza."

"You will never get it out of her," Papa insisted, "particularly if she knows it will be a favor to me!"

"I can manage," Ellen said quietly. "Hush, Horry. If your face gets splotchy, Edwin might reconsider."

Horatia gasped and ran to the mirror in the hall, turning her head this way and that to survey the ravages of tears on her face.

"You will look all of twenty, if you keep crying," Ellen said, her face devoid of all expression.

Horry gasped. "Twenty! Horrors!"

"Twenty," Ellen repeated, her voice firm. "Now, dry your eyes, Horry. I can solve this problem."

With a tight little nod and one last teary-eyed entreaty of her papa, Horatia summoned her little brother to help her from the room. She smiled bravely and allowed him to lead her away.

The squire turned to his remaining daughter and grasped her by both hands. "Ellen, if you can carry this off, I will get you anything you want," he declared.

Ellen stood on tiptoe and kissed her tall parent's cheek.

"Done, Papa, done. Better yet, I will return with two bottles of Fortaleza."

Papa closed his eyes in relief, hugging her to his ample chest. He picked up his riding crop again and dashed out the door, leaving it wide open. In another moment, Ellen saw horse and rider thundering in the general direction of the last siren call of the hunting horn.

Ralph returned and flopped down on the window seat. "El, they wear me out," he complained when he could manage speech. "I think Horry is a perfect lamebrain to moon over that spotty Edwin. You would never do such a thing, would you?"

She shook her head, the laughter back in her eyes.

Ralph sat up, resting on one elbow. "Why did you promise Papa two bottles of that dratted sherry? You know that Aunt Shreve has not spoken to him since the reading of that will four years ago. When I was but a child," he added.

Ellen burst into laughter. "And what are you now, my dear?" she teased and took him by the hand, pulling him to his feet. "Come. Let us do our best."

It meant retracing their steps from manor to village again for the second time that morning, but neither Grimsley objected. The air was crisp with autumn; the tantalizing fragrance of burning leaves made brother and sister take a deep breath and sigh together.

They looked at each other and laughed. There wasn't any need to speak; they understood the Grimsleys too well. Papa saw no further than hounds and horses; Mama darted from anxiety to crisis; Horry was twined all around herself and her darling, noddy Edwin.

"There is hope for Martha," Ralph said finally, giving voice to what his sister was thinking. "We shall give her a few years and see if she improves."

"'A few years,'" Ellen mimicked. "By then you will have abandoned me for Oxford and will not have a thought to spare for either sister!"

"If Papa doesn't stick me in an office in the City with one of Mama's brothers first," he said quietly and took her by the hand. "You know Gordon is supposed to be the Oxford-educated one."

They walked a moment in silence. Ralph squeezed her hand. "Whatever the outcome, I will always have a thought for you, El."

They continued in companionable silence. *And I for you*, Ellen Grimsley thought as she looked down at her little brother.

He strode along at her side, his face half turned to the sun, a smile in his eyes. His hair looked as it always did, as if he had bounded out of bed, rushed to the stable, and combed it with a pitchfork.

But his freckles were fading. Mama had remarked over breakfast only this morning that his wrists were shooting out of his cuffs and he was overdue a visit to Miss Simpson, who made all the children's clothes.

Papa had come out of his hunting fog long enough to peer closer at his son. "Nay, wife, not this time," he had boomed out. "'Tis time for Ralph to visit my tailor. He's too big to wear nankeen breeches anymore."

Ellen nodded, remembering the glow of pleasure on Ralph's face. Papa had noticed him. Perhaps when he wore long pants and a gentleman's riding boots, Papa would acknowledge that his younger son could be a scholar as well as a rider to hounds.

On a day as glorious as this autumn morning, anything was possible, Ellen decided. Perhaps Aunt Shreve would relinquish two bottles of Fortaleza without a murmur; perhaps Horatia would reconsider and let her be a bridesmaid after all, even if her small stature did upset the symmetry of the other, taller cousins and friends. Perhaps when the wedding was over and Horatia shot off, Mama would relax for a season and not scold and berate her younger daughter because she made no push to secure a husband for herself among the eligibles of the district.

I am too short for a Grimsley, and I have no hunting instincts, she thought as they stood still and watched Papa race toward the hounds and riders that milled about on a distant, smoky hillside, waiting for the dogs to recapture the scent.

Brother and sister stood close together and watched the hunters. They leaned forward and listened and then smiled to each other when the hounds began to bay again. Soon the pack, followed by the pink-coated riders, disappeared over the hill.

The field was theirs again. Ralph sat down on a sun-warmed rock. "I will wait for you here, El," he declared, and then made a face. "After this morning, I haven't the fortitude for the scold Aunt Shreve is going to give you."

Ellen grinned. "Coward!"

Ralph nodded, unruffled. "Shakespeare would call me a 'whey-faced loon.'"

Ellen waved to him and hurried toward the village.

When she was out of sight, she slowed her steps. *Why did I promise Papa that dratted Fortaleza?* she thought.

She remembered the reading of Grandfather's will, with all the relatives assembled, black and sniffling, or at least holding handkerchief to nose in a show of sorrow.

Not that anyone had loved Grandfather overmuch before he cocked up his toes. He was a testy old rip who pinched the maids, scandalized his daughter, and infuriated his son by outliving his usefulness. To the best of her recollection, Ellen was the only grandchild to mourn his loss. She missed his stories of battles fought, creditors outrun, and fortunes won and lost and won again.

She missed him still, even four years after his death. At eighteen, she still mourned the loss of the only relative who had not gawked and gasped when she did not fulfill the promise of her Grimsley heritage and grow to elegant heights. He had not scolded her, as if complaints would add one inch to her stature. He had thoughtfully matched his stride to hers, and they had walked and talked over the Cotswold hills until he died.

She thought again about the will, written in Grandpapa's crabbed handwriting and changed and changed again as relatives fell short of the mark. In a final show of pique against her father, Grandfather had evenly divided all his possessions except land between his only surviving son and daughter, right down to the half case of Fortaleza.

Ellen closed her eyes, seeing again Papa storming out of the solicitor's office, cheated out of entitlements he felt were rightfully his, muttering about the perfidy of a sister he could name. Aunt Shreve, stung by his anger, had taken instant exception to his blathering and closed her door to him.

"And mind you, Ellen Grimsley," Aunt Shreve said a half hour later as Ellen sat in her aunt's cozy sitting room on Porter Street. "Your father sets too great a store by Horatia's wedding to that peabrained excuse of a son and heir to Sir Reginald Bland. A baronet!"

She spat out the word, as if the tea she sipped suddenly displeased her. "What is that to anything? Grimsleys have managed for centuries without titles in the family and done quite well, thank you. Does my brother do this so he can smile and nod and play the fool and introduce his son-in-law, the son of a baronet, to his horse-dealing cronies? I ask you."

Ellen knew better than to interrupt a Grimsley tirade, even if this particular Grimsley had long been wedded and widowed by a Shreve. She folded her hands patiently in her lap.

"And such a collection of foolish parts is our dear Edwin!" Aunt Shreve said, not failing her niece. "Does anything ever go on behind those blue eyes of his, Ellen?"

"Oh, Aunt Shreve, you know that Horry loves Edwin. And if he is not over sharp, what is that to anyone in my family? They'll never notice."

Aunt Shreve took another sip of tea. "No, I suppose they will not. As long as he can sit a horse, I suppose everyone will overlook his other deficiencies." She peered over her spectacles at her niece. "Not for the first time have I wondered how you and Ralph came to be dropped down in the midst of that ignorant family, my dear. One could accuse your mother of shady dealings."

Ellen laughed. "Aunt Shreve! You know that my mother is perfectly respectable!"

Aunt Shreve managed a smile. "Respectable to the point of numbness. Setting all that aside, I trust you will do better than Edwin Bland, my dear."

Her niece sighed. "Mama claims that all I can hope for is Thomas Cornwell, particularly now since I have driven off the vicar."

Aunt Shreve winced. There was a long silence, which she finally broke when she had drained the rest of her tea. "Dear me," she said finally, "he of the protruding ears?"

"The very same," Ellen replied.

"Goodness, a lowering thought," Aunt Shreve murmured. They regarded each other, and Aunt Shreve shuddered. "Now there is a young man with nothing to recommend him but his height!" She leaned forward. "I charge you to find some tiny little man. It will drive your father into bedlam."

"Aunt Shreve, you are absurd!" Ellen protested, laughing.

Her aunt smiled. "I know it. We can safely say that your father only got a half-share of the eccentricity too! But seriously, my dear, you must get out of this place."

"How?" Ellen asked and helped herself to another biscuit. She studied the tray in front of her, remembered the reason for her visit, and cleared her throat.

When she said nothing, Aunt Shreve snorted in impatience. "What errand has your ridiculous father sent you on, child?" She chuckled and rubbed her hands together. "One would suspect you had come to me on some nefarious expedition, sent by my brother!"

Ellen was silent as the embarrassment spread up her shoulders and onto her face like a contagious disease.

"You have hit upon it, Aunt," she murmured. "Papa made an extravagant promise at the last Assembly Ball that he would toast the happy couple with Fortaleza sherry, and now Sir Reginald won't rest unless it actually happens. You know what a connoisseur of wines he thinks himself." Ellen looked away, suddenly ashamed of her relatives. "You would think that the fate of nations hung upon this single issue."

Aunt Shreve was silent for a long moment that stretched into minutes. She poured herself another cup of tea and took it to the mantelpiece, where she sipped it and regarded her niece thoughtfully.

"My dear," she said finally, "what would irritate your father the most? I mean, what would really get his goat?"

Ellen smiled in spite of her own discomfort. "Probably to be forced to dance to your tune, Aunt. You know how he hates that." She laughed out loud, her embarrassment overcome. "He must have been a dreadful little brother."

"The worst," Aunt Shreve agreed absently, her mind intent upon the question she had posed.

"Papa even told me that he would give me anything I wanted, if I could talk you out of one dusty bottle of sherry," Ellen said, joining her aunt by the fireplace.

Aunt Shreve mused a moment more and then looked her niece in the eye. "My dear, what is it you want more than anything?"

"Well, I would like to be one of Horry's brides-maids, but even wishing won't help me grow six inches." She blushed at her aunt's shocked stare. "I . . . I upset the symmetry, Aunt."

"Upset the . . ." Aunt Shreve paced the length of the room and back.

"I don't mind, truly I don't," Ellen said quickly, her heart pounding at the look in Aunt Shreve's eyes. "I was thinking about teasing Papa for some hair orna-ments." She fingered her cropped hair. "I don't need anything else, really. Oh, Aunt, don't look like that!"

Aunt Shreve was silent. When she spoke, her voice was even, serious. "We can do better than that, much better. Did I not see you this morning, trailing in the wake of our vicar, one of organized religion's greatest jokes upon the Church of England? Are you in trouble again for correcting him in Ralph's lessons?"

Ellen nodded. "He insisted that Boston was the capital of the United States of America." She shook her head. "Papa assured him that New York City was the capital, and that is how the matter stands."

Aunt Shreve rolled her eyes and returned the teacup to the table with an audible click. She took her niece's hands in both of her own.

"Do I recall a conversation last week over tea where you told me your greatest wish was to go to Oxford like your brother Gordon?"

Ellen stared at her aunt, remembering her words. "Yes, but that was only in jest! It's impossible. Just wishful thinking. Besides that, Papa told me only an hour ago that I had all the education I needed and that my duty now was to find a husband. He would never permit it." Ellen laughed. "Not to mention the entire English educational establishment! Really, Aunt Shreve."

Aunt Shreve went to the bell pull and gave it a tug.

"Do you think he would change his mind for two bottles of Fortaleza? What about four bottles?"

Ellen stared at her aunt. "That would be the half case that Grandfather left you. Even the Prince Regent doesn't have four bottles of Fortaleza, I vow."

"I never could tolerate the stuff," Aunt Shreve confided, "although I would never tell your father that." She clapped her hands together. "I would love to see the look on your father's face when you present him with my half case and tell him that his sister will take it all back unless he allows you to go to Oxford!"

Ellen sat down. "What do you mean?"

"I know that Oxford University itself is out of the question, and more's the pity. I ask you, what possible polluting effect would females have upon the quadrangles of Oriel or Balliol? But setting that aside, as we must, have you not heard of Miss Dignam's Select Female Academy? Miss Dignam is an old and dear friend of mine, for all that we have not seen each other in years. And I believe the academy is even located on the High Street. You could admire any number of spires and crockets and see that clever round library from your window."

"Do you mean the Radcliffe Camera?" Ellen asked, her eyes wide. "Papa would never . . ."

"I believe he would, my dear, for four bottles of

Fortaleza, and relief from Horatia's endless tears." Aunt Shreve went to her escritoire and took out paper and pen. "'Dear Charles,'" she began, and then crumpled the paper. "He has never been 'Dear Charles.' 'Charles' will suffice." She thought another moment, smiled, and wrote a note, sealing it with wax and handing it to her niece.

"Take that to your ridiculous father and start packing, my dear!"

Chapter 2

I AM A PERFECT BEAST, ELLEN thought as she leaned back against the cushions in the post chaise and rested her eyes on the late October scenery. *I should be missing them all so much, and I am not.*

She thought a moment and then smiled to herself. *I will miss Ralph.* He had hugged her for a few moments longer than the others. "I shall think of you often, El," he had whispered when the others had already turned back to the house, and Mama and Horry had resumed their argument over hothouse flowers or potted plants for the wedding.

"I will miss you too," she replied. "I will write you and tell you all about the colleges."

"About Oriel, if you please," he urged, letting go of his sister and straightening his new waistcoat, sewn by the squire's own tailor.

"Do you wish to be an Oriel man someday?" she teased, keeping her tone light to discourage the tears that threatened to fall.

"I do, above all things," he replied fervently. "And then I will hope for an appointment to All Souls, where I will read literature and eventually become a scholar of renown."

Ellen kissed him on both cheeks. "And I will be your secretary?" she teased.

Ralph shook his head. "No, El; you will be *my* teacher." He looked across the fields stripped bare by winter. "At least, that is how it should be."

"But it is not, my dear," she said.

He stood on the front steps, waving good-bye until he was only a small figure. "I will write you often," she whispered to the glass.

Horatia had been properly appreciative of the Fortaleza, although she did not change her mind about her bridesmaids. "You are a perfect dear to do this, Ellen, and I am fully aware of what I owe you," she declared, tears glistening on the ends of her lashes as she clutched the dusty bottles of sherry to her breast. "After the wedding, I will tell you just where to stand so that you may catch my bouquet. Mama will be so thrilled."

Papa had turned shades of scarlet, crimson, and a deep magenta that worried them all when Ellen brought the Fortaleza to him and declared that she would spend the winter at Miss Dignam's Select Female Academy in Oxford as her reward. Horatia sat him down, and Mama loosened his waistcoat, while Ellen propped his feet on the hassock and Ralph stood close by with a pillow for his neck.

When he had control of his faculties, the squire fired off a fierce note to his sister in the village, demanding an explanation of Ellen's strange request, and declaring that it was absurd and out of the question. Aunt Shreve sent her reply in the form of her footman, who demanded the return of the Fortaleza. He stood there, his hands outstretched, while Horatia sobbed and Mama scolded. Papa had no choice but to relent and then collapse in his armchair, overcome by the rigors of maintaining domestic tranquility.

"You are the most unnatural Grimsley!" he declared for the next two weeks, each time he encountered her in a hallway or at meals. He even began to eye his wife askance, as if to accuse that virtuous and boring woman of some misdeed that had landed someone else's child in the Grimsley bassinet some eighteen years previous. The result of his mutterings had been a lively argument between the parents that kept everyone tiptoeing about the manor until a truce was declared and the squire readmitted to his bedroom.

Ellen bore it all calmly, ignoring Papa's pointed stares and Mama's torrent of advice, larded with admonition and foreboding. "You know, Ellen, that Dr. Spender Chumley over in Larch lectured on the subject of females damaging their brains with overmuch study," Mama warned. "He claims that the brain enlarges and creates a curiously shaped head that is not attractive in any way."

This information sent Horatia rushing to the mirror to examine the shape of her own head.

Ellen laughed out loud. "Horry, you haven't a fear in the world," she said. "I don't think two consecutive thoughts have ever encountered each other in that space between your ears."

"Thank goodness for that," Horatia declared. "I would not wish to risk deformity." She looked at her mother, her eyes filled with anxiety. "Mama, surely dancing lessons do not come under the category of study that Dr. Chumley speaks of?"

"They wouldn't dare," Ellen replied.

Ellen was packed by the end of the week, but the November rains came early that year. She was forced to fidget and pace about the house another week until the roads were passable again.

She endured one final visit from Thomas Cornwell, who dropped by after a day at the Grain Exchange in Morely, full of news about the price of corn and the effect of war on his bankbook.

No use in telling Mama to send down the news that she had a headache.

"Ellen, you never have a headache," Mama said. "Now go downstairs and do your duty!"

"But Mama!" she protested.

Mama only stared at her as her lower lip began to quiver. "If I have to play the hostess and sit for hours in the parlor while he talks on and on about rye and barley, I will go distracted."

Ellen dug her heels in. "Mama, this is the man you paint in such rosy colors for me! Now I find that you can scarcely tolerate his conversation!"

"My dear Ellen," said Mama as she held the door open for her daughter. "Once you are married to Thomas Cornwell, you needn't listen to him!"

And so she had listened until the rains began again and darkness settled in, and she had no choice but to invite him to dinner. By the time he left after a game of whist in the sitting room, she knew everything about this year's rye and barley crop (the most promising in the last ten years) and the total number of pigs transported to market.

And now my head does truly ache, Ellen thought as she walked Cornwell to the door, careful to keep her distance, dreading the moment when he would clear his throat and look at her expectantly.

So far she had managed to avoid his kisses. For a small stipend from her quarterly allowance, Ralph usually presented himself in the front hall in time to dampen the Romeo in Thomas Cornwell.

But this time Ralph had been dragged to the sewing room to try on the new waistcoat Horry had commissioned just for the wedding. Cornwell cleared his throat on cue.

"I will miss you dreadfully, Ellen," he said and gazed at her, his eyes hopeful.

This is my cue, Ellen thought. Instead, she held out her hand and smiled up at the big farmer. "Mr. Cornwell, I am sure that your rye and barley will keep you feverishly busy this winter."

He dropped to his knees in front of her as she grabbed his elbow and tried to tug him to his feet.

"Marry me, Ellen, and make me the happiest man in Oxfordshire!"

"Get up," she hissed. "This will never do."

"Only say yes and I will get up," he pleaded, following her on his knees across the hallway.

Mama, her arms full of deep green fabric, hurried into the hall. She stopped, her eyes enormous, and stared at Thomas Cornwell. Ellen looked at her in desperation.

Mama sighed. "Mr. Cornwell, this will never do! I cannot possibly contemplate another wedding right now! Do get off your knees and save this for the spring."

His face red from his exertions, Cornwell scrambled to his feet. "Yes, Mrs. Grimsley," he said as he accepted the hat and coat that the wooden-faced butler was holding out. "Ellen, I will write," he declared, hand to his heart, as she opened the door and ushered him into the rain. He stuck his head back in the door, his face redder still. "Provided that is not too forward."

Ellen shook her head. "I think it is, Mr. Cornwell," she said, her voice low, even though Mama had already retreated from the front hall. "I will see you at Christmas." She closed the door on his protestations of love.

Ellen endured another week of Mama's tears and good advice. "You will be sharing rooms with Fanny Bland, our own dear Edwin's sister. That is the only thing about this havey-cavey business that sets my mind at ease. Fanny is all that is proper, and she will keep an eye on you."

"Yes, Mama."

"And you will not go out of doors unaccompanied or have anything to do with the students in the colleges."

"No, Mama."

"You will do nothing to call attention to yourself."

"Never, Mama."

She spoke so quickly that Mama looked at her and frowned, but made no further comment beyond a martyr's sigh and a sad shake of her head.

Ellen found herself walking to the road during that interminable week of impassable roads, testing the gravel, willing the sodden skies to brighten.

The postman met her one morning with a letter of welcome from Miss Dignam and a list of her classes. *I will take French and embroidery?* she asked herself, letter in hand, as she walked slowly back to the house. She turned the letter over, hopeful of further enlightenment. Surely there was some mistake. She wanted to take geography and geometry too, if it was offered.

She folded the letter. *Surely I can discuss this with the headmistress when I arrive*, she thought.

Mama could spare none of the maids to accompany her to Oxford. Papa was forced to prevail upon his sister to act as escort. Aunt Shreve accepted with alacrity, declaring it a pleasure and presenting the squire with two more forgotten bottles of Fortaleza, to his great amazement and grudging approval.

"There now," she declared. "Charles, you have enough Fortaleza to toast Horatia, and her first child, and Ralph's entrance into Oxford—if you have the unexpected good sense to send him there instead of to

a beastly counting house in the City. You can also celebrate Gordon's leaving of Oxford eventually, if that
should ever happen before we are too gnarled to pop
a cork."

Brother and sister had declared a wary truce and
were sitting knee to knee over the tea table in Aunt
Shreve's house. Ellen cast anxious glances at her papa
throughout the interview.

He surprised his daughter by managing a ponderous joke. "What, no bottle for Ellen?" he asked. "She
may marry someday, if we can force her nose out of
books, or if she is not off exploring the world in a birch-
bark canoe."

Aunt Shrive smiled at her favorite niece. "I wasn't
going to tell you this, Charles, but years ago, Father
gave me a bottle of Palais Royal brandy."

The squire choked on his tea. "My word, sister," he
exclaimed when he could breathe again. "I doubt there
is another bottle in England!"

"Quite likely," his sister agreed as she poured more
tea. "I am depending upon Ellen to make a fabulous
alliance." She set down the cup and fixed her brother
with the stare that had probably made him writhe
when they were growing up. "*When* she is good and
ready, Charles. Then I will open the Palais Royal."

Thinking back on that artless disclosure, Ellen
laughed softly to herself. *Mama declares that since I
scared off the vicar, the best I can hope for is Thomas
Cornwell. Horatia claims that she can find me someone among her darling Edwin's circle of rattlebrained
acquaintances.* She shook her head. *None of these*

paragons would be worth Palais Royal. I suppose I must make the exertion on my own.

Aunt Shreve joined her in the village, and they continued east across rolling fields shorn of sheep that dotted the landscape in other seasons. The trees had all molted their leaves in great piles, leaving skeletal branches that bore no promise of spring in the near future. *"Bare ruined choirs, where late the sweet birds sang,"* she thought, her mind upon Ralph and his everlasting Shakespeare.

"Perhaps I should study Shakespeare, in honor of Ralph," she said out loud. She dug in her reticule for the letter from Miss Dignam and held it out to her aunt. "See here, Aunt, they have me down for nothing more strenuous than French and embroidery; I believe that I will request geography and Shakespeare, at least. I am not afraid of scholarship."

Aunt Shreve put on her spectacles and read the letter. She leaned back, the look on her face telling Ellen that she was choosing her words with care.

"My dear, I hope you will not be too disappointed if Miss Dignam's falls short of your expectations," she began. "I have never been there, but I do not know that study for women is serious anywhere."

Ellen waved her hand and reclaimed the letter. "Oh, that is all right, Aunt. If they only teach the tragedies of Shakespeare and not the more ribald comedies, I can be forgiving!"

The sun broke through the weight of autumn clouds by late afternoon and their entrance into Oxford. The post chaise had slowed to the movement of farm carts that trundled toward the ford of the Thames called, in true scholar's eccentricity, the Isis, while it wound around the university town.

"It is only when I travel this road behind loads of potatoes, onions, and pigs that I wonder why anyone saw fit to establish a university in this place," Aunt Shreve grumbled. "If this is the center of the universe, then I am Marie Antoinette, head and all!"

Aunt Shreve was poised to say more in the same vein as they inched along, but the look on her niece's face stopped her complaints. She tapped on the glass and rolled it down as the post chaise stopped.

"Mind that you pause and pull off when you reach the top of this hill, Coachman," she ordered.

They continued in silence broken only by the squawk of geese in the cart ahead. In a few minutes, the carriage pulled out of the line of traffic and stopped.

"Get out and stretch yourself," Aunt Shreve suggested. "And do go to the top of that rise."

"You needn't let me slow you down," Ellen protested. "Surely the view can wait."

"No, it cannot," Aunt Shreve insisted. She motioned to the carriage door, where the post boy stood to open it.

Ellen stepped out, grateful—even though she had objected—for the chance to walk about for a moment. She walked to the top of the gently sloping rise, looked toward the east, and loved her aunt all the more.

The sun was going down over Oxford, throwing streams of molten fire upon honey-colored walls and spires. Ellen held her breath at the sight and then let it out slowly, There was Great Tom, and the spires of Magdalen, grace notes to the elegant architectural humor of the Radcliffe Camera, and behind it, the Bodleian Library. The river flowed under bridges as inspired as the buildings that lined it on both sides.

From her elevation, Ellen gazed, hand to eyes, into college quadrangles where the grass was still green, protected by the warmth of centuries-old stone. She clapped her hands in delight. Oxford was a city the color of honey, and a veritable honeycomb itself of colleges, quadrangles, and churches.

The sky turned lavender as she watched and then a more somber purple. *We will have rain tonight*, she thought, *but it will be special rain because it falls upon Oxford.*

"Excuse me, miss, if I appear forward, but are you in some trouble with your post chaise?"

Ellen whirled around. Papers in hand, a man sat upon a rock near the crest of the hill where she stood. She had not noticed him in his black student's robe because he blended in so well with the shadows that were lengthening across the copse.

"Oh, no, sir. We are fine," she said, putting her hands behind her back as though she had been caught pilfering a candy jar. "My aunt merely wanted me to have a look at the city before we drove in."

The man got to his feet. He was taller even than the tallest Grimsley. His hair was ordinary brown and untidy, and the wind was picking it up and tousling it further. Ellen felt the need to put her hand to her bonnet.

The breeze caught the student's gown and it billowed about him, making him appear larger yet. The wind tugged at the papers in his hand. As she watched, he tore them up and held them in both palms to the wind like an offering. The scraps swirled up and out of sight.

"Good riddance," he said and came closer.

He had an elegant face, at odds with the untidiness of his hair, with high cheekbones, a straight nose, and eyes as dark as his gown. She noticed that his ears lay nicely flat against his head, and she smiled as she thought of Thomas Cornwell.

"I amuse you?" he asked, giving her a little nod that passed for a bow.

"No, it is someone else. You have excellent ears, sir," she said and then put her hand to her mouth. "I mean, I was thinking of someone who is not so blessed. Oh, dear, that was a strange thing to say!"

He laughed and tossed away the remaining scraps of paper that still rested in his palm. He gave her a real bow, and he was more graceful than she would have thought, considering his height. Suddenly, she felt out of place and much younger than eighteen.

"Do you come up here to commune with nature, sir?" she asked.

He shook his head. "I come here to walk off my letters from home."

She thought of her own home and found this reasonable. "I expect I would like to do the same thing," she said. "Do your parents smother you too and worry and prose on and on?"

He gave a shout of laughter, grabbed her hand, and kissed it, bowing again. "Are you a Sybil, or perhaps a Cassandra, to divine this? I would not have thought there were other parents in all of England like my mother, but perhaps I was wrong. James Gatewood at your service, miss."

She smiled and withdrew her hand from his. "I am Ellen Grimsley, sir."

"Ellen?" he asked. "Prosaic name, but lovely."

"I do not mind that it is ordinary," she replied, twinkling her eyes at him for no reason that she could discern. "It could have been much worse." She hesitated, looking at the student. Something about his open countenance seemed to invite confidence. "It could have been Zephyr."

"Zephyr?" he asked in amusement. "Oh, surely not!"

"Zephyr indeed. It happens that a horse named Zephyr won at Newmarket the day I was born. My papa is horse mad, sir." She sighed, and then grinned as he laughed. "But Mama, who seldom prevails, prevailed from her bed of confinement, for which I am grateful."

He nodded in perfect understanding. "As it is, I suppose now you have brothers who tease you and call you Nellie, but that must be preferable to Zeph."

"Indeed, it must be," she agreed. She looked around at the carriage and made a motion to leave.

He grabbed up his books by the rock, falling in step with her as she retraced her way to the carriage below. She glanced at his books, noting North's

Treatise on Government and a copy of Paine's *The Crisis.*

He followed her glance. "I should be studying, but it looked like a fine afternoon."

"And you are 'a summer soldier and a sunshine patriot,' when the weather is mellow?" she teased.

He raised one eyebrow. "You are a spy, sent by my don," he teased in turn, "come to find out why I am not buried in scholarship."

She shook her head. "I am no spy, and that's all I know of Thomas Paine," she confessed. "I found the pamphlet at a church rumble sale, but Mama snatched it away and told me it was wicked."

"And well she did, Miss Grimsley," he said with a smile. "You might have attempted a nursery room revolt. But wicked? No."

"You're teasing me," she observed. "Sir, I do not joke about books."

"*Touché.* Nor do I, Miss Grimsley," he replied. "Perhaps I can loan you my copy. Are you staying in town?"

She nodded. "I will be matriculating at Miss Digman's Select Female Academy."

"I never heard the word *matriculation* used in the same breath as Miss Dignam's," he said. "I had thought the most strenuous course there to be French knots."

"I am sure it is not so," she said quickly. "I have great plans." She was silent a moment. "I have greater plans than my brother, and he is a student here . . . under duress."

"That happens to some," he replied. "And what is this scholar's name?"

"It is Gordon, and he is in his first year at University College," she replied. "He does not know how lucky he is."

"They seldom do," Gatewood murmured. He was silent then as they continued down the hill together.

As they came closer to the carriage, Ellen stopped in confusion. "Excuse me, sir, for being so forward. I really shouldn't be talking with strangers."

"Neither should I," he said and twinkled his eyes at her. "But as I did not think you would do me any harm, I chanced it. Good day, Miss Ellen Grimsley. I trust you will find Oxford to your liking."

She nodded and smiled up at him. "I am sure that I shall." He continued toward the main road. Ellen looked at the post chaise and called to him.

He turned, a look of interest in his lively eyes.

"My Aunt Shreve was teasing me a moment ago, but tell me, sir, is Oxford really the center of the universe?"

He came back to stand beside her. She noted the shabbiness of his coat under the student gown and his collar frayed around the edges. He did not appear to have shaved that morning, and his eyes were tired. He was silent a moment, considering her question, and then the good cheer reappeared. He shifted his books to his other arm and touched her arm lightly.

"I will give you an Oxford answer, Miss Grimsley," he said. "The answer to that question depends entirely upon where you are standing."

"Well, then, sir, where are you standing now?" she persisted. "I really must know."

He looked down at her, his expression hard to read. "I would say that from where I am standing right now, yes, and yes again, Miss Grimsley. Good day."

And then he was gone, taking long strides down the hill toward the town. She thought he whistled as he hurried along.

Ellen watched him for a moment and then returned to the carriage. "I just met the strangest man," she said to her aunt, who had been admiring the view from the other window. "A student, I think."

Aunt Shreve turned and followed Ellen's gaze. "That fellow over there? He certainly has a broad set of shoulders to recommend him."

"Aunt!"

"I may be a widow twenty years and my children grown, my dear, but I can admire," Aunt Shreve replied. "Come, come, Ellen. You have had your look at Oxford. What do you think?"

"His ears are flat."

Aunt Shreve stared at her in consternation and then burst into laughter. "My dear, I do not open bottles of Palais Royal for flat ears!"

"I am only teasing, Aunt," Ellen replied. "I think Oxford is splendid. I also think that words do not describe it." She leaned forward and touched her aunt on the knee. "Thank you, Aunt Shreve. Even if Papa only allows me to stay here until Horry's wedding, it will be enough."

As they drove across the bridge, the clouds

settled lower, resting on the highest spires as the honey-colored buildings turned gray again. When the cold rain began, Ellen wondered if the tall student had reached his chambers in time. Then she put him from her mind as the magnificence of Oxford surrounded her.

Gordon Grimsley, black-gowned and even handsomer than she remembered, paced in front of the fireplace in Miss Dignam's sitting room. Ellen shook the rain from her cloak and only had time to lay it aside before her brother grabbed her in a bear hug and kissed her soundly on both cheeks.

He had an appreciative audience. As he whirled her around and she shrieked in protest, Ellen made the observation that Gordon Grimsley rarely did anything without an audience.

The sitting room was occupied by young ladies who had all suspended whatever activity they were engaged in to watch—cards clutched tight in nerveless fingers; stitches dropped; pages unturned; words arrested in midsentence. As she stood in the circle of his arms, Ellen Grimsley noted that her brother had lost none of his effect on females, even the select females of Miss Dignam's Academy.

"Gordon, really," she whispered. "You've never been so glad to see me before!"

He winked at her and nodded to a dry husk of a woman bearing down on them from the other side of the room. He spoke out of the side of his mouth. "I do not think she will suffer me much longer in her sitting room."

"And no wonder," Ellen whispered back. "Gordon, you are incorrigible."

"Yes, thank the Almighty," he agreed. He turned then and bowed to the lady approaching. The bow was so elegant that several of the young ladies sighed. Ellen put her hand to her mouth to smother her laughter. Trust Gordon to put his best foot forward.

"Ellen," he was saying, "it gives me great pleasure to introduce to you Miss Dignam, your headmistress. Miss Dignam, this is my little sister, Ellen."

Ellen grasped the woman's cool, dry hand, opened her mouth to speak, and then closed it when the woman only touched her hand and then hurried past her to embrace Aunt Shreve.

"Eugenia, how long has it been?" she exclaimed, lips stretched tight over protruding teeth in what must be a smile.

The students in the room continued to gape. Gordon looked at them in amusement. "Perhaps they never knew a dragon to have friends," he whispered to his sister.

While they watched the reunion, Gordon took his sister by the arm. "I have spoken a meal for the three of us at The Mitre." He grinned. "Providing you can fork over the blunt."

"Gordon, it is only just past the quarter. Are your pockets to let already?"

"Always," he agreed cheerfully. "I was hoping you would be bringing some reinforcements from home." He looked around to make sure that his aunt could not hear him. "I am planning to toddle over to London this weekend with a new friend of mine."

"Gordon, that is a long way to go. What about your studies?"

He shrugged and flashed that lopsided grin of his that only made her more wary. "I'll get by."

There wasn't time for a reply. In another moment, Aunt Shreve, her arm about Miss Dignam, had returned to her side. "Come, my dears," she announced. "Miss Dignam has given us leave to go to—The Mitre, is it, Gordon? I promised to have you back here by nine o'clock, and indeed, Gordon has his own curfew."

Again that careless shrug. Ellen frowned, dreading the uneasiness that was already stirring her stomach around.

"I am entirely at your service, ladies," Gordon said as he made a final bow, to the accompaniment of an entire row of sighs from the students grouped on the sofa.

"Gordon, you are utterly shameless!" Ellen scolded as they bundled up against the drizzle and hurried along the street to Cornmarket. "I think you are a dreadful flirt."

"I must second the notion," Aunt Shreve agreed as they entered the inn and surrendered their cloaks to the serving girl. She smiled at her handsome nephew. "And I also must acknowledge that you received an unfair amount of the Grimsley charm." She took him by the arm as they walked into a private parlor. "I would advise you not to waste it on your aunt and sister. We know you too well."

The first course was ready as soon as they were seated. They ate in hungry silence, and then Gordon pushed back his plate. "Sister, I could not believe my

47

own eyes when I received that letter from Mama, telling me that you would be attending Miss Dignam's Academy. Have you let your brains leak out? If Papa offered me anything I wanted for two bottles of sherry, this place would be low on my list."

He smiled at the waiter, who set the next course in front of him. "I can't imagine anyone comes up to Oxford without vast coercion, El."

"You're a dunce, Gordon," she said without missing a bite.

He slammed down his fork. "Don't keep me in suspense, sister! Did or did not Papa say something to you about my joining that cavalry regiment?"

Ellen stared at her brother. "He did no such thing, Gordon, and you know it. I remember well the terms of the agreement he forged with you when you came up here only one month ago. You are to acquit yourself at Oxford for a year, through all the terms, and then he would think about it."

Gordon picked up the fork again and dragged it around the food on his plate. "Think about it!" he burst out. "While he's thinking about it, the war will end in Spain and I will have missed all the fun!"

"It cannot be otherwise," Ellen replied. "Now tell me what you have learned thus far at your college."

He gave her a blank stare and continued picking over his food, his lips tight together and the frown line between his eyes deeply pronounced.

Aunt Shreve picked up the ball of conversation. "My dears, whenever I see you two together, I am struck by your resemblance to one another."

48

Ellen smiled at her aunt and took a closer look at her elder brother. They had the same fair hair and blue eyes, but to her mind, there the resemblance stopped. She observed her brother in profile, admiring the regularity of his features, and wondering why they were so different in temperament, inclination, and goal. *I would give the world to walk these halls and quads, and Gordon cannot wait to leave it.*

Her own pleasure in the meal dissolved. She ate what was put before her and wished herself elsewhere. Gordon, when he recovered from his sulks, kept up a witty conversation with Aunt Shreve that earned him a kiss on the cheek as he escorted them back to the school and a handful of guineas.

"Your mother thought you might be in need," Aunt Shreve said. "She says that is all you will have until the quarter, so practice economy, my dear."

Gordon grinned and kissed them good night. The bell in Magdalen Tower tolled, and then another and another. "I'll be in touch, Ellen," he said as his lips brushed her cheek.

Aunt Shreve watched him go. "I worry for him," was all she said as they opened the door and were greeted by Miss Dignam.

"I will show you to your room," she said, handing Ellen a candlestick.

"One moment, Miss Dignam, if you please," Ellen said. She set down the candle and reached in her reticule for the letter. "Miss Dignam, if you please, could I change these classes in embroidery and French for geography and perhaps geometry? I would like that, and I know that I can keep up."

Miss Dignam blinked. "We do not offer such things here! We find that a little Italian and a little French, and watercolors or embroidery are enough. Geometry? Goodness, child, these subjects are not for females."

"Do you mean I cannot study them here?"

"Precisely." Miss Dignam permitted herself a smile. "If you continue with us next year, the older students study the improving poetry of John Donne. But only with their parents' approval," she emphasized, "and only if it does not excite them."

"I had no idea," Aunt Shreve said in a faint voice.

"Oh, yes, my dear Eugenia. We follow the same pattern with the modern composers such as Beethoven." Miss Dignam gestured toward the stairs. "Come, my dear, you will have a strenuous day tomorrow. We have been studying the different shades of blue and green in watercolors, and you must attempt to catch up with us. I recommend that you retire."

Ellen kissed her aunt good night and quietly climbed the stairs behind the headmistress. Miss Dignam opened a door and peered in.

"You are sharing chambers with Fanny Bland," she whispered. "She is an unexceptional girl, and all that is proper. I believe you are already acquainted?"

Fanny made no sound. Ellen said good night to Miss Dignam, undressed in the dark, and crept into bed. The sheets were cold and stiff, as if Miss Dignam had added starch to the rinse water. Ellen huddled into a ball and ducked her head under the covers as the tears began to fall.

When she finished crying, she blew her nose quietly and tucked her hand under her cheek. "Things always look better in the morning," she said, her voice soft.

As she drifted toward sleep, she thought again of the student on the hill. She had already forgotten his name, but she could not forget the independent way he strode down the hill. *You look so free*, she said to herself as she watched the shadows cross the window and the moon change. *I want to be free too.*

Ellen was almost asleep when she heard the sound of pebbles hitting against the window. She did not move, imagining that the sound came from some other part of the hall. She closed her eyes.

The sound continued, little scourings of sound against the window. After debating with herself another moment, she rose silently from her bed and tiptoed to the window. She opened it and leaned out.

Gordon stood below, his hands cupped around his mouth. "I thought you were deaf, my dear."

Ellen leaned her elbows on the windowsill. "What on earth do you want, Gordon? Don't you have a curfew?"

He laughed softly. "I can climb the wall, silly! We're leaving for London in the morning. Loan me three pounds. I know Mama must have sent you some money. Be a sweet thing, Ellen."

She leaned farther out. "I dare not!" she called down to him.

"I'll win it back at faro," he assured, his voice sharpening with that impatient edge that reminded her of Papa. "Don't be so missish, El."

"Oh, very well," she grumbled as she groped about on the dressing table. She counted out some coins and tossed them down to her brother one story below. He caught the money expertly and pocketed it. He bowed elaborately and walked backward down the deserted street, facing her.

"I'll win it back, and with interest, El. Don't you worry about a thing."

Ellen stayed at the window until he was gone. She turned to her bed. The girl in the other bed was sitting up, watching her.

"Why, hello, Fanny," Ellen said, smiling. "I'm sorry I woke you."

Fanny rested herself on one elbow. She squinted into the gloom and then smiled, showing all her teeth. "I'm telling Miss Dignam in the morning."

Chapter 3

THANKS TO GORDON'S LATE-NIGHT entreaty and Fanny Bland's spite, Ellen spent her first morning at Miss Dignam's Select Female Academy sitting on a hard chair, writing, "I will practice decorum as a virtue whilst I reside in Oxford," one hundred times.

No matter that she had pleaded with Miss Dignam that Gordon was her brother and in need of assistance. Miss Dignam only pursed her lips in a thin line. "We have a front door," she said and held up her hand when Ellen opened her mouth. "And he can plan ahead next time before curfew!"

When Ellen tried to speak again, Miss Dignam forgot herself so far as to put her hands on her hips and exclaim, "Miss Grimsley, are you always so difficult?"

Ellen closed her mouth and glanced at Fanny Bland, who had pounced on her as soon as Aunt Shreve had said her farewells with hugs and kisses. Fanny was smiling.

Ellen raised her chin higher. "I have been told I am rather more trouble," she said in her clear voice. "You can ask anyone in the district. I am certain Fanny would be happy to furnish you with names and directions. She takes such an interest in me."

The smile left Fanny's face.

Miss Dignam chose not to pursue the conversation. "Fanny, please conduct Miss Grimsley to an empty classroom, where she can pursue her morning's labors," she said.

Ellen waited until Miss Dignam had closed her office door behind them. "Fanny Bland, you are a fine friend!" she declared. "And to think I was looking forward to being your rooming companion."

Fanny sniffed. "I don't know why you ever entertained that notion. You might have fooled me, except that Edwin wrote to warn me that you were a coming little snip who thought nothing of correcting people like our good vicar."

With a sinking feeling, Ellen remembered that Vicar Snead was a distant cousin to the Blands. "Lead on, Fanny," she said, eyes ahead. "I will take my punishment."

Fanny blinked in surprise at Ellen's unexpected capitulation but led her into the empty classroom. She supplied her with pen and ink and moved to the door. Ellen stopped her.

"Tell me, Fanny, what is the capital of the United States?" Fanny fiddled with the doorknob, a look of intense concentration troubling her face for a small moment. "I do believe it is Philadelphia," she replied. "Yes, I am certain of it."

Ellen only sighed and turned to the blank page before her. "I am sure you are right," she murmured.

She finished writing her sentences before noon and was composing a letter home, begging someone to come and get her, when Miss Dignam swept into the room. She held out her hand for the sheaf of papers and checked them, her eyes growing wider and wider as she scanned the closely written sheets. She jabbed the offending papers with her fingers and thrust them under Ellen's nose.

"My dear Miss Grimsley, I do not know why I ever allowed your dear aunt to enroll you here!"

Mystified, Ellen took the sheets and stared at them, her cheeks growing rosy. From number fifty on, when her mind began to grow numb, she had written, "I will practice boredom as a virtue whilst I reside in Oxford."

Without a word, she accepted another sheet of paper and bent her head over her labors once more. Miss Dignam watched in silence for a moment. "And while you are at it, compose an essay on the folly of disobedience," she said before she made her majestic progress from the room.

The dinner hour came and went. As her stomach rumbled, Ellen breathed in the fragrance of beef roast and gravy, boiled mutton and the sharper odor of mint sauce. Never mind that she had always regarded boiled mutton as penance; she could have eaten a plateful and held out her dish for more.

But no one else came to rescue her from her sentences. "Ellen Grimsley has been sentenced to starvation," she said out loud and giggled, despite her misery.

There was a tap at the door, scarcely audible, and Ellen stifled her laughter, fearful that too much enjoyment during punishment would lead to more sentences, and perhaps a thesis on the folly of mirth.

"Yes?" she asked.

A maid stuck her head in the doorway. She looked around, and seeing no one else in the room, whisked herself inside and closed the door behind her quickly. She held out a small package, done up in white paper and tied with a silver bow.

"For you, miss, at least, if you are Miss Grimsley," said the maid, when Ellen made no move to take the gift.

"I am Miss Grimsley, but tell me, who is this from?" The maid looked about her again and came closer. "He was a tall gentleman, a student I am sure, but older than some. He came to call, but Miss Dignam had left word with the footman that you were in the middle of an 'improving punishment.'" The maid leaned closer, cupping her mouth with her hand, in the event that the walls had ears. "At least, that is what she always calls it. I don't know that it ever improved anyone."

"Did he leave his name?" Ellen asked, thinking of Gordon. "Was he tall and blond, and rather fine to look at?"

The maid shook her head. "No, miss, not a bit of it." She perched herself on a desk. "But that's only the half of it. I shoved him out, and then who do I see poking about the kitchen door a half hour later but the same gentleman!"

"And?" Ellen prompted.

"And he handed me this package and told me to sneak it to you, and mind that I was not to let the dragon see it."

Ellen slid the ribbon off the package and opened it. Inside was a box of chocolates. "Wagoner's Chocolates," she read and looked at the maid. "Tell me, is that a local emporium?"

The maid nodded. "It's the best candy shop in Oxford." Ellen opened the box, inhaling the comforting odor. With ink-stained fingers, she picked up the small card.

"'Courage. Jim,'" she read out loud. She turned the card over. Nothing more.

"How singular," she said, as she popped a chocolate into her mouth. She held out the box to the maid, who protested at first and then took a piece. They sat in companionable silence in the room that had somehow become less depressing.

Ellen sighed. "I am sure it is a mistake, but oh, how pleasant," she said as she selected another piece. "I love nougat centers." She wiped her fingers on the wrapping paper. "I suppose we should not eat any more. I am sure these are intended for one of the other students. If we do not stop soon, that will mean another hundred sentences." She laughed out loud. "I will remember that gluttony is a deadly sin whilst I reside at Oxford."

The maid giggled and shook her head when Ellen offered her another candy. "It's no mistake, miss," she said, accepting a second piece when Ellen continued to hold out the box to her. "He said it was for Ellen Grimsley."

Ellen shrugged. "How many Ellen Grimsleys can there be in Oxford?"

Then she remembered the tall gentleman on the hill yesterday afternoon. "Tall, and with brown hair and . . . and . . ." she said, trying to think of how to describe that look of interest in his eyes.

"Wondrous broad shoulders," the maid continued and then blushed. "At least, that's what I noticed."

"You and my aunt! James . . . James Gatewood," Ellen said, her mind full again of the student with the easy air about him. "I don't suppose you ever wrote sentences, James Gatewood," she said under her breath.

"Beg pardon, miss?" the maid asked, her hand poised over the open box again.

"Oh, nothing, nothing. Although I do not think he should waste the ready on such expensive chocolates. Do have another. I intend to. What is your name?"

"Becky, miss. Becky Speed."

"Well, Becky Speed, thank you for rescuing me from starvation. Let us each take one more, and then hide this box behind that row of books. I would hate for Miss Dignam or the odious Fanny Bland to suspect we had enjoyed a pleasant moment."

When Miss Dignam entered the room ten minutes later, Becky Speed was gone, the chocolate was hidden, and Ellen was finishing the last sentence of her essay with a flourish.

Miss Dignam sniffed the air. "I smell chocolate," she accused.

Ellen looked up from her work. "I cannot imagine," she exclaimed with an air of wide-eyed innocence that would never have fooled Gordon but seemed to suffice for Miss Dignam.

The headmistress accepted the essay and additional sentences and then arranged her lips in some semblance of a smile. "Very well, Miss Grimsley. Virtue is as virtue does. Come along with me now. It is time for embroidery."

An hour later, Ellen looked up from a tangle of embroidery threads, filled with the desire to return to the sentences and the hidden box of chocolates. Miss Dignam had introduced her to a roomful of Fanny Blands, students who, from the whispers behind their hands and the looks they gave each other, had already been introduced to Ellen by Miss Bland herself.

Ellen dug her toes into the carpet during Miss Dignam's introduction, accepted the basket of tangled threads with the admonition to make order out of chaos, and scurried to the remotest corner of the room.

The whispers reached her then, and her ears burned, even as her heart ached. "She thought to study Shakespeare and geometry. Imagine that!" "A petty squire's daughter with no more breeding than to lean out her bedroom window and toss money down to someone she claims is her brother." "Dreadfully fast." "Frightfully wild."

The tangle of threads blurred as she worked on them. In another moment, they disappeared altogether.

She folded her hands in her lap, bowed over the threads, and cried.

The others in the room were silent then. When they began to speak again, it was to each other, as though they had effectively shouldered her aside and cut her off from all further notice. She might not have been in the room.

The afternoon dragged on. Doggedly, Ellen kept her head bent over her work, unraveling twisted strands and wishing herself elsewhere, anywhere. She longed for a seat by the window, where at least she could look out occasionally. As it was, she saw nothing except the backs of the other girls and heard nothing except the impartial tolling of Oxford's bells. The clamor thrilled her to the bone, even as it mocked her and reminded her that she had no part of it.

After a cheerless dinner of boiled mutton and potatoes, she longed for Gordon to return. She sat in the parlor with the others, her head down, her eyes politely neutral.

Gordon had never been her favorite brother, although they were so close in age. He had teased her, bullied her, and tormented her throughout their shared childhood. But sitting there in misery in Miss Dignam's parlor, she would have given the earth for a glimpse of him.

When the clock struck seven times and still he had not made his appearance, Ellen remembered that he had taken himself off to London. *Where you will likely get into huge trouble*, she thought, *and cause Papa such misery that you will get no closer to the fighting in Spain than the pier at Brighton.*

Gordon, why are you not more prudent, she thought as she shifted in her chair, careful not to draw attention to herself, but weary beyond words with sitting.

Visitors arrived and were admitted to the sitting room. Some of them were parents, and others were young men from the different colleges. Parents chatted amiably enough with their offspring, but the young men writhed and squirmed under the cold eye of Miss Dignam, who sat in one corner and played solitaire.

Ellen observed the couples with some compassion, despite her own misery. While she did not exactly wish herself back in the company of Thomas Cornwell and his big ears and stupefying conversation, she wished that someone would come for her.

After another hour of quiet observation, she was grateful that no one had chosen to visit her. With increasing amusement, she watched how Miss Dignam slapped her cards down and cleared her throat whenever any young man went so far as even to gaze over-long into the eyes of one of her select females.

It would take a man of supreme courage to carry on a courtship under such daunting circumstances, Ellen decided as the evening drew to its weary conclusion. *I wonder that anyone attempts it*, she thought. *The desire to perpetuate the human species is stronger than I imagined.*

For one tiny moment, she wished that James Gatewood would announce himself to the butler and drop in long enough for her to thank him for the chocolates. When he did not, she realized that his kindness had been an impulsive whim, now forgotten. *And I had better forget it*, she thought.

At last the final guest left. Miss Dignam nodded to Becky Speed, who bolted the front door and took the Bible from the bookcase. Miss Dignam accepted the Bible and then peered slowly around the room until her eyes lighted on Ellen, sitting in the corner and trying to make herself small. The headmistress thumbed through the pages, stopped at Ecclesiastes, and cleared her throat.

While the other girls knotted fringes, crocheted, or embroidered, Miss Dignam read chapter one, slowing down on the last two verses: "'And I gave my heart to know wisdom, and to know madness and folly. I perceived also that this is vexation of spirit. For in much wisdom is much grief: and he that increaseth knowledge increases folly.'"

Miss Dignam closed the book. Ellen looked up at the sudden sound in the quiet room to see Miss Dignam's eyes boring into her.

"And that, my dear Miss Grimsley, is how the preacher disposes of wisdom. It brings only sorrow and grief. I am certain that we can all echo the sentiments of Ecclesiastes."

She looked around the room as the girls nodded. Her eyes fell again on Ellen. "And you, my dear?" she asked.

Ellen considered the question. She thought about the dreadful day she had endured, relieved only by the kindness of a servant and a box of chocolates. She thought of Gordon, likely making a cake of himself in London and ignoring the riches that were here at Oxford. She took a deep breath and threw herself into the breech once more.

"I am equally certain, in this instance, that Ecclesiastes could not be further from the truth, Miss Dignam," she replied quietly, her hands tight together in her lap.

Miss Dignam gasped and gathered the Bible closer to her, as though Ellen would spring from her chair, snatch it from her, and trample the Holy Writ underfoot.

"And now you will criticize the Bible?" she said as the other students looked at each other with varying expressions of amusement and horror.

Ellen, her face pale, stood up. "No, I do not argue with the Bible!" she declared, her voice low and intense. "I merely put forward the suggestion that in the many years and years of its translation that possibly, just possibly, there might be an error in the text? Surely God does not wish us to glory in ignorance."

She looked around her and slowly sat down, numbed by the blank expressions of the select females of Miss Dignam's academy. *Don't you ever have a thought that is original?* she wanted to ask but did not.

Instead, Ellen rose again and went to the door, her back straight. She paused in front of Miss Dignam, who still clutched her Bible. "I suppose this will mean more sentences," Ellen said, her eyes straight ahead.

"Two hundred more," snapped Miss Dignam, "plus an essay on 'Why I Have Decided to Follow the Teaching in Ecclesiastes.'"

As she went slowly and quietly up the stairs, candle in hand, Ellen smiled as she reflected that with her sentences and essay, she was possibly getting a better education than the girls who untangled yarn and fretted over watercolors.

She looked back down the stairs where the other girls stood, whispering to each other. "I shall think upon this assignment and create a truly masterful essay," she said quietly.

Fanny Bland treated her to prickly silence as they both prepared for bed. Ellen sighed, said her prayers in mutinous fashion, and leaped between chilly sheets, pulling the blankets up tight around her chin.

Fanny remained where she was beside her bed for another pious five minutes while Ellen lay with her hands behind her head, staring at the ceiling. She was drifting off to sleep when Fanny finally crawled into her own bed, muttering something about those who don't take much time for God.

Ellen only gritted her teeth and resisted the urge to declare that she kept her prayers economical so the Lord God Almighty could spend His valuable time helping the troops in Spain or guarding sailors on the high seas. She lay quiet, her eyes shut tight, composing another letter home in her mind, pleading with them to rescue her from her own folly. In a moment, she slept.

The tedium of that weekend was unparalleled in Ellen's memory. Her hopes of at least a walk beyond the front door of the academy were dashed by Miss Dignam's upraised eyebrows and the assignment of one hundred more sentences, on top of the two hundred, at her suggestion of a stroll down the High Street. "'I will remember to conduct myself with decorum at all times,'" Miss Dignam had pronounced, and left her to the empty classroom and the chocolates.

The other young ladies were permitted a repairing lease around the extensive gardens behind the academy. Her head bent over the paper, Ellen smiled with unholy delight at the sudden rumble of thunder, followed by the drumming of rain and the shrieks of the select females assembled outdoors to walk about. She popped another chocolate in her mouth, raised her pen high in salute to the soggy students, and labored on, finishing each sentence with a flourish that bordered on insolence.

Becky Speed joined her, scooting into the room and closing the door quietly almost before Ellen realized that she was not alone. She smiled and held out the chocolate box. Becky accepted with a curtsy and sat on the desk, her legs swinging, as she nibbled around the nougat center until the chocolate was gone.

"I wish that I could write," she said at last, shaking her head over the last chocolate in the box and then changing her mind when Ellen insisted.

Ellen tucked the empty box behind the bookcase again. "It would be an easy matter to teach you," she said.

Becky shook her head and got down off the desk. "Miss Dignam says I don't have any need to learn how. She says it would put me above my station."

Ellen eyed her thoughtfully. "I suppose it would,

but where would be the harm in that?" She perched herself on the teacher's desk. "Perhaps you could become a bookkeeper's assistant, or run your own shop. A candy shop."

The girls giggled together.

"I would like that," Becky said. "I could help my mum provide for us."

Ellen took out the remaining sheet of paper. "Then sit yourself down, Miss Speed," she said, raising her eyebrows in an imitation of Miss Dignam that made Becky smile. "You could become rich at the Female Academy, writing sentences for the wicked!"

They were part way through the alphabet when Ellen heard Miss Dignam's measured tread in the hallway. Becky leaped to her feet and began to ply the feather duster around the bookcase with such vigor that she sneezed. Ellen grabbed up the pages of the letters and words A through K, sat upon them, and continued with her sentences.

Miss Dignam opened the door slowly. She did not hurl it open as she had the day before, intent upon surprising Ellen at some misdeed. The expression on her face as she peered over Ellen's shoulder, while grim, had not yesterday's suspicion. Ellen held her breath, too afraid to look at Becky, who continued to dust with all the energy of a troop movement.

Miss Dignam cleared her throat, and Ellen looked up, biting her lip to keep from exclaiming. Miss Dignam was smiling. She handed Ellen the essay on Ecclesiastes that had been part of yesterday's punishment.

"Well written, Miss Grimsley, well written,

indeed," she said, "even if I do not precisely agree with your argument."

"Why thank you," Ellen stammered, taking the paper in trembling fingers, amazed at Miss Dignam's sudden about-face. "I have marked a few places where it might be improved upon," Miss Dignam continued, "but it was an excellent piece of expository writing. You are to be commended."

Ellen could only stare as Miss Dignam took a seat beside her.

"I believe we can continue to expect writing of a similar quality from you, Miss Grimsley." She paused, as if composing herself for an apology. Ellen waited, holding her breath.

The apology did not come, but Miss Dignam continued in a voice that was almost human. "My dear, I had no idea of your family's connections here at Oxford," she said at last, and paused, obviously waiting for some comment from Ellen.

Ellen racked her brain for an Oxford connection other than Gordon, who, if suspicion served her right, was setting no records at University College.

But Miss Dignam expected some response. Ellen swallowed the lump in her throat, hoped fervently that no stray chocolate still clung to her teeth, and smiled. "Yes, Miss Dignam, our ties here are exemplary," she said, crossing her fingers behind her back, totally at sea.

Miss Dignam only nodded and smiled back. "I have never before had the honor of admitting Lord Chesney to my sitting room, but there he was this morning, for a quarter hour and more, telling me about your abilities! I could only agree with him, of course," she said and reached out a bony hand to pat Ellen's knee. "Naughty girl! You should have told me of such an illustrious connection!"

Ellen continued to smile, even as she searched her brain. Lord Chesney? *Surely she has me confused with someone else*, was her first thought. *No one in our entire family knows a lord*, she thought. *The only titled gentleman of her acquaintance was Fanny Bland's insufferable father, and he was only a paltry baronet.*

Her own confusion was amply covered by Miss Dignam. "Goodness, child, Lord Chesney is one of All Souls's most distinguished Fellows! Surely you are aware of that?"

"Well, no, ma'am," Ellen said honestly. "Lord . . . er . . . Chesney is a modest man. I have never once heard him to sound his own horn," she finished. That, at least, was honest enough.

"How true that is," Miss Dignam agreed. "He is the epitome of good breeding and all that is correct."

In the small silence that followed, Ellen ventured a question.

"Tell me, did he explain yesterday the nature of his visit?" she asked, hoping that any information Miss Dignam would drop would give her a clue.

"He said that he was interested in your progress and hoped that I would have good reports to make of you."

"How . . . kind," Ellen said faintly. "Of course, Lord Chesney has always been kind. He is probably one of the kindest gentlemen of my acquaintance," she offered, fervently praying that a just God would not strike her dead on the spot.

Miss Dignam managed another indulgent laugh and rose. She shook her finger at Ellen, but there was no malice in the gesture. "Naughty girl!" she said again. "We will see that you are not a disappointment to his lordship."

"Yes, certainly. Of course," Ellen said, hoping for a quick and merciful end to this strange interview.

Miss Dignam gestured toward the papers on the desk. "When you have finished those silly little sentences, bring them to me, and we will discuss your future plans here at the academy. Lord Chesney assures me that he is deeply interested in your progress."

Miss Dignam overlooked Ellen's openmouthed amazement and left the room in all her majesty, closing the door quietly behind her.

Ellen stared at Becky, who stopped dusting and hurried to her side. "I get the feeling that you have no idea who Lord Chesney is," she said, as Ellen continued to stare at the closed door.

"You are right enough," Ellen said finally. She frowned and drummed her fingernails on the desk. "Although I have my suspicions. I think it is my brother Gordon, up to some trick."

"But hasn't Miss Dignam seen Gordon?" Becky asked.

"Then it must be a fellow student he has coerced into this little prank," Ellen said. "Gordon, when I see you . . ."

She took her time over the sentences, in no hurry

to see Miss Dignam again so soon. Lord Chesney? Father had never mentioned such a personage. Papa's cronies were other well-heeled squires like himself, men dedicated to the hunt and little else. And Aunt Shreve prided herself on her small circle of friends, all of them well known to Ellen.

Her interview an hour later with Miss Dignam left her shaking her head. Gone was the animosity of yesterday. The formidable headmistress might have been a different person as she informed Ellen that, beginning on Monday, she would study geography with the older students, and that perhaps a scholar could be found to tutor her in one or two of Shakespeare's more proper plays.

Ellen hurried from the headmistress's office when the interview ended. She closed the door behind her and leaned against it for a brief moment, baffled by Miss Dignam's startling bonhomie. *I shall ask Gordon*, she thought as she hurried to her room. Surely he will be back tomorrow. Her heart warmed toward him. *Can it be that he has done something that will make this dungeon tolerable for me? Gordon, you are a dear.*

Sunday came, but no Gordon. Marching in ranks of two, the students traveled at a slow and decorous pace down the High Street to St. Mary's for church at eleven of the clock. It was the parish church at Oxford's center, and there were many students in attendance. Ellen looked them over, wondering which man was Lord Chesney. Miss Dignam had mentioned All Souls College. "Rare air, indeed," Ellen murmured as she listened to the priest's responses. "What does it all mean?"

Surely Gordon would return on Monday. The next morning she sat politely through a lecture on geography, her mind wandering about, as the instructor, a spinsterly don with a permanent blush, spoke at length on the products of the Low Countries and What It All Meant to England.

Evening came and still Gordon did not make his appearance.

Ellen stood at her bedroom window, looking down into the street, willing him to appear. Her uneasiness grew until her head began to ache. What kind of trouble had Gordon gotten himself into in the middle of London? She had heard tales of Newgate, and Bow Street Runners, and flats and cheats and gaming hells, and assorted lowlife on the prowl for young men less wise in the ways of the world than they thought themselves.

She thought too of James Gatewood. Already she was having difficulty remembering his face, seen only briefly that afternoon of her entrance into Oxford. He had not returned after delivering the candy. She had told herself that she would not think about him anymore, but she did as she stood at the window and chafed after Gordon.

"And what would you do if James Gatewood were here?" she asked herself. "Tumble all your troubles into his lap?"

She would never do that, but as she considered the matter, she had a feeling that his lap was big enough to carry them all. How she had come by this knowledge, she could not tell, but it was the one warm thought in an evening of fret and worry.

She was walking from geography next morning, chewing on her lip and wondering where she had misplaced her pathetic bit of embroidery for the afternoon's class, when she heard someone hissing at her.

Startled, Ellen looked around. There was no one but Becky Speed, watering the plants by the stairwell. She came closer.

"Thank goodness, miss," Becky said. "There's someone here who wants to see you in the worst way."

The maid set down the watering can, looked both ways, and darted for the door that led belowstairs. Ellen followed, after a careful look of her own.

And there was Gordon, sitting at the servant's dining table, rubbing his head as though it hurt. He looked up when Ellen came clattering down the stairs, and winced as she shrieked, "Gordon!" and threw her arms around him.

"Have a care, sister," he pleaded, holding his head with both hands. "My head is screwed on upside down."

Flashing a grateful look at Becky, Ellen sat down close to her brother. She sniffed the air around him and drew back slightly. He smelled as though he had not changed his linen since their last meeting. His face was a rough field of whiskery stubble, and he smelled of gin, sweat, and stale tobacco.

He acknowledged her presence with a gusty sigh and then rested his head on the table again. "Ellen," he croaked, "you don't know what I have been through."

His eyes were red puddles in his pale face. Ellen waited for him to speak, waited for some explanation. The realization of what had happened dawned on her. "Gordon," she said, her voice overloud. She shook his arm. "You didn't lose all your money?"

"Softly, softly," he pleaded, clutching his hair this time. "Every farthing, El. And then there I was in the gutter, looking up at this huge watchman." He sat up at the memory and groaned.

Ellen stared at him, her eyes wide. "Papa would be aghast," she said.

The look he fixed on her had nothing in it of exhaustion or alcoholic muddle. "He's not going to hear about it from me *or* you," he said, clipping his words off and then sinking his head to the table again, as though gathering strength for his next thought.

She waited for him to speak. Becky plunked a cup of tea on the table and pushed it close to his nose. "I found him out by the back door," she whispered to Ellen. "I thought he was your brother."

Ellen gave her a grateful look. "Becky, you're a wonder."

Becky only smiled. "I . . . had a brother once, miss." Ellen pushed the cup closer. In another moment, the odor reached Gordon's nostrils. He sat up and took a sip. "You're as bad as Mama," he grumbled. "El, tea doesn't cure everything."

Ellen touched his arm. "It helps, Gordon. Now you have merely to tighten your belt until the next quarter rolls around and . . ."

Gordon let out a sound between a wail and a moan and turned his face away. "El, you don't know the half of it," he said. "I needed that money to pay the student who has been writing my essays for me. He

73

won't continue without more blunt, and I lost it all!"

Ellen stared at him as the words sank into her brain. "Good heavens, brother, do you mean . . . ?"

Wearily, Gordon propped his head on his hand. "Every week he writes the essay that I read on Saturday mornings. He wrote the last one on credit, and said he wouldn't write any more until I coughed up the guineas." He fumbled in his pocket and pulled out a wrinkled letter. "And what do I find under my door but this note from the warden himself! I missed last Saturday's essay, and if I do not produce an acceptable essay this Saturday, he will write Father."

The silence stretched between them. Gordon took another sip of tea. "Then Papa will summon me home and I will never be any closer to Spain than I am right now!"

Ellen sat in silence, thinking to herself that it was no time to trot out her childhood scolds and remind him that it was only what he deserved. She touched his hair, matted and dirty from the London gutter. "Can you not write your essay now? It is only Tuesday. Surely . . ."

He groaned again and drained the rest of the tea. "El, you dolt," he said. "I am trying to tell you that I have never written an essay in my life!"

As tears filled his eyes, she realized it was also not the time to vent her own anger at his good fortune in an Oxford career. *For he will not see it that way*, she thought.

"You have attended the lectures," she began. "That ought to be some help in writing an essay."

"Yes, I attend the lectures," he said. "I take notes while that dreary don drones on about this or that, and then I turn my notes over to my friend and he writes the essay."

He eyed his sister, and as she stared back, the look in his face changed and became more thoughtful. He brushed the hair back from his eyes, but his glance did not waver from her face.

Ellen had seen that expression before, but not in years. She shook her head. "I don't care what you are thinking, but the answer is no, you provoking brother."

He did not appear to hear her words. A grim smile played about his lips. "I have just had a brilliant idea, El. It's a real hayburner, and I am astounded that I could think of it, considering how I feel right now."

She knew better than to say anything but pursed her lips into a thin line.

When she made no comment, he took her by the arm. "Ellen, you're going to attend that lecture in my place and write my essay."

"I am not!" she declared. "You can go to your lecture and . . ."

He shook his head. "Not like this, El. It starts in half an hour, and I can't even hold up my head. Can you fathom the trouble I would get into from the warden if he saw me like this? No, Ellen, you'll be as safe as houses."

"You can't possibly be serious," she said, her voice soaring into the upper registers.

He winced. "Trust me, El."

Chapter 4

I WOULDN'T TRUST YOU IF YOU WERE the last Grimsley alive," she declared indignantly, even as Becky Speed put her finger to her lips and Gordon flinched at her bracing tones. "Especially if you were the last Grimsley alive."

She moved closer to her brother, her face inches from his. "We are not children in the nursery anymore, and I cannot be coerced! You must think I am fearful stupid," she hissed.

To his credit, Gordon shook his head vigorously, which only caused him to moan and clutch it in both hands, as though he wished to wrench it off. "No, never that," he gasped. "I ask you to help because I am fearful stupid," he continued, changing his tack as he watched the suspicion grow in her eyes. "You owe me no favors. And I am certain you can think of countless injustices that would render such sisterly goodwill impossible."

"I can," she agreed with feeling. "If you give me leave of twenty seconds or so, I will name ten or twelve, brother."

He shook his head more carefully this time and took her by the hand before she could get out of his vicinity. "Ellen, I am desperate," he said, his voice soft, pleading.

"Well, I suppose you are," she replied, at a momentary loss over his apparent abandonment of the argument. She regarded him in silence for a long moment.

That they did resemble one another, she would not deny. Her fingers strayed to her own blond hair, cut almost as short as his, and just as curly. She sighed. Even this similarity would fool no one.

"It won't work, Gordon," she began. No sooner were the words out of her mouth than she knew she would do what he asked.

After a lifetime of careful strategy with his little sister, Gordon knew it too. He sat up, still cradling his head, his eyes alert for the first time.

"Under ordinary circumstances, I would agree with you," he said, his tone normal as he watched her closely for adverse reactions. "But we are dealing with my don, who is probably more ancient than the Magna Carta, and nearsighted to boot."

Ellen bit her lip, but she listened, wondering why she was listening even as she did so. *Drat all brothers*, she thought to herself. *They should be buried at birth and dug up at twenty-one.*

"You need merely to swathe yourself in my student's gown," Gordon said. He took another sip of the refilled teacup that Becky had placed at his elbow, along with a plate of gingersnaps. "Sit away from the window, where the room is lightest, and he will never know."

"Gordon, when I walk in, he will observe how short I am!" Ellen insisted.

Gordon was calm now, in control. "No, he won't, sister. You will be seated long before he arrives. I swear he forgets every week where our assigned meeting place is. All you have to do is take notes now and then, say 'hmmm' and 'ahh,' in all the right places, and remain seated until he leaves. Nothing could be simpler."

"The gown will not be sufficient," she grumbled, casting about for argument. "You know very well I will be found out the moment I attempt to cross the quad-rangle in my dress and your gown."

"I already considered that," he replied and nodded gingerly toward a bundle near the back door. Becky hurried to fetch it. Gordon opened the bundle and pulled out a pair of trousers and a frilled shirt.

Ellen shook her head. "I couldn't possibly," she said. "Besides, Gordon, I will not fit into your clothes!"

He eyed her patiently, fondly. "These belong to the chap I share my quarters with, El. He's a little taller than you, but not by much. And here are his shoes and stockings. Come on, El, what do you say?"

She snatched the clothes from him and held them to her. "I should leave you to your fate, brother," she began. "You brought this all upon yourself, you know."

"I know," he agreed, his voice contrite. He got down on one knee and looked up at her.

Tears started in her eyes, and she touched the top of his head.

Why should I "wink at your discords," she thought. *And here I am, quoting the Bard like Ralph. Why should I be an instrument to hurry you ultimately to Spain?* She straightened her shoulders and turned to Becky.

"Becky, can you get this bundle to my room? I must beg off from embroidery with Miss Dignam."

Becky nodded and dashed away with the bundle. Gordon rose, resting his hands on the table. "Just this once, Ellen," he said. "Then perhaps you can show me how to write a scholarly essay."

"Perhaps I can. Wait for me here."

She met Miss Dignam in the hall and made no effort to disguise her agitation. Her heart in her shoes, she hoped her face looked as pale as it felt. She put her hand to her forehead, gratified that her fingers shook.

"Miss Dignam, I must beg your excuse from embroidery," she said. It was an easy matter for tears to stand out on her long lashes. It was an art she had learned from Horatia. Her chin quivered and Miss Dignam succumbed.

"My dear! You must go lie down!" the headmistress exclaimed. "Are you well?"

Ellen shook her head. She looked about to make sure that no one lingered to listen and stood on her tiptoes. "It is a female matter, Miss Dignam."

The headmistress colored and patted Ellen's arm. "Go lie down, my dear," she repeated. "Shall Becky create a tisane for you?"

"If she will bring me a warming pan for my feet,

that will suffice," Ellen said, her voice faltering as she considered the enormity of her deception. *And dare I drag Becky into this mess?* she thought as she walked slowly up the stairs.

With Becky's help, she dressed quickly in the shirt and trousers. The shoes were too large, but Becky stuffed them with tissue paper.

While Ellen fiddled with her hair, biting her lips and scarcely daring to look herself in the eye, Becky arranged her pillows and extra blankets into a facsimile of a person and puffed the comforter up high. She went to the window.

"Thank the Lord it is raining," Becky said. "You will have the hood up over your face." She sniffed the air. "If only you did not smell of lavender, Miss Grimsley."

Ellen turned away from the mirror. "That is the least of our worries." She strode up and down the room. "Oh, Becky, I cannot begin to walk like a man."

"Turn your toes out more," suggested the maid. "Let your arms swing."

"I look like Jack Tar!" Ellen protested after several more trips up and down the small chamber.

Becky shrugged. "Better that than a schoolroom miss. Now throw out your chest. No, no, you had better not do that, Miss Grimsley!"

"I will clutch Gordon's gown tight about me, I assure you," she said, and then sighed and pulled on a dress over the shirt and trousers. She swung an engulfing shawl of Norwich silk about her shoulders. "Lead on, Becky Speed," she said, her eyes straight ahead.

The students had all taken themselves to the class-rooms on the main floor. With Becky in the lead, Ellen hurried down the back stairs.

In the servants' hall, Gordon sat up when he saw her. He watched in appreciative silence as she removed the shawl and dress and held out her hand for his student's robe. He draped it around her slim shoulders. "One could wish you had broader shoulders," he began but shut up when she glared at him. "It was only a wish." He sniffed at her hair. "Perhaps Old Ancient of Days has no more sense of smell than of sight," he said, more to himself than to her. "He will think me Queer Nabs indeed."

Ellen opened her mouth for a retort but thought better of it. She waited a moment until she had command over her voice. "Tell me what it is we are studying today, Gordon, if you can think that far."

The wounded look he fixed upon her was small recompense for the murder in her heart. "It is to be Shakespeare, of course."

"Could you not narrow it down at least to the comedies, tragedies, or histories?" she snapped, grabbing the tablet and pencil he held out to her and stuffing them in one of the deep pockets of the gown.

"It is the one about fairies and donkeys' heads and a chap named Puck. I suspect it is a comedy," he said, opening the back door for her. "Of course, come to think of it, that sounds like government, and so it could be a history."

"How wise of you, dear brother," she said.

He returned her frown with the smile that had

always caused Mama to indulge him. Ellen laughed in spite of herself. Filled with more charity, she followed him into the street and took his arm.

He stopped and removed her hand from his arm. "Really, my dear, how does this look?" he asked. "That sort of thing will never do in public."

They hurried across the High Street. Swept with rain, it was nearly devoid of all students. Ellen glanced back at the Female Academy. No one watched from the windows. She could only breathe a sigh of thanks to the patron saint of students, whoever he was, and hurry after her brother.

He slowed down for her on the curb and ushered her into one the narrow alleyways that led into the heart of the university. Gordon kept his head down against the rain, but Ellen raised her face to the sky, looking about her at the spires and ancient walls.

"I never thought to be here," she said and stopped to admire the high walls that dripped rain. "Where does that little door lead?" she asked, pointing.

"To All Souls, El, holy ground indeed. Now hurry up and keep your face down. I never thought a beautiful sister to be a handicap before."

She stopped again and smiled up at him. "Gordon, that's quite the nicest thing you ever said to me!"

"Well, it's true," he replied gruffly, his eyes on the street ahead of them. "Once you got rid of your baby chins and freckles, you were the prettiest chit in the district. And I'm not just saying that," he hastened to add. "I mean it. Now, quit gawking and step lively."

They hurried down another narrow lane and

another, robes clutched tight against the wind and rain. Gordon paused for a moment, waved her off, and was quietly sick down another alley.

As she waited for him, a group of students passed, looked at him, and winked at her. Her heart in her stomach, Ellen grinned and winked back. *Mama will flail me alive*, she thought, when the students offered some ribald advice to Gordon, pale and shaken.

Mama must never know, she thought and rubbed her arm in the unfamiliar linen shirt. Gordon had tied the neck cloth about her, and it seemed to tighten like a hangman's noose. *Surely I will not be sentenced to appear before a firing squad if I am discovered*, Ellen thought. *Perhaps they will only transport me to Botany Bay.* She tugged at the collar, wishing her imagination less lively.

Another brisk five minutes brought them to University Quadrangle. Gordon stood outside the door and turned to his sister. "El, go up the first flight of stairs, down the hall to your left. It's the last room on the left." He took her hand. "He'll do all the talking. He always does."

She squeezed his hand. "Gordon, I think I do owe you a favor."

"What?" he asked, surprised.

"Silly! For sending someone called Lord Chesney to Miss Dignam. You certainly convinced her that we have high connections here, and he—whoever he was—saw to it that I was moved into geography instead of watercolors. And she says I will have a Shakespeare tutor."

He continued to stare at her. "El, have your wits

gone wandering? I don't know any Lord Chesney. Must be one of Aunt Shreve's eccentric connections. You know how she is about not letting her left hand know what her right hand does."

"Yes, but . . ."

"But nothing, El." He grinned at her suddenly. "Besides, El, you know I never exert myself for my sisters! Perhaps you have a benefactor. I wish I had one. Now, go on."

He opened the door for her and leaned against the frame, his expression warning her that in another moment he would be on his hands and knees by the gutter again. She hurried inside the quad and shut the door after her.

She held her breath and looked about her. The rain had turned the honey-colored stone a dismal gray. The trees were bare, the grass the faded tan of autumn. The only sound was the rain that rumbled through the gutters and gargoyles and spewed onto the ground. She sighed and clutched her gown about her. It was the most beautiful place she had ever seen. "University College," she whispered, unmindful of the rain that pelted her. "Founded by Alfred the Great. Home of scholars these thousand years."

With a laugh in her throat, she ran across the quad toward the hall, remembering to keep her toes turned out. The steps to the second floor were worn and uneven. She mounted them slowly, not so much fearful of her footing as mindful of the thousands who had trod them before her. She breathed deep of air that smelled of old wood, new ideas, candle wax, and somewhere, books in leather covers.

The room was empty, as Gordon had predicted. A fire struggled in the grate. She spent a moment in front of it, warming her hands, and then tugged the straight-backed chair into the shadow and away from the window with its wavy panes of leaded glass that admitted little light anyway. She took out her pad and pencil and waited.

In a few minutes, she heard someone climbing the stairs slowly, as she had done, a step at a time. The steps down the hall were measured and sure, as if they had walked this way for centuries at least. She smiled to herself as the person stopped frequently, as though to peer into each room. Gordon had said that his don was forgetful. *I wonder how many students he has misplaced over the years*, she thought. *I wonder, are they still waiting?*

She saw a mental image of rows and rows of dusty skeletons waiting in each room, pencils still caught in bony fingers. She laughed out loud and then stopped when Gordon's don crossed the threshold and stood there, peering at her.

She would not have thought such a thing possible, but the man was shorter than she. His scholar's gown swept the floor as he entered the room. He raised his shoulders at the sound of the fabric dragging along the floor, rather like a barnyard fowl attempting flight and then thinking better of it. He had no hair on his head, and drops of rain glistened there and on his spectacles.

Still observing her, he brushed his hand across his head and dried his glasses on the hem of his dusty robe.

The results did not satisfy him, so he removed a hand-kerchief from some inner pocket and tried again.

"Better, much better," he murmured and then sniffed the air in Ellen's general vicinity. He frowned and peered at her, squinting through nearsighted eyes.

"Lavender, eh?" he asked. "The new mode at University College? How odd is this younger generation."

Ellen cleared her throat and returned some non-committal reply, careful to utter it in lower tones, with some semblance of Gordon's style. She sat forward, ready to capture his every word.

The don perched himself on the room's only table and gathered his robes about him like a crow folding its feathers. Ellen looked on in fascination, waiting for him to turn around and around and settle himself. She smiled at the absurdity of this, her fear gone.

He frowned. "My dear Grimsley, is this some special occasion? Is there something particular you wish from me?"

Ellen stared at him, her eyes wide, her fear returning. What had she done wrong?

"See here, sir. This is the first time you have come to drink from the font of knowledge with pencil *and* paper." He withdrew a slim volume in red morocco from another pocket. "Dare I to hope that you have even read *Midsummer Night's Dream*?"

"I have, sir," she answered, grateful that only two weeks ago she and Ralph had hidden themselves in the buttery and read the play aloud to each other while Horry sobbed over the fit of her wedding dress, Mama lamented the dearness of beeswax candles, and Papa, booted and dressed in his hunting clothes, shook his fist at the heavens because of the rain.

"For we need a good laugh, El," Ralph had insisted. "And what could be funnier than lovers?"

"I have indeed, sir," she repeated. "It is a favorite of mine."

The don grabbed his book to his meager chest in a gesture of extreme surprise. "Next you will tell me something profound, Grimsley, and then I will know I am in the wrong room."

Ellen had the wisdom to be silent.

The don waited another moment, then opened the book. "Very well, then, since you have no more profundities, let us begin this romp, Grimsley. Let us see 'what fools these mortals be.'"

When she set down her pencil two hours later, sighing with satisfaction, Ellen was in complete charity with her brother. For two hours, she had listened to the undersized, scrawny don transform himself into all the characters wandering about in that enchanted forest.

She regarded the little man with a feeling close to affection. He was Pyramus; he was Chink; he was the haughty Hyppolita, the confused Helena. He was lover and rustic; fond father, foolish maid. He was an absurd little bald man, undeniably prissy, and stuffy with old ideas. He was the very soul of education, and she would have followed him anywhere.

"I understand this play," she said softly, her words not even intended for his ears.

He heard her, though, and smiled. "Then, Grimsley,

you can tell me what it is about, can't you? You can be the first scholar I have instructed this day who is not more concerned about his stomach, or his imagined injuries, or his paper due, his book unread. Tell me then, sir."

Ellen took a deep breath. "It is about the absurdity of love."

The don closed his book and whisked it out of sight in his pocket. "Grimsley, you astound me. Yes, yes! It is about the absurdity of love." He pointed his finger at her. "Do you understand the absurdity of love?"

"I know nothing of it, nothing at all, sir," she confessed, and hesitated, looking up at him.

"Yes?" asked the don, leaning forward. "What else?"

"Perhaps I was wrong. I confess that I know even less than when you began to read," she said, looking down at her hands. "I said I understood the play, but I do not. My ignorance is nearly complete, and somehow, this does not bother me." Ellen looked at him. "Have I failed?"

Her heart nearly stopped when the don hopped off his perch and strode to the window, throwing it wide. He leaned out for a deep breath, a beatific expression on his face, and turned toward her again. "Grimsley, my lad, you have succeeded! Such ignorance is the essence of education. I must have misjudged you."

Ellen looked at him in confusion.

"My dear Grimsley, armed as you are with this supreme ignorance, and an obvious love for the play, what should you do about it? Think hard, lad, and we will see if there is hope for you."

She thought hard. *I could answer this odd question with a smile and shrug, as Gordon would, or I could be honest.*

"I would seek to find out more, sir," she replied quietly.

"Why?" he challenged.

The word hung in the air and seemed to settle on her shoulders.

"Because I wish to know more, even if for no other purpose than to satisfy myself," she replied.

The don smiled and nodded. "Then education is served, lad," was all he said as he adjusted his gown and went to the door. "I can recommend a course to follow."

"Sir, please do," she said, rising to her feet and following him.

"Grimsley, how short you are today," the don said.

Ellen held her breath, but he did not pursue this line of reasoning.

"In the Bodleian you will find a book. It is called *Commentary and Notes on* A Midsummer Night's Dream. I suggest you read it and make it the basis of your paper for Saturday's reading." He shook his finger at her. "Which, I must add with sorrow, you neglected to attend last week. I am certain the gods mourned. Redeem yourself, lad, with this little work of Lord Chesney's."

She sat down again. "Lord Chesney? *The* Lord Chesney?"

"There is only one from that shatterbrained family." The don shook his head and bowed his head.

"Sad what happened to him. England has lost a great Shakespeare scholar."

"He is dead?" Ellen gasped, her mind filled with even more confusion. Was that the mysterious Lord Chesney who sat in Miss Dignam's parlor only two days ago and changed the course of her Oxford stay? "I do not understand."

"He is dead in English literature, Grimsley! What could be worse? I hear he is even now a fellow at All Souls and reading history." The don made a face, as though he had uttered a foul word. "I fear he will become a Philistine after all."

He brightened then. "But he is young, Grimsley. Perhaps there is hope. Such wisdom! Such sagacity! We can only pray that he will yet return to his own special analysis of the Bard. Such piquancy! Such wit!"

He paused, as if so much exclamation had wound him down like a top. His voice was milder when he spoke again. "Good day, Grimsley. I await your paper this Saturday with something close to bated breath." He cast his eyes upon Ellen, squinting at her. "I hope you will leave off the lavender. And do grow, Grimsley, between now and Saturday."

He closed the door behind him. Ellen stared after him, shaking her head and then smothering her laughter with her hands. *Such a funny stick*, she thought, recalling Gordon's dire warnings.

She went slowly down the stairs, trailing her hand along the banister. *How many have done this before me*, she thought, as she felt the years of polish, the roughness of the wood worn smooth by hands and time. No matter that no one believed any longer that Alfred the Great himself had established this seat of learning. She lowered herself to the bottom step and leaned against the railing, content to summon the sight of king and scholars, gathered together at this oxen ford, thirsty for knowledge in an age when few knew anything.

"Not so different from now," she said and rose.

The rain pelted down, drenching the quadrangle, driving the few remaining leaves to the ground and the students indoors. She tucked her tablet into her pocket and walked slowly toward the door in the wall. She looked back once at the hall she had left and raised her hand. It was an absurd gesture, but there was no one around to see her salute to stones and wood and scholarship.

Ellen peered about her, but Gordon was nowhere in sight. She had not expected to see him, especially with the rain pouring down and his inner workings in such a muddle. She was glad of the solitude. She wanted to think for a moment of what she had learned. Her own inclination ran more to geography, cartography, and mathematics, but she had read Shakespeare to humor Ralph. The scrawny little don—*I don't even know his name*, she thought—had awakened her to the vigor of Shakespeare. She clasped her hands together and looked down at them. "Like Adam, I have been touched by the finger of God," she whispered.

The rain did not let up. She walked faster. *I should return to Miss Dignam's*, she thought, *but I must go to the Bodleian for that book by the mysterious Lord Chesney.* Ellen glanced at the little door that led into All Souls quadrangle. The don said Lord Chesney was a fellow there. She paused a moment and then hurried faster. The mystery would keep for drier weather.

A quick run through deepening puddles brought her to the Bodleian Library. She stood at the entrance a moment, amazed at what she was about to do, took a deep breath, and entered. The odor of books was over-powering. It made her mouth water as she stared about her, admiring row upon row of handsomely carved bookshelves, busts of Oxford's better-known graduates, and the plastered, ornamental ceiling that seemed to go on forever.

All was silent. She tiptoed into the main reading room and let out her breath in a sigh of relief. The library was almost empty. A few students sat here and there, some studying, more sleeping, others gazing out the window with thoughtful expressions. The smell of wet wool competed with the odor of books.

I should remove this cloak, she thought, *but I dare not.* She clutched it tighter about her, sloshed in soggy shoes to the librarian, and in her gruffest voice, asked for Lord Chesney's book.

It was brought to her in a moment with the admonition to keep it dry. Keeping her head down, she nodded her thanks and looked for a safe place to read. Beyond the rows of shelves that flanked the main room's middle section was an area with tables and small desks lining the walls. She hurried to one of the desks, sat down, and began to read, careful to keep her sodden cloak high around her face.

She was deep in the first chapter when she heard

footsteps behind her and felt a firm hand on her shoulder. She stiffened, not daring to turn around.

"That's my carrel, lad," said a familiar voice. "Best you move into the center tables."

She knew without even looking over her shoulder that it was James Gatewood. There was just the trace of London in his voice that she remembered from their brief meeting on the hill. Without a word, she got up and moved to a table.

From the corner of her eyes, she watched as Gatewood took off his cloak, draped it over the back of his chair, and looked with a sour expression at the wet chair she had vacated. He removed a neck scarf and dried off the seat. In another moment, he was tipped back in the chair with his feet propped up on the desk.

Ellen put her hand to her mouth to hide the laughter. *Mama would cough up nails if I sat like that*, she thought. *Oh, what am I saying? She would twirl about and expire if she knew I was sitting in the Bodleian Library in borrowed trousers.*

She looked down at herself. Her legs were primly together, as she always sat. After a quick glance about, she pulled back the cloak and crossed her legs, resting her ankle on her knee and leaning back slightly in her chair. Her face flamed. *I am vulgar*, she thought, *but my goodness, this is comfortable.*

She picked up the book again and in another moment was captivated by Lord Chesney's remarkable wit and cynicism as he deftly skewered the young lovers in *Midsummer Night's Dream* and served them up to the reader on a platter of impeccable scholarship.

She laughed out loud at Lord Chesney's description of Helena as "Befuddled, bemused and outwitted by love, that great leveler. Why should she be different than we? Do we laugh at her, or ourselves?"

"Shhh!" said James Gatewood, finger to his lips. "Lad, this is a library, not a theatrical amusement," he whispered.

"But it is Shakespeare, sir," Ellen replied, lowering her tones, hoping she sounded more masculine than she felt as she clutched the cloak more tightly about her face.

Gatewood only smiled and nodded, to her relief, and returned to his reading.

Ellen dug the paper and pencil from her pocket and bent her head over her notes, writing as rapidly as possible. The rain had stopped. Soon scholars would be returning to the library. She wrote faster.

She did not notice the mouse until it ran right by her hand, took a quick glance at Chesney's *Commentary*, and scurried off the end of the table.

Ellen gasped, screamed, and leaped onto the chair, grabbing her cloak about her. Starting in surprise, Gatewood tipped too far back in his chair and tumbled himself to the floor. He lay on his back, his face red, his eyes indignant.

He scrambled to his feet and gripped her tight by the arm.

"Scared of a little mouse, eh, lad?" he declared as he yanked her off the chair. "Is this 'the gift and flower' of English youth? Merciful heaven, help us!"

She stumbled against him. Gatewood flinched and

drew back, gaping down at her with open-mouthed amazement. Before she could say a word, he ripped the cloak from her face and stared at her.

"Blast it, Ellen Grimsley," he said in a voice much too loud for the Bodleian Library. "Grimsley, Grimsley, Grimsley," echoed in the vault overhead.

He hastily released his hold on her, touched her face with the back of his hand in the oddest, most tender gesture, and then looked up as the librarian bore down on them.

She remained silent as he whirled her about and clamped his arm around her shoulders, quick-marching her toward the exit.

"Smartly now, Miss Grimsley, you rascal," he whispered. "I think we can beat him to that door!"

Chapter 5

I T WAS A NEAR-RUN THING. AS HE propelled her toward the side door, she pushed it open and stumbled through. Gatewood slapped her sharply on the hip and turned to face the librarian, who was red-faced from his pursuit of them across the main floor.

"I can deal with this upstart noisebox," Gatewood said and closed the door behind him. Without another word, he grabbed her by the hand and tugged her along the alley into the nearest doorway, where they stood as the rain began again.

Ellen couldn't bring herself to look at James Gatewood. She stared down at her hands, embarrassed beyond words.

Gatewood cleared his throat. "Miss Grimsley, in my wildest imaginings, I never thought to be ejected from the Bodleian."

She looked up, fearful of his wrath, into smiling eyes. "I am so sorry. Will your reputation suffer damage?" she asked in all seriousness.

"Probably." He laughed and leaned against the wet stones. "Miss Grimsley, you look like a drowned rat. Or mouse, in your case. Which reminds me. I must brave the Bodleian again." He stepped from the protection of the doorway and into the rain.

Ellen grabbed for his hand. "I must have my notes, sir. Oh, please, can you fetch them?"

He kissed her wet hand and dashed back into the library. Ellen drew her gown around her again and huddled in the doorway. She thought at first she would run. In another moment she could be across the High Street and safe in the kitchen belowstairs at Miss Dignam's. But that would mean abandoning her notes and leaving Gordon to his well-deserved fate on Saturday, and she could not do that.

Since when have I become so scrupulous about casting Gordon to the fates? she asked herself. *Let us be honest, Ellen. You want your notes back. You want to write that paper.*

Gatewood was back then, his cloak draped about his shoulders this time and her notes in his hand. He glanced at them as he handed them to her. "I noticed Chesney's *Commentary* on the table."

She accepted the notes. "I wish you could have smuggled that out for me, sir. I had only just begun it."

"Please call me Jim," he said promptly. "And I will call you . . ." He paused and looked her over as she blushed. "Somehow, Miss Grimsley, or even Ellen—it

97

is Ellen, isn't it?—sounds misplaced for someone in trousers."

She grimaced as she pocketed the notes. "I am supposed to be Gordon Grimsley."

"'Worse and worse it grows,'" he quoted, his eyes twinkling again. "I scarcely need remind you that women, even women in their brothers' trousers, are not allowed to undertake serious scholarship in the Bodleian. Or any scholarship, for that matter."

When she made no reply, he looked beyond her into the rain, the smile gone from his eyes. "And more's the pity, I suspect."

She looked at him then. "Well, thank you, sir." Her teeth began to chatter and she shivered.

He put his arm around her and pulled her into the rain again. "Bundle up, Mr. Gordon Grimsley," he said, speaking loudly to be heard about the thundering downpour. "I feel the need of a pint."

She stared at him, her eyes wide. "Sir, I have never been in the taproom of a tavern!"

He only laughed and tugged her along. "Then you should not have got yourself into a pair of trousers, Miss Grimsley!"

She pulled back. "Sir! I should think that you could wish to see the back of me, after the embarrassment I just caused you."

He released her and they stood regarding each other in the pouring rain. "I suppose you are right," he said slowly. "After all, scholarship is a stodgy thing, is it not? No?" He did not put his arm about her again but started walking toward the High Street.

The fact that he did not look back to see if she followed piqued her own interest, and she trailed after him. In another moment, he slowed down and walked by her side.

"I confess to curiosity, Miss Grimsley," he continued. He seemed unaware of the turn their brief acquaintance had just taken in the rain and the narrow alley. "From my knowledge, I have never before encountered a female in the Bodleian. As you are the first, and I may claim some slight acquaintance, I thought I should ask you."

"Yes, but a tavern?"

He continued his slow meander down the alley, unmindful of the rain. "If I escort you to Miss Dignam's, I fear you would be in the suds indeed, unless that dragon's ideas of females and academe have changed. I would have no leave to find out more." He bowed. "And as a student, is not my task to find out more? I ask you, Miss Grimsley."

"Ellen," she said involuntarily.

"Not a chance," he replied as quickly. "I will call you . . . oh, let me see, how about . . . I will call you Scholastica."

"Please don't," she said. "Surely you cannot call that an improvement over Ellen."

"Does Ellen need improving?" he asked. "Ah, well, since you were deep in Chesney's *Commentary* on the fairies and lovers, I will call you Hermia."

She stopped in the middle of a puddle and clapped her hands. "Do you like *Midsummer Night's Dream* too?"

He took her by the elbow and steered her down another alley.

"I am excessively fond of it, fair Hermia. As I am also excessively wet, let us discuss this indoors."

In another moment, she was seated in a high-backed settle in a smoky corner, her hands wrapped around a battered pint pot. Gatewood sat next to her, turning himself to face her, and effectively shielding her from others in the room. He twitched the cloak back from her face and just looked at her until she turned away and took a deep quaff of the ale.

She coughed as the fumes rose and circled through her brain. "This is a vile brew!" she gasped when she could talk.

"Yes, isn't it?" Gatewood replied. "You would be amazed how inspirational it can be in the eleventh hour before a paper is due." He leaned closer, lowering his voice. "I have it on good authority that Lord Chesney himself wrote much of his *Commentary* at this very table."

Ellen opened her mouth to ask him about Lord Chesney, but Gatewood was off and running. "My dear Hermia, please tell me—if it isn't too much trouble—what you were doing in the Bodleian? I suspect that Miss Dignam's is slow indeed, but isn't the Bodleian rather a risk?"

Ellen nodded and frowned into the ale as she swirled the pot around and around. "I told Gordon it would not work, but he was suffering the ill effects of a weekend in London, and I said that I would write his Saturday paper for him." She laughed and shook her head. "I should never listen to Gordon."

Gatewood only smiled and took another drink. Ellen took him by the arm. "But think, Jim! I actually attended his tutorial!" She let go of his arm, but she could not keep the enthusiasm from her voice. "I have been merely a dabbler in the Bard—it is Ralph who is enamored of him—but never before did I realize that Shakespeare could be such fun!" She subsided then, her face red. "I suppose I get carried away."

"Not at all," Gatewood said. "I like the way enthusiasm makes your eyes shine. Most chits only look that way when you pay them a compliment, and, even then, they are not sincere." His voice trailed off, and he leaned back against the settle, staring at the wall straight ahead. "How on earth did you fool your brother's instructor? And by the way, who is Ralph?"

"He is my younger brother," she said, the animation coming into her voice again. "He is taking lessons from the vicar, a prosing bagwig who thinks the capital of the United States is New York City."

"Ignorant clergy," Gatewood said. "They should all be lined up and shot. Your brother would be better served at Winchester or Eton."

"Papa will not hear of it. He says Ralph can do well enough with Mr. Snead." She sighed and took another cautious sip. "He has plans to send Ralph into the City to work with one of Mama's brothers—she has prodigious many. Gordon is here at University College because he is the oldest son, and Papa wants him to be a gentleman."

Gatewood laughed and then sobered immediately. "No, no, go on," he said. "From what I already suspect of the infamous Gordon, this is not his inclination."

"Indeed, no! He wants more than anything to take up with a cavalry regiment in Spain. But he promised Papa a year at Oxford, and provided he acquits himself well, he may yet buy his colors." Ellen set aside her cloak, wringing water out of it under the table. "Have you ever noticed, sir, that life is not fair?"

"It has come to my attention on occasion," he said. "Are there others in your family? Are they satisfied?"

Ellen smiled. "Horatia is prodigious happy, sir."

"Jim," he said automatically, not taking his eyes from her face, which she considered somewhat forward. She put his manners down to the ale he was steadily consuming.

"Jim, then," she amended. "She is soon to marry the son of a baronet." Her eyes widened as she looked at Gatewood. "He is worth almost four thousand a year. Imagine!"

"I cannot," Gatewood replied, his eyes as merry as hers. "So Horatia is happy."

"And what about Ellen?" he asked, when the silence stretched on and she returned to her own pint pot.

"Mama is determined that she will do as well as Horry, but Ellen is not so sure. She would prefer to map unknown continents," she said, her voice subdued. She thought a moment more and then set down the pint pot with some force. "Is marriage the destiny of women, sir, I ask you?"

"I fear it must be, Hermia," James Gatewood said, a smile playing around his lips. "We all have our little duties."

"Even you?"

"Even me."

Ellen sighed and reached for her cloak again. "I thought as much." She paused and stroked the sodden material. "But I have had my afternoon at University College, sir—Jim, and I have learned so much about Shakespeare!"

"Ah, yes, we have returned at last to the issue. How did you fool your instructor?" he asked again.

She peered at Gatewood, the admiration strong in her voice. "My goodness, sir, you are so good at keeping the thread of the conversation."

"Jim," he said again. "Well, of course, fair Hermia. That is what they teach us here at Oxford, don't you know. We learn to detect false argument, to build an unassailable case, and to be, above all else, objective." He ran a lazy finger down her cheek, even as she leaned away from him. "Not in a million years could any man alive mistake you for your brother."

"Do you know my brother?" she asked. "I am sorry for you."

"I . . . well, I know who he is now," he said.

If he was evasive, she overlooked it. Her eyes were merry as she also overlooked his forward behavior. "I sat in the shadows, sir, and to tell the truth, I think the old man was remarkably shortsighted. And, sir, he was so small!"

Jim sat up straight again, his eyes filled with remembrance.

"You can only be describing Hemphill. No bigger than a minute, and with a funny way of hunching up his shoulders to keep his gown from dragging?"

"The very same," she said, as she eyed the pint pot and pushed it away from her. "He was all the characters for *Midsummer Night's Dream*."

"And his Pyramus has a lisp," Jim continued, draining the rest of his ale. He struck a pose in the narrow booth. "'Thuth die I, thuth, thuth thuth.'"

Ellen joined in his laughter. "Yeth, you have hit it, thir," she said, a twinkle in her eyes to match his. "And now I must go."

He inclined his head to her. "So you should."

She reached for her cloak, draping it about her shoulders again and feeling the pocket to make sure that her notes at least were dry. "I could wish for Chesney's *Commentary*, but I believe that I can recall enough to write Gordon's paper."

Gatewood edged his way out of the booth, keeping between Ellen and the other patrons while she gathered her cloak tight about her again. She had taken no more than one step toward the door when Gatewood propelled her back into the booth, put his finger to his lips, and practically sat on her.

Mystified, she craned her neck around to see what had caused this strange behavior, spotted her brother, and ducked her head until only one eye peeked out from under Gatewood's arm.

She held her breath as Gordon crossed the floor, listing about as though the tavern itself moved. Supporting him was another student, dressed also in black and no more able to navigate the perils of a public house. Ellen let out a gusty sigh.

"Oh, if I could only wring his neck," she muttered. "Do get off me, Jim."

Gatewood moved slightly. "Wring his neck?" he whispered. "You are much too kind."

She only looked at him, noting that his eyes were the warmest shade of brown and quite close to her own. They even had little gold flecks in them.

"He is a ridiculous brother," she whispered back.

"I suppose he is." He turned around and watched the two young men cross to a distant bench and throw themselves down like rag dolls. He moved over to give her more room. "And here I have just rescued him and that other young chap—he is, regrettably, a relation of mine—from the pitfalls of London. Ingratitude."

They looked at each other. "It appears that my brother and your relative are keeping low company."

Gatewood smiled. "It does. That was where I was this weekend, by the way, Hermia. I went on a rescue mission to London to wrest two rascals from the Watch. Did you wonder why I did not follow up that clandestine box of chocolates?"

She took another glance at her brother, who leaned over the table, head resting against the wood, eyes closed. "They were delightful and you were very kind," she said as he ushered her from the tavern and into the rain again.

"But I do not understand why you did it," she added as he threw an arm over her shoulders and steered her around the larger puddles.

"I came to pay a visit, and a cheeky little maid informed me that you were suffering the indignity of

Miss Dignam's personal attention. In situations like that, only chocolates will do."

Before she could ask any more questions, he was hurrying her across the High Street. He paused under the awning of a greengrocer's to shake the rain from his gown. He held out his hand to Ellen, and she grasped it.

"I had better leave you here," he said. "I must return to the Bodleian where Machiavelli awaits." He made a face. "I confess to no love for the labyrinthine mind of the politician."

"Then why do you study him?" she asked. "Surely you can do whatever you wish. You are a man."

"No, actually, I cannot," he replied, after a moment's reflection. "I have made my own bargain with my late father." He sighed. "And my mother, who likes to worry." He shook her hand but did not release it. "Perhaps your brother and I are more alike than you know. Good day, my dear. Do stay dry."

She watched him cross the street again and ran after him. "Oh, wait!" she called.

He turned. "If you get a putrid sore throat or a racking cough, I will refuse to claim any responsibility beyond a posy or two on your grave."

She stopped in front of him, shy suddenly, wondering why she had pursued him. She held out her hand this time. "I just wanted to thank you again for the nicest afternoon I have ever spent," she said, her voice low. "Thank you for not betraying me in the library."

He bowed over her hand, and the rain from his hood dripped onto her wrist. "I will advise the librarian to engage the services of a good mouser. I will even return poor Chesney's *Commentary* to the stacks for you."

A cart rumbled by, splattering them both. Without a word, he lifted her onto the sidewalk and closer to him. "I can think of no greater misfortune to a father than that his dear daughter Ellen be struck and killed by a passing poultry cart when he thought her safe and bored at Miss Dignam's. It is not the sort of news that parents thrive on, I suspect," Gatewood said, his voice lively with amusement. "I suppose I must pay a visit to Miss Dignam's horrible sitting room when we are both dry and you do not look like a heroine out of a bad novel!"

"Promise?" she asked, releasing her grip on his hand.

"If I am able. I wish to read your paper before that ungrateful brother of yours acquires it."

"I will begin it tonight," she said and looked both ways before stepping into the street. "I have other questions, sir, many others! Who is Lord Chesney? I have something perfectly diverting to tell you about him, and I don't even know who he is." She leaned forward for one last confidence. "I think he is my benefactor. Imagine that!"

"I cannot. Of course, Chesney is a raving eccentric." Gatewood held up his hand to stop her flood of questions. "Even Chesney can wait, fair Hermia. Good day, for the second or third time."

Ellen laughed and waved her hand to him as she splashed across the street again and hurried to the shallow steps that led to the servants' entrance. When she looked back across the High, he was still standing there, watching her. He blew her a kiss as she ran down the stairs.

Becky Speed was watching for her at the window. When Ellen clambered down the stairs, the maid flung the door open wide and pulled her into the pantry. She thrust a bundle of clothes at Ellen and whispered at her to hurry and change.

"It is almost dinnertime, Miss," she said as she closed the door to the pantry and helped Ellen off with her soaking wet cloak.

Without a word, Ellen hurried out of her clothes. She gathered them into a sodden bundle and tiptoed up the back stairs. She just had time to throw them under her bed and rearrange herself and the pillows before Fanny opened the door.

Ellen snapped her eyes shut, wishing that she could look pale and interesting, instead of rosy from her exertions. She was mindful of her damp hair that curled so outrageously around her face. *My heart is pounding loud enough for Fanny to hear it*, she thought. She patted the lump of papers under her pillow, grateful that her notes were dry.

She made no comment as Fanny came closer to the bed. Even with her eyes shut tight, Ellen could almost see Fanny peering at her down the length of her long Bland nose. *And probably regarding me with vast suspicion*, Ellen thought. For a small moment she considered her years of diligent honesty and cast them aside.

She opened her eyes slowly. "Fanny, is that you?" she asked, her voice cracking as she sought for just the right tone between mere discomfort and Fatal Illness.

"Of course it is," Fanny snapped. "Who else would it be?" she said, her voice still harsh, but troubled now with a faint uncertainty. "Ellen?"

Ellen sighed and tugged at her damp hair. "Fanny, 'tis laudable perspiration. Thank heavens the fever has broke," she said.

Fanny took it all in. She gaped at Ellen's damp hair and the red spots of color in each cheek. "I had no idea," she said, lowering her voice. Her tones took on a reverent quality that almost made Ellen choke. "Are you feeling more the thing now, Ellen?"

Ellen nodded. With a gesture that she hoped was casual, she tugged the blankets up higher around her throat, covering her day dress. "Thank you for your concern, Fanny dear," she replied. "Please assure Miss Dignam that I will be right as a trivet by morning."

Fanny Bland was all solicitation. "Can I get you a tisane?" she offered. "May I bathe your temples with lavender water?"

Ellen shook her head and touched Fanny's hand. "Just let me rest in peace," she said, careful not to look Fanny in the eye. She coughed for good effect and closed her eyes again.

She could hear Fanny by the bed. She heard the rustle of skirts, a sudden sniffling, and was thoroughly ashamed. In another moment, Fanny closed the door quietly behind her.

Ellen, how can you stoop so low, she thought as she sat up in bed. *Depressing, boring, vindictive old Fanny Bland is actually worried about you.*

After a moment spent in minor repentance, Ellen stripped off her dress and leaped into her nightgown. She retrieved the notes from under her pillow and smoothed them out. She toweled her hair dry, felt pangs of hunger, and decided that her penance would include no dinner that night.

Besides, she considered as she flopped back on the bed with her arms flung wide, *I have such food for thought.* She lay there in the semidarkness, her mind busy on *Midsummer Night's Dream* and the whimsy of love.

Morning brought Miss Dignam to her bedside. Dutifully, Ellen—her fingers crossed under the covers—stuck out her tongue upon command and coughed as directed.

"You seem to be recovering nicely," Miss Dignam assured her. "Goodness, but you certainly gave our dear Fanny a start yesterday!" She shook her finger playfully in Ellen's face. "Now, you rest today. I am sure you can catch up with your embroidery tomorrow. We are exploring the variety of the French knot today. I feel that one of your mental acuity can easily conquer that subject tomorrow while we go on to daisy chains." She held up her hand when Ellen tried to speak. "No protests, my dear!"

"No, Miss Dignam," Ellen said.

After Miss Dignam left the room, Fanny followed in her wake with her bag of neatly arranged embroidery threads. When the door closed, Ellen sat cross-legged on her bed and spread out the closely written notes she had taken during the tutorial and in the library. Pages in hand, she bit back her disappointment about the *Commentary*. Her notes were thorough, as far as they went, but the page was blank after the mouse scare, when her pencil drew a line like a startled eyebrow across the rest of the sheet.

"I suppose Vicar Snead would tell me that is what comes of spurious scholarship," she muttered.

As she sat wondering what course to take now, a servant scratched at the door.

Becky Speed opened the door, a parcel in her hands. Her eyes danced with excitement as she held out the package to Ellen.

"Here you are, Miss Grimsley," she said, her voice breathless as though she had run up three flights of stairs. "You cannot imagine who this is from!"

"Lord Chesney?" Ellen asked.

Becky shook her head. "Oh, I do not think so. He didn't look much like a lord. No, it was that student who brought you the chocolates last week. There I was, beating out the hall rug over the front railing, when he runs across the High, saying something about being late for a tutorial, and tossed me this package."

Ellen pushed aside her notes. "It must be James Gatewood." She leaned toward Becky. "He is an original item, Becky, and heavens, I caused him such monstrous trouble yesterday."

Becky frowned and backed toward the door. "Perhaps it is some sort of incendiary device, ma'am. Perhaps you should not open it."

Ellen tugged off the brown paper. "Goose! He wasn't that angry!" She paused, the wrapping in her hands. "Goodness knows he could have been. No, he was rather sweet about the whole thing. Heavens knows why. When I think . . ."

She stopped, embarrassed, and looked at the books that came spilling from the wrapping. "Becky, it is Chesney's *Commentary*!" She opened the slim volume. "And look, it hasn't even been cut yet!"

A note fell from the book. "'Fair Hermia, if Miss Dignam's Select Female Academy is as disapproving of mice as it is of all forms of scholarship and original thought, you will not be interrupted as you study this work,'" she read. "'The other book should provide further insight.'"

"What a kind man," Ellen said as she opened the other volume in her lap. "Becky, I do not think he can afford to give me books. He does not appear entirely prosperous."

"There is more writing on the back of that note," Becky said. Ellen turned it over. "'I hope you have not discarded your breeches and student gown. The larger volume must be returned to me at All Souls. Behave yourself. Jim.'"

Becky sucked in her breath. "Cheeky sort, Miss Grimsley."

"Not at all," Ellen protested. "I would say that he is more like a big brother." She considered Gordon in all his drunken splendor, sprawled across the table in the tavern. "At least, the kind of big brother that does one some good."

The servant came closer again and looked about the room. "Do you still have . . . ?"

"The breeches and cloak? Oh, my, yes. I hung them in the dressing room far in the back. Fanny will only find them if she pokes her long nose amongst my possessions, and why should she?"

Ellen put the books on the desk and turned back to her notes. She rested her cheek on her hand. "I will return the book, Becky, but then I will be done with this business. It can only get me in trouble of the worst kind. Then I would be dragged home to a purgatory of addressing wedding invitations and listening to Horry moan and groan each time some piddling little detail went awry."

Becky's face fell. "But don't you love weddings, Miss Grimsley?"

"I daresay I might someday, but Horatia's is rather a trial." She opened the book, but her mind was far away. It was more than just foolish, brainless Horatia. The trial was also Mama, looking her over so carefully when she thought Ellen was not aware, wondering if there was such an advantageous alliance in her younger daughter's future.

"Bother it," she muttered as she pulled out her letter opener and slit the pages of Chesney's *Commentary*. In another moment, she was deep in Shakespeare's enchanted Athenian forest, smiling over Lord Chesney's wise remarks and wondering about the man who wrote them. By the end of the day, when Gordon's essay had become a rough reality, she had created in her mind a picture of her benefactor.

He must be a kindly older man, probably someone with children of his own that he had seen through the trials of love, she thought as she lit the lamp and continued copying her draft onto better paper. *He can only be one of Aunt Shreve's friends. Papa doesn't know anyone this intelligent.*

She put down her pen. *James Gatewood says that Lord Chesney is a fellow at All Souls, so how can he be old? It is all too strange,* she decided.

She sat in her room, waiting for Gordon to announce his presence below. James Gatewood had promised he would visit her and read the paper, so she waited for him too. No Gordon, no Gatewood.

"Men are selfish beasts," she decided as she tied on her sleeping cap and blew out the candle.

Chesney's *Commentary* lay on the desk beside her bed. Moonglow streaked across it, setting the gold lettering on the spine shimmering. Ellen picked it up, settling the book on her stomach. "But for this excellent bit of insight, I forgive you, Jim Gatewood."

Gatewood did not darken Miss Grimsley's door the next day. Ellen's mind wandered through her geography teacher's tightlipped description of the French countryside. During the interminable lecture, which dealt more on the evils of Napoleon than on the geography of France, she was tempted to ask why it was necessary to be so censorious about flora and fauna. *Surely one cannot blame flowering shrubs for the rise of That Beast From Corsica,* she thought.

She fared no better in embroidery, tangling her threads until Fanny was forced to desert her own neat

114

sampler and help her. Ellen gritted her teeth, smiled sweetly at Fanny, and edged her chair closer to the window. She could see the spire of All Souls, located as it was just across the street. She was no wiser about the whereabouts of James Gatewood.

His gown rumpled as though he had slept in it, his eyes bulging from the exertion of running, Gordon darkened her door that evening. She met him in the sitting room under the agate eyes and wooden countenance of Miss Dignam. Without a word of greeting, he snatched the manuscript from her lap. He rifled through the pages and then sighed with relief, flinging himself into a chair.

"Ten pages! Thank the Almighty!" he exclaimed. "I had forgotten to tell you that the paper had to be between eight and ten pages." He counted the pages again, smiled, and stuffed them in his pocket.

Ellen started forward in her chair, mindful of Miss Dignam's eyes on her. "But don't you wish to read what I have written, Gordon?"

"Heavens no," he said and shook his head. "I am sure I could not understand one word, anyway. All that matters is that it is ten pages long." He leaned forward then and tugged at the short curls framing her face, curls she had spent all afternoon taming, in the hopes that someone would arrive to appreciate them. "Someday, I will do you a great favor, sister," he said and then laughed. "I'll start by telling you that your curls make you look like a poodle! Really, El."

She stuck out her tongue at him, and he laughed and leaped out of his chair in pretend fear. He dashed to the door, ignoring the quelling look Miss Dignam cast in his direction as she smacked down her playing cards.

Ellen hurried to his side. "At least let me know how it goes when you read the paper, you beast! You owe me that."

He tweaked another curl. "I will report promptly. El, did you do all those curls for me, or do you have a beau already? Someone stuffy and studious?"

"Of course not," she denied, her face rosy. "I did them for . . . for Lord Chesney!" She laughed at the look on his face and pushed him. "I am beginning to wonder if my benefactor really exists. Well, go on, if you must."

He left, after a kiss in the air by her cheek and a wave in her general direction. Ellen walked slowly back to her room. *I will never compose another page for so ungrateful a brother*, she thought as she ran her hand along the stair railing. *I wonder how many other select females have felt so full of the dismals.*

She would never attempt the Bodleian again, as much as it beckoned. She sat at her desk, chin in hand, and gazed across the street to the spires of Oxford.

It might as well be on the moon, she thought, *for all the good it does me.*

Chapter 6

ELLEN STEELED HERSELF FOR AN-
other dreadful weekend. She lay in bed and
watched Fanny primping in front of the mirror,
raving on about the treat in store for her.

"Really, Ellen, if you had paid more attention
to your embroidery this week, I am sure that Miss
Dignam would have permitted you a stroll down the
High Street with an unexceptionable beau."

She paused and turned around, her smile arch.
"Provided you could find an unexceptionable beau,
Ellen. I have my doubts."

She turned back to the mirror, and Ellen stuck her
tongue out. "I am not sure that it is to my taste to be
shepherded about in the company of a beau and a servant, not to mention the other couples in attendance,"
Ellen replied, keeping her voice light.

Fanny refused to be ruffled. She shook her head

and clucked her tongue at her reflection. "Ellen, you are a faster little piece than I ever thought. Countenance, Ellen, countenance."

With a wave of her gloved hand, she was gone. Ellen threw her pillow at Fanny as the door closed and then pulled the covers over her head. She thought about home and even about Thomas Cornwell. At least if she were home, they could stroll about the gardens or play cards in the library without the ubiquitous presence of a maid or footman. And if he was poor company, well, at least he was company, and she knew his faults.

She could ride when she chose and walk to the village with Ralph, talking about Great Ideas. Here there was nothing but the prospect of another day spent at the embroidery hoop.

She was almost asleep again when Becky Speed knocked and stuck her head inside the room. "Miss Grimsley, come quick! You have a visitor."

"Go away," Ellen said, her voice muffled under the bed clothes.

"It is Mr. James Gatewood, and he has never looked so good," Becky said. She ran into the room and pulled the covers off Ellen, who sat up in surprise.

"You mean his hair is combed?" she asked and then laughed. "Well, I suppose such a momentous event calls for my presence, if for no other reason than to verify it."

She dressed quickly, running a comb through her tousled curls, grateful for once for naturally curly hair. She patted on her lavender cologne while Becky buttoned her up the back. "He said he didn't have much time," the servant said.

Ellen hurried down the stairs and threw herself into the sitting room.

James Gatewood whirled around from his contemplation of the view out the front window and put up a hand to stop her. "Whoa, fair Hermia! Where's the fire?"

Ellen twinkled her eyes at him. "Becky said you did not have much time, and I wanted to see how you looked with your hair combed."

He threw back his head and laughed until Ellen blushed. He turned around slowly, for her benefit. "Every hair in place, my dear. Note that the gown is pressed and I have on a starched collar." He put his hand over his heart. "I promised my mother that I would go to such exertions occasionally. It was one of the terms of the agreement."

"Agreement?" she asked.

It was Gatewood's turn to blush. "I did not really mean to mention that, but here it is: I promised Mama a year only at All Souls, and then I would go into the . . ." He paused and frowned, as if searching for the right words. He brightened. ". . . into the family business."

Ellen sat down and patted the seat beside her. Gatewood joined her, and she noticed that he smelled quite pleasantly of French cologne. "And what, sir, is the family business?"

"Horse trading," he replied, not batting an eye. "And window dressing," he added.

"Such odd occupations," she said.

"Someone must do them," he replied. "It is my lot

in life to be a horse trader and a window dresser."

He regarded her for a moment, and she was aware how patched-up was her own hurried appearance. "I slept late," she said in self-defense.

But there was nothing in his eyes of complaint. It was a warm expression he fixed on her, one that made her stomach jump a little.

"I think you are charming," he said, "even with the wrong shoes on, and the marks of the bedspread still on your face." Ellen gasped and looked down at her feet, where one brown shoe and one black one peeked out from under her dress. She touched her cheek. "Oh, dear!"

He leaned back on the couch, stretching out his legs, enjoying the moment. Without thinking, Ellen socked him in the stomach. "You are no gentleman!" she protested, laughing. "You remind me more of my brothers, and I will treat you that way."

"Brothers, eh?" he teased, when he could breathe again. "I don't know who to pity more: you or them."

The bells of Oxford sounded the hour. Gatewood glanced out the window. "I would love to discuss your family, but I am late. Do you have a copy of your *Midsummer Night's Dream* paper? I would love to read it."

"I did not have time to make another copy."

Gatewood shook his head. "My dear Miss Grimsley, always keep a copy. That is the first rule of the writer."

"It is only a paper for Gordon," she protested.

"Still and all, madam, scholarship demands it,

and there is no telling who might try to gyp you." He rose and put on his gloves again. "I shall be forced to attend Gordon's University College reading this morning then, won't I?"

Ellen stood up too, careful to keep her shoes under her dress. "I wish I could accompany you."

He looked down at her, a lazy smile playing about his face. "I wish you could too." The smile vanished. "It seems unfair."

He took her hand and squeezed it. She looked up at him in surprise and then smiled her sunniest smile.

"It doesn't matter." She let him hold her hand. "I am going to cry uncle soon and ask Papa to come and get me." Unexpected tears filled her eyes, replacing the smile. "Oxford is not what I thought it was, and I was a silly nod to harbor expectations."

"You are leaving?" he said, his voice as serious as hers. He only tightened his grip on her hand. "Do reconsider, Hermia. The Bodleian will be so dull with only the mice to entertain me."

She smiled then and turned loose his hand, which she was gripping just as tight. "Still, sir, it has made me wiser."

He was standing so close that she could have kissed him. The thought made her blush again, even as she wondered where such an idea had come from. She stepped back and clasped her hands behind her.

"You'll be late to the lecture, Jim," she said, her voice soft.

"So I shall be." He kissed her cheek. "Courage,

fair Hermia," he said, and quoted, "'Do not doubt that saints attend thee.'"

"*Hamlet*," she said, "and badly altered, I might add."

He laughed and touched her cheek where he had kissed her. And then he was gone. She stood in the doorway until he vanished down the alley that led to the interior of Oxford and University College.

Fanny and the other students returned before noon from their stroll about Oxford, rosy from the cold and glowing with news. Ellen looked up from her embroidery as Fanny entered the room. Fanny removed her hat and unbuttoned her pelisse. She went to the fireplace to warm her hands.

"Guess who we saw running and jumping about on Cornmarket Street like a rabid dog?" she said at last.

"The Duke of Wellington," Ellen said promptly, her eyes on her embroidery.

"Silly! It was your brother!" Fanny shook her head in disapproval at the memory. "He accosted me, Ellen, and grabbed me by the shoulders and said he had news for you. Imagine." She looked down her long nose at Ellen. "Perhaps someone taught him how to write his own name or tally beyond his fingers."

Ellen tightened her lips, counted to ten, and then smiled sweetly into her roommate's smug face. "Capital! Perhaps we should recommend Oxford to your brother Edwin, so he can learn these skills too. It must be grievous indeed for Edwin to have to take off his shoes to do higher math at the Grain Exchange."

Fanny turned white about the mouth. "You're

going to wish you hadn't said that," she exclaimed and then cast about for something else. She raised her chin. "At least I, unlike you, am to be a bridesmaid for my dear Edwin and your featherbrain of a sister. Too bad such ignorance seems to run in your family!" She grabbed up her own embroidery and flounced from the room, slamming the door after her.

"Sticks and stones may break my bones," Ellen muttered. She refused to let her mind dwell on Fanny's rudeness. "Or my own," she said out loud, grinning to herself. "That was a repartee worthy of Ralph."

She looked out the window, wondering when Gordon would appear, wondering if her paper had really been such a success.

In a few moments, she saw him meandering along, hands shoved deep into his pockets, whistling. She tapped on the window to get his attention. When he looked up, he pointed down the street. Ellen shook her head, but he only shrugged his shoulders and grinned at her, pantomiming a pint of ale in one hand.

"Drat you, Gordon," she said as she ran down the stairs and out the front door. She took him by the arm. "Not one step farther until you tell me how it went," she said, out of breath.

Gordon looked around him. "Really, El, how does this look?" he complained. "I was merely going to celebrate the successful outcome of this morning's work," he said. "And then I was going to come back to Miss Dragon's Female Hothouse and tell all."

Ellen tugged him back to the academy. "That

won't do, Gordon. I know you too well. Tell me first, and then go to the Cock and Hen."

He gave her a look of compounded suspicion, surprise, and hurt feelings. "Really, El. How did you know it was the Cock and Hen?" he accused, assuming that exalted air he used on occasion when he wanted to remind her that she was the younger sibling. "El, one would think you had been there yourself. You're not keeping low company here in Oxford, are you?" he asked on the attack. "On the sly from Miss Dignam?"

Even though his dart hit home, she refused to acknowledge it to him. "The lowest company I keep is yours, brother," she said. "Now come in here. You owe me that."

When she released her grip on his gown, Gordon Grimsley carefully shook out its folds and followed her into the school, muttering something about little sisters who haven't a penny's worth of dignity to their name.

He followed her into the parlor, head high. When she closed the door behind them, he grabbed her and whirled her about, setting her down again and kissing her cheek with a loud smack. "We did it, El. My paper was a smashing success!"

"Whose paper?" she asked quietly, but he did not hear her as he continued to dance about the room with her. He stopped finally and flopped down on the settee.

"El, you should have been there. I rose to read my paper, and everyone was rummaging around and making vulgar noises. You know, the usual bits of nonsense at the Saturday readings."

She didn't know, but she nodded. "Go on."

He rose to his feet and struck a pose by the fireplace. "By the second page, everyone was silent," he said, his eyes bright. "Even the dons and fellows were hanging on my every word."

Ellen sighed with pleasure. "Magnificent, Gordon," she said.

He bowed. "It was, rather." He hurried forward then and grasped her hands. "But the best part was the end, El. When the last word died away, the room was dead silent. And then everyone began to applaud."

"No!" she gasped, her eyes wide, the color rushing to her cheeks.

"Yes! And they stood up!" He threw himself in the chair across from her. "I never knew I could do so well!"

She frowned at her brother, who lolled in the chair, head back, eyes closed, a silly smile on his face. "I am the one who wrote the paper, Gordon," she reminded him.

He opened his eyes. "Oh, yes, quite," he said. "Wish you could have been there, dear, to see my triumph."

She chose to overlook his enthusiasm and wondered for only a moment about the depression that settled over her.

It lasted only long enough for Gordon to sit upright and leap to his feet again. "El, here's the best part! Lord Chesney was there, and he singled me out for a conversation!"

"No!" she exclaimed again, her hands to her face. "Gordon, for heaven's sake, tell me what he looks like. What did he say?"

Gordon looked at her and shrugged. "Well, he was tall and had brown hair."

Ellen pounded the armchair. "Can't you be more specific? That could be almost anyone in England!"

"I suppose you are right," he said and smiled. "He really looked like a lord."

Ellen sighed and took a turn about the room. "Gordon, you have never met a lord. How would you know?"

"Well, he had a certain air about him."

"So does the village tannery back home, Gordon."

He tried to stare her into capitulation, but he blinked first. "He had a Londoner's accent, I think. Sounded like a real aristo." He frowned and tried to think. "Black robe . . . what else is there?" He brightened. "He did have a rather magnificent gold watch fob."

Ellen sat down beside him. "So does James Gatewood, Gordon, and he is nothing out of the ordinary. Far from it, in fact."

Gordon grinned and tweaked her curls before she could draw away. "Silly! What do you expect here at Oxford? That Lord Chesney will wear his House of Lords getup or employ slave girls to dance in front of him and toss out rose petals? Ellen, sometimes you are almost as ridiculous as Horatia. Or me," he added, to soften the blow.

She took his words in good grace and considered their merit. What did she expect, after all? "And I suppose you will tell me that he puts his trousers on one leg at a time."

"He probably does, El," he said and put his arm around her. He leaned closer. "I think he must tie his own neckcloths too. Between you and me, it didn't look so expert."

He glanced toward the door that led to freedom and the tavern, and ran his tongue over his lips. Ellen tugged on his arm. "One thing more, Gordon, before you abandon yourself to the Cock and Hen—or whatever that place is called—you said he had some conversation with you."

He slapped his forehead. "Oh, my, did he ever!" He took both of her hands in his. "El, you need to write me another paper."

She withdrew her hands from his grasp as though they burned.

"Not this sister, Gordon! I swore I would not do that again." She eyed him until he blinked again. "Particularly since you seem to forget who wrote that first paper."

She might as well not have bothered to speak. "El, he told me I should write a paper on *Measure for Measure.*" Gordon rose and took his stand by the fireplace again. "He wants to know what I think about it! El, is it a play?"

"Yes, you block, it is a play," she said quietly. "Perhaps it is time you learned to write your own papers at University College."

His eyes grew round as he stared at her in horror. "Ellen! Don't abandon me now! It's just one more paper, and soon the winter vacation will be upon us and maybe, just maybe, Papa will change his mind and buy me a pair of colors."

When she made no reply, he fell on both knees and

clasped his hands together. "Sister, have a heart!" He thought a moment and sidled closer to her on his knees. "Didn't you just tell me that you owed Lord Chesney for your own improved treatment here?"

"I suppose I did, Gordon," she said at last. "Although what that has to do with . . ."

Gordon Grimsley had no time for sisterly riders. He let go of her hands and leaped to his feet. "I knew you would not fail me! I promise to attend my tutorial and take exemplary notes this time."

She nodded, already regretting her decision. "At the very least, you can give me back my *Midsummer Night's Dream* paper."

He shook his head. "I wish that I could, but Lord Chesney asked me for it, and what could I do?"

"What indeed?" she asked. "Gordon, you are the biggest flat that ever drew breath. Yes, I will write your stupid paper for the honor of the Grimsleys, and you had better hang on to the original this time."

He kissed her cheek. "Ellen, you are a great goer! Remind me to do something nice for you sometime."

The look she gave him sent him backing toward the door. He had almost escaped into the hall when she called to him.

"Gordon, I want you to take a note to James Gatewood at All Souls," she said, hurrying to the escritoire. She wrote quickly. "Tell him that I will return that one book that he loaned me, and tell him that I have a few questions about *Measure for Measure*. Maybe he will help me."

"I don't know, El," he said doubtfully, the letter

between his fingers. "Gatewood doesn't sound at all the thing. Didn't you tell me that he comes from a long line of horse traders? I know that Papa is horse-mad, but I am not sure he would approve."

"Find someone to deliver that note, or I won't write your paper," she said.

He gave her a wounded look. "Lord, El, you can be difficult. Why did I never see this before? Very well, I will deliver it to the porter at All Souls, but that is all. Suppose I run into Lord Chesney there? He would ask me something about Shakespeare, and then we would be in such a fix."

"No, Gordon, *you* would be in such a fix," she amended pointedly.

He could not have heard her. He opened the door and stood there in the hallway, shaking his head over the perfidy of sisters until she wanted to yank the hairs out of his head one at a time.

As he regarded her, the gleam came back into his eyes. "El, you should have heard the applause I got," he said as he closed the door behind him.

"Ungrateful wretch," she muttered under her breath.

She took the noontime meal in thoughtful silence, considering *Measure for Measure*, and wondering why Lord Chesney would request a paper on that play, of all plays. She had never read it and had only the vaguest notion of the plot.

After luncheon, she hurried to the academy library, a skimpy affair with one rack of books that were all split leather bindings and moldy paper.

Measure for Measure was not numbered among the Shakespeare collection.

Miss Dignam, noting the library door open—a rare thing in her academy—came into the room with a glare of suspicious inquiry in her face.

Ellen had perched herself on a stool, her knees drawn up to her chin. She brightened to see Miss Dignam and got down off her roost.

"Miss Dignam, tell me please, does the academy possess a copy of *Measure for Measure*?"

Miss Dignam had shut the door behind her. "Miss Grimsley, that is most decidedly not a play for select females," she said, lowering her voice to a hiss. She gestured toward the bookcase. "I will tolerate *Romeo and Juliet* because, heaven knows, young girls need to see what happens when they disobey their parents . . ."

"I don't think that is precisely the message Shakespeare intended," Ellen murmured.

Miss Dignam frowned down at her. "It is the message I intend, Miss Grimsley!" she declared. "*Hamlet* is tolerable, I suppose, because who among us will ever actually meet a Dane? And *Macbeth*, well, *Macbeth* is questionable, what with ladies walking about in their nightgowns. But there will be no *Measure for Measure* in this academy," she concluded, shaking her head vigorously at the thought. "I honestly do not know where you get your ideas, Miss Grimsley."

Ellen threw up her hands in exasperation. "Miss Dignam, have you ever read *Measure for Measure*?"

Miss Dignam sucked in her breath as though she had been shot. "Of course not! I have it on good authority that it is no play for a lady to read, and that is enough for me!"

Ellen was forced to listen to the improving tirade that followed. With her fingers crossed behind her back, she promised never to stray into those less-accepted works of the Bard and beat a hasty retreat when Miss Dignam paused for breath.

Miss Dignam followed her into the hall. "Miss Grimsley, I recommend a turn about the garden to work off your excess zeal for scholarship of a questionable sort."

"Yes, Miss Dignam," she replied and hurried upstairs before Miss Dignam dredged up another argument.

Fanny was seated at the dressing table, examining the spots on her face up close in the mirror. She leaped back when Ellen bounded into the room.

"Can't you knock?" she protested.

"It's my room too, Fanny," Ellen said over her shoulder as she hurried into the dressing room she shared with her roommate.

She pulled aside her clothes to find the scholar's gown and the shirt and breeches. She peered closer, a frown on her face. Surely she had not left that shirt all bunched up like that. She thought she remembered shaking it out before putting it on the hook behind her other clothes, but there it was, thrown in a ball on the floor of the closet. She put it on the hook again and grabbed up her sewing basket.

To her relief, Fanny was gathering up her embroidery. "Some of us have been invited to Lady Willa

Casterby's apartment to complete our assignment." She smiled in triumph. "Too bad that you were not included."

"Yes, a pity," Ellen agreed, flopping down on her bed. "I do not know how I shall endure this slight." She laughed and rested on one elbow. "Think how convenient this will make it for you to talk about me. Think how I would retard the conversation, were I there."

Fanny uttered an unladylike oath she never learned at Miss Dignam's Select Female Academy and slammed the door behind her. Ellen was off the bed and back into the dressing room as soon as Fanny's footsteps receded down the hall. She took off her dress, pulled on the shirt and breeches, and put her dress on again.

Ellen looked in the mirror and laughed. "I am as fubsy as Fanny, with all these clothes on," she said. She threw a shawl around her shoulders to hide the lumps and then folded the scholar's robe as small as she could and stuffed it in her embroidery basket. She snatched up the book she was to return.

Becky Speed was polishing silver in the servants' quarters when Ellen tiptoed silently down the stairs. She looked up in surprise. "Miss Grimsley! I thought you said you were not going to try that again!"

Ellen made a face as she struggled to unbutton her dress. "I was not, but Gordon has found himself backed into a corner and needs my help. This one last time," she finished, biting off each word.

Becky finished unbuttoning her. "You may say that, but I think you like writing those papers."

Ellen nodded. "You have found me out, Becky. I suppose I do."

In another moment, she was wrapped in the scholar's gown and across the High Street. She took a deep breath and turned the handle on the small door that opened onto All Souls quadrangle.

She crossed the quad quickly, head down, hardly allowing herself a look around at the peaceful grandeur that was All Souls in early December. She ran into the hall and stepped up to the porter's tall desk, standing on tiptoe and keeping her head down at the same time.

If the porter was surprised to see an undergraduate before him, and one so short, he did not let on. He scarcely glanced up from the paper he was reading and inclined his head in her direction.

"Yes, young master?" he inquired mildly.

"The way to James Gatewood's apartment, please," she said, her voice gruff.

"Gatewood. Gatewood. Oh, yes, Gatewood!" the porter said, a smile wreathing his face. "Up the stairs and to the right. Look for the nameplate."

Ellen nodded and ran up the shallow steps, holding her breath when a group of scholars passed her. They were speaking in Latin. She rolled her eyes. *I have died and gone to heaven*, she thought. *Surely there is no place in all of England like All Souls, maybe not in all the world.*

One of the men said something in Latin and the rest laughed.

Ellen hugged herself. Only Ralph would

understand how exciting it was to be in a place where scholars joked in Latin.

She took the hall at a half-trot, looking at the nameplates, exclaiming to herself over the viscounts and earls and other distinguished names she recognized from the scraps of London news that occasionally made their way into the Grimsley household.

James Gatewood. There it was, an ordinary piece of paper stuck in the holder. She peered closer. The ink looked hardly dry. *Trust James to forget about such details*, she thought as she timidly knocked.

The door opened and James stood there, dressed in a shabby shirt without a neckcloth and breeches that looked slept in. His waistcoat was unbuttoned and his shoes were off.

"Hermia," he said, keeping his voice low. "To what do I owe this pleasure? Come in, come in."

She hurried into the room. "I sent Gordon with a message," she stammered, her face red.

He shrugged, a smile on his face. "I think we know Gordon well enough to suspect the outcome of that, my dear. I am glad I am here."

Ellen looked about her in delight. Books filled the room, filling each bookcase to overflowing. They rested on the broad window ledges and jostled each other on every flat surface. The desk was covered with papers, the wastebasket crammed to capacity.

"You are fearsome untidy," she said, clutching the book she was returning, as if afraid to turn it loose in this room.

"It is the despair of my mother," he agreed. "But

what is the point of putting away a book, when you know you will only be needing it again sometime next week, or the month after?"

She laughed. "I can't imagine, James." She held out the book to him. "I wanted to return this book, as you requested. I have kept Chesney's *Commentary*, because you said I should."

"So I did," he said, taking the book from her and adding it to the pile on the chair by the desk. "By the way, I heard your brother's presentation this morning. That essay was something fine, indeed." He shook his head. "You should have seen Gordon basking in all that acclaim."

He noted the mulish look in her eyes. "Acclaim that should have been yours?"

She nodded and then laughed in embarrassment. "But that wasn't why I wrote the paper, Jim, and not why I have come now."

James gestured to a chair by the fireplace, removing the books in it and sitting down across from her. "Why have you come, Hermia? I hoped you would, but I did not expect to see you, not really."

She clasped her hands in front of her. "I know I should not be here, but the worst thing has happened, James."

"There was an earthquake, and no one told me?"

She laughed, despite her agitation. "Are you never serious?"

"I am usually too serious," he said firmly, "except where you are concerned. And if I get too serious, I will send you into the Bodleian again to hunt for mice so I can have another laugh."

135

"It is Lord Chesney, James," she said when he had fallen into his familiar pattern of just looking at her in silence, his eyes appreciative. "He was at the lecture too, and he has asked my looby brother for another paper!"

"Such a troublesome man is Lord Chesney," Gatewood commented. "It is a wonder that any of us tolerate him."

He went to a cabinet by the fireplace and removed some cheese. He sliced it and put it onto a cheese fork and handed it to her. "Turn that slowly while I toast the bread."

She did as he asked, watching the cheese change color and begin to bubble. In another minute, she slid the cheese onto the toast he held out to her and accepted it gratefully. He poured her some tea and then toasted some cheese for himself.

"Now, is that better?" he asked when she finished and was sitting cross-legged by the fire.

"Oh, much, Jim, but it has not solved my problem. I am supposed to write a commentary on *Measure for Measure*, and I daren't chance another tutorial, or try the Bodleian. I don't even have a copy of the play, and there is not one at Miss Dignam's. In fact, she was aghast that I would think of reading it." She looked at him as he sat beside her in front of the fireplace. "What is the matter with *Measure for Measure*?"

He went to a particularly abundant bookcase and stood there a long moment, his eyes skimming each row. He pulled several more books from the shelf.

"You may borrow these, Ellen, and this copy of the play. They might answer some of your questions." He chuckled. "Knowing your mind, though, I expect they will only raise more questions, but that is the essence of scholarship, so we shall be satisfied."

She opened the first book, which was stenciled with a heavy crest and the word Chesney scrawled across the top. She looked at him, her eyes puzzled.

He took it from her, swallowed, and returned it without batting an eye. "Dear me, it appears that I have acquired some of the mysterious Lord Chesney's books. We have been known to raid each other's libraries."

She opened another book and another. All were stenciled with the same crest. She closed the books and raised laughing eyes at him. "You are a bit of a rascal, Jim! Don't you think you ought to return his books?"

He crossed his heart. "As soon as you have finished with them, I pledge that they will be returned to Lord Chesney. There, is that good enough, you little Puritan?"

She nodded. "I would hate for Lord Chesney to lose track of his books. Perhaps you should check his shelves for books of your own, James. Ralph and I are forever getting our books mixed up."

"I will do it this very afternoon," he said. "Of course, Chesney is such a raving eccentric that he probably won't even remember that he loaned them."

She laughed and hugged the books to her. Her eyes grew troubled then, and he sat down beside her on the floor again.

"What's the matter, my dear?" he asked, his voice soft.

"I am so tired of getting all my information

secondhand. What am I supposed to look for in *Measure for Measure*?" she asked. "What is there that Gordon is supposed to discover?"

Gatewood settled himself against the dressed stones of the fireplace, where he could see her better. "Merely whatever speaks to you about the play, fair Hermia," he said. "It is called one of Shakespeare's 'problem' plays. It is the story of sexual blackmail, simply put. See if you can uncover a new way of looking at it, something no critic has ever even considered." He shifted slightly, resting his arm on his knee. "I wonder that Lord Chesney would choose such a topic, but then, he is a different sort of fellow."

"You know him well?" she asked, her face fiery red from Gatewood's plain words.

"About as well as one person can know another," he replied, moving away from the warmth of the fireplace. "We have always been friends. He's a bit of a rascal, I think, but harmless enough."

She was silent a moment, staring into the flames. "I will write this one paper, and then no other, as I am leaving," she said. "One would almost think that Lord Chesney engineered this to keep me here, with the assignment of this paper to Gordon."

"I did not know you were leaving," he said quickly. "Didn't you tell me that . . . that Lord Chesney had smoothed things over at Miss Dignam's?"

She shrugged. "I am enjoying my geography class, thanks to his lordship, but I want more, Jim. The other girls laugh at me, and I begin to think I am as much a raving eccentric as Chesney himself."

He smiled and took her hand. "What is it you really want, Ellen?"

She looked around from habit, to make sure that no one was listening, and he chuckled. "I want to map the world, Jim! I want to ride in an ascension balloon all across Europe and visit every country there is, learning languages and customs. And when I am done, I am going to write the most marvelous books about what I have seen. Books for young ladies who aren't as fortunate as I am." She stopped, embarrassed. "Well, you did ask."

"So I did," he replied and gazed into the fireplace. He looked at her, his eyes piercing. "And what if you cannot do any of these things?"

Ellen rested her chin on her knees. "I will probably just return home and marry Thomas Cornwell, or someone else my Papa has in mind, someone with horses and property and a seat on the Grain Exchange. That's probably what will happen. I'm not a fool."

Gatewood was silent then, his face unreadable. Ellen watched him for a moment and then got to her feet. She touched the books in her arms. "But right now, I will write about Shakespeare and probably remember these days as the best of my life. Thank you, James Gatewood."

She went to the door and let herself out while he still sat on the floor. She was at the top of the stairs when he bounded out of the room, grabbed her around the waist, and kissed her.

She didn't struggle to get away, because she didn't want to. She let him kiss her and kissed him back, wishing that her arms were not full of Shakespeare.

He stepped back from her. "That is for luck, Ellen," he said, his voice unsteady. "Make it a wonderful paper."

Hands in his pockets, he backed down the hall and into his room again. She heard him whistling before he closed the door.

Chapter 7

HE BEGAN *MEASURE FOR MEASURE*
in earnest the following morning. When geography was over, and she had learned all she
cared to know about the exports of Portugal, Ellen ignored the summons to luncheon and seated herself at
her desk.

Chin in hand, she gazed out the window to the
spires of All Souls across the street. *If I were to tell James
Gatewood that I had just come from an hour's enlightenment on the kinds and varieties of cork and its implications in the society we live in, I could probably have
heard him laughing from here to All Souls*, she thought.
Scholarship is strangely served at Miss Dignam's.

And then she thought no more of James Gatewood,
because thinking of him made her blush.

How extremely odd it was that he had kissed
her. She could fathom no reason for it, not really. He

knew she was the daughter of a squire, a man of some substance in the shire. Ellen stirred restlessly in her chair and opened the play before her. Wasn't James Gatewood descended from a long line of window dressers and horse traders? Surely he could not think himself in any way eligible. She knew that a certain number of openings in some of the colleges were saved for poor students, but he was not in the same class with her.

She closed the book again, considering the matter. As she had created her own fiction about Lord Chesney, she could do the same for Gatewood. He was probably an only son, whose proud but respectable yeoman family had scrimped and saved for years to afford him this one year at All Souls. She sighed. Perhaps it was a parish effort. She knew that appointments to All Souls were rare, indeed. Perhaps Gatewood's entire parish had banded together to see that he received this chance to make something of himself.

She frowned. It did not fadge. Although he generally looked undeniably rumpled, his clothes were of excellent quality, and there was nothing seedy about him. His personal library was huge, and he was a friend of Lord Chesney.

Ellen brightened again and reopened the book before her. Perhaps James Gatewood was another of Lord Chesney's projects. It would be so like Lord Chesney in his bounteous eccentricity to help a poor but honest son of his retainers.

Lord Chesney. Now there is an unknown quantity, indeed, she thought. *I know only that he is a peculiar eccentric who loves the plays of Shakespeare. He has taken it upon himself to interest himself in the Grimsley family. Beyond that, I have nothing but idle speculation. I don't even know what he looks like*, she thought, as Lord Chesney crossed the stage of her mind and followed Jim Gatewood into the wings.

The boards were cleared for Shakespeare.

She read rapidly, almost finished the play while the others were at the dining table, and then stretched out for the repairing nap that Miss Dignam considered essential before her minions tackled the intricacies of embroidery.

Fanny Bland had eyed her with vast suspicion as she flounced into the room they shared and laid herself down. Ellen ignored her, beyond a glance and an unvoiced question at Fanny's self-satisfied expression.

It was an expression she remembered from their shared childhood, when the older Fanny had taken such delight in seeing that Ellen was constantly in trouble. Horatia had always been content to follow after the insufferable Edwin and listen to him prose on and on about horses and the proper management of a Cotswold farm. Fanny had made her own fun by tripping up Ellen with her infernal tattling.

The memory rankled, even though they were too old for that sort of childish devilment. Pointedly, Ellen turned her chair slightly to avoid Fanny's smirk.

She was unprepared for embroidery and had to endure Miss Dignam's icy stares and the laughter of the other girls as she struggled to follow the simplest instructions. Her mind was full of the trials of Isabella and her impetuous brother, Claudio, arrested by Angelo, a petty bureaucrat. As her eyes paid attention to Miss Dignam's explanation of feather-stitching, her mind was full of Isabella's awful dilemma and the price Angelo wanted from her for Claudio's life.

I would never surrender my virginity for the safety of my brother, she thought, red-faced, as she fumbled with the threads and knots in her lap, not daring to raise her eyes to Miss Dignam's barely banked wrath.

Well, not for Gordon, anyway, she concluded as, tongue between her teeth, she hurried through another lopsided row of daisy chains.

For Ralph? Well, possibly. The thought made her laugh out loud and brought Miss Dignam over to stand in front of her, staring down.

"You find this abomination of a sampler amusing?" Miss Dignam thundered as the room grew quiet.

Ellen paled and swallowed. "No, Miss Dignam," she whispered. "I was merely thinking of something else."

"Shakespeare," Fanny offered and then laughed at Ellen's discomfort. "One of those questionable plays, I do not doubt."

Miss Dignam snatched the sampler from Ellen's nerveless fingers and waved it about the room as the other girls laughed. "Miss Grimsley, it is a continuing mystery to me why Lord Chesney is so interested in your progress here," she said as she picked out the offending threads and thrust the project back in Ellen's lap.

"It is a mystery to me too," Ellen said and then flinched when Miss Dignam frosted her with a head-to-toe stare.

"I'll thank you not to add impertinence to your numerous and growing list of character deficiencies, Miss Grimsley," the headmistress said.

Ellen raised startled eyes. "I meant no impertinence," she stammered. "I . . . I don't understand his interest, either, Miss Dignam. I meant nothing more."

But Miss Dignam had turned her back on her and was admiring Fanny's beautiful row of daisy chains.

Ellen sighed and vowed to do better. By the time the endless class was over, her back ached and her head was pounding.

In the peace of her room, a quiet contemplation of the armload of books that James Gatewood had loaned her did nothing to restore her confidence. It was as he had said: they raised more questions than they answered. She stared hard at the books, willing them to tell her more about *Measure for Measure*. Her scrutiny yielded nothing except a greater headache, and the gnawing discomfort that she, or Gordon, at any rate, was about to be weighed in the balance and found wanting.

She leaned back in her chair and stared at the ceiling. "What is it that Lord Chesney—bless his quirky heart—expects that Gordon will discover from this play?" she asked out loud.

The answer came to her so fast that she thudded all four chair legs back onto the floor. Her heart pounding, she looked at the books of commentary on the desk in front of her and closed them one by one. She stacked them to one side and took out a piece of paper. *Lord Chesney expects more from Gordon—the wonder scholar—than stale, revisited ideas. And James Gatewood expects more from me*, she thought, opening the play again and dipping her pen in the inkwell. *I will not merely shake my head over this frank and enormously engaging play and declare it a "problem" like other Shakespeare students. I will turn it on its head.*

She wrote steadily until the dinner bell chimed in the hall. With a yawn, Ellen got to her feet, stretching her arms over her head and then pressing her hand to the small of her back. *Scholarship is tedious business*, she decided as she went slowly down the stairs, her mind full of *Measure for Measure*.

The small talk at the dinner table flowed all around as she ate thoughtfully, chewing over Isabella's plight and Shakespeare's intentions with the same interest that she awarded the beef roast and kidney pie. She sat impatiently through all the courses, with their accompanying dreary gossip about the royal family and Beau Brummell's latest witticisms, eager to be back at her desk.

After Miss Dignam finally released the diners, Ellen scurried into the library and surveyed again with dismay the pitifully few copies of Shakespeare's plays. "This will never do," she declared firmly as she hurried upstairs.

In another moment, she had composed a hasty scrawl to James Gatewood, fellow, All Souls. It was a plea for a copy of Shakespeare's complete works, if he possessed such a volume, plus the return of his commentaries. "'I have decided to attempt original scholarship,'" she wrote. "'Should you wish to know more, then don't miss Gordon's Saturday recitation. Regards, El.'" She signed her name with a flourish.

She summoned the footman and sent him downstairs with the books, the note, a shilling, and the admonition to jettison the books and swallow the note if Miss Dignam should happen by. The footman merely grinned and bowed.

Ellen expected no reply that evening, but she waited anyway, hopeful that the footman would find Gatewood in his quarters and possessing just the volume she required.

Her wishes were rewarded an hour later by a tap on the door. Fanny looked up from her contemplation of her face in the mirror but turned away with a sniff when Becky Speed came into the room.

"Miss Grimsley," she said breathlessly as Fanny turned to regard her again. "The footman said I was to give this to you." She handed Ellen a cumbersome folio edition of Shakespeare's complete works.

It was a beautiful work in and of itself, bound in soft morocco leather, with gold leafing. She carried it to her desk and took out the note stuck into it.

Jim had returned her own note and added his own scrawl to her words. "'I can hardly wait to hear the pearls of wisdom that will drop from Gordon's lips. Yrs., Jim.'"

She laughed and followed the arrow at the bottom of the page. "'P.S.,'" she read silently. "'I suppose I shouldn't have kissed you on the stairs like that, but it seemed like a good idea at the time.'"

She blushed and read the postscript again, wondering for the first time if James Gatewood was as wild an eccentric as his friend Lord Chesney. She crumpled the note in her hand, putting it in the back of her desk drawer. She looked over her shoulder to see Fanny regarding her thoughtfully.

"Little secrets?" was Fanny's only comment as she began to dab witch hazel on her face.

Ellen's eyes were as wide and innocent as Fanny's. "Fanny, you know my life is an open book," she said as she gathered together her papers and arranged them neatly on her desk. "Besides, I have never known a time when you could not find out my business. I have no secrets, Fanny."

Fanny turned an unhealthy red and set her lips in a firm line.

Ellen prepared for bed, retrieving her flannel nightgown from the chair close to the fire where she had draped it. She climbed into it quickly in the chilly room, grateful for its warmth, not caring that Fanny thought her tacky for leaving her gown on the chair for all to see.

In perfect charity with God, she knelt longer beside her bed for prayers this time. *And God bless Jim Gatewood and his wonderful library*, she prayed silently. After a moment's consideration, Ellen rested her cheek on the bed. *And help him to find someone who doesn't mind a little disorder and who is not above scolding him to dress tidy occasionally. Heaven knows, he shows to advantage when he does.*

Ellen raised herself up on her knees and clasped her hands together again. There was no sense in bothering the Lord Omnipotent about James Gatewood's less-than-perfect personal habits. *And bless Mama and Papa and Martha and Horatia and Ralph, and even Gordon*, she concluded, and then hopped into bed.

Fanny blew out the lamp. Ellen sighed and closed her eyes, grateful to be away from her desk, even as her mind tossed about scenes and plots from Shakespeare's plays to support the theory that was going to startle University College on Saturday.

"Did you hear me, Ellen?"

She opened her eyes. Fanny was speaking in her usual querulous tones.

"No, I'm sorry, Fanny. What did you say?"

"Merely that I was going home this weekend to be fitted for my bridesmaid dress."

There was an edge of triumph in Fanny's voice. Ellen felt tears sting at her eyelids, and she scrubbed them away. Horatia had chosen the most beautiful deep green for her bridesmaids. Ellen had lingered over the bolts and bolts of specially dyed lawn that Mama had purchased, wishing that she could grow six inches and be symmetrical enough to march in the bridal procession.

Ellen raised herself up on one elbow and looked through the gloom at Fanny. "I hope you have a good time," she said softly. "I wish I could be a bridesmaid too. Good night, Fanny."

"Oh, well, thank you, Ellen," said Fanny, the surprise showing in her voice. She cleared her throat in a way that sounded vaguely like embarrassment to Ellen. "Is there . . . is there anyone you want me to say hello to for you?"

Ellen thought a moment and remembered her conversation with James Gatewood in his chambers. She took a deep breath. "If you should happen to see Tom Cornwell, tell him hello for me."

"I will, Ellen."

She closed her eyes again, surprised at the tears that still threatened, even though her artless words had disarmed Fanny for the time being. Tom Cornwell was likely her destiny. She had said as much to Jim. She clutched her pillow in her arms, enjoying the comfort of it, and wishing for the briefest moment that James Gatewood's arms were still around her and that silly armload of books on the All Souls stairwell. *Perhaps Thomas will hold me like that someday*, she thought, and dabbed at her eyes. *Maybe, if and when we are married, he will become someone I can love and respect.*

Soon she would be returning for Horatia's wedding, and she could see him again. Perhaps he would be more to her liking, then, if she looked at him seriously in the light of a possible husband. *Someone to share my bed with*, she thought as she rested her head against the pillow. *Someone with enough money for Papa, and living close by for Mama.*

What about me? she thought. *What does he have that I will need?* Her tears flowed faster. *Would he understand if I wanted to travel, and learn to make maps, and write guidebooks? Would he loan me books, and give me chocolates when I was desperate, rescue me from the Bodleian, and make me a little tipsy in a tavern?*

She turned her face into the pillow so Fanny could not hear her. *Will Thomas Cornwell, with his big ears and horse talk, and conversations about the Grain Exchange, even have a clue about me, Ellen Grimsley?*

When she heard Fanny breathing slowly and evenly, Ellen left her bed and sat at her desk again, parting the curtains so she could see the moon rise over the spires of Oxford. Her hand gripped the curtains. "It is only across the street, but I can never reach it," she said softly. "Oh, mercy, it is so unjust."

She touched the pages in front of her. There would be this final paper for Gordon, and no more. She would go home before she made a fool of herself and tell Mama that she was ready for Thomas Cornwell and his clumsy attentions. If she had any regrets, she would bury them in the back of her mind, stuffed out of sight like the shirt, breeches, and scholar's gown that hung in the dressing room.

Fanny left after morning classes in the company of a maiden aunt who was returning home to the Cotswolds from London. "I will remember you to your family," she told Ellen over her shoulder as she followed the footman downstairs with her trunk.

"Thank you, Fanny," Ellen said. She waited impatiently by the front door while Fanny stood there, trying to remember if she had forgotten anything.

As soon as Fanny left, Ellen darted upstairs again, spreading her pages and notes across both beds and walking around them, rearranging ideas as she considered what she was doing. Using *Measure for Measure* as her starting point, she would prove, play by play, that many of the plays of Shakespeare were written by a woman.

"Surely no man can know the mind of a woman so well," she said out loud and then repeated her words as she wrote them down. "I will prove it and prove it until there can be no argument," she said, looking around her at the garden of notes planted everywhere.

"What do you think of my idea?" she asked Becky Speed later when the maid came in.

"I think you are going to find yourself in the middle of a muddle," the maid said frankly. "How long will it be until someone asks Gordon an intelligent question—begging your pardon, ma'am—and he stands there like a half-wit?"

"There is that risk," Ellen agreed. "But what is that you have there?" she asked, eager to change the subject, because Becky had hit on the target of her own fears.

From her contemplation of the clutter about her, Becky brightened and held out the box. "More chocolates, Miss, and don't we know who they are from?"

Ellen clapped her hands. "Jim Gatewood is probably spending money he does not have, but oh, how thoughtful!" She opened the box, sniffing the contents, and pulled out a note. "'If chocolates be the food of scholarship, eat on,'" she read and laughed. "He is never serious where Shakespeare is concerned. What a mangle of a quote."

Ellen popped a chocolate in her mouth and held out the box to Becky. "I am to be interrupted only if the building is burning down," she told the maid. "If Miss Dignam should cut up stiff that I am missing embroidery, tell her . . . oh . . . tell her that Lord Chesney has given me a particular assignment that I must fulfill. She won't believe it for long, but at least I should have the paper in hand before she gets too suspicious."

She was back at Shakespeare before Becky let herself out quietly.

That evening, Gordon delivered his notes to her from his weekly tutorial. "We discussed *Measure for Measure*," he said, stretching out his hands to the sitting room fire. "I do not know how Shakespeare comes up with such rattlebrained plots. I am sure I do not have a sister like Isabella, who would surrender her . . . well, you know . . . for me."

Ellen only glanced up from his notes and smiled her best gallows smile, the one reserved for brothers. "You are absolutely right, Gordon."

An uncomfortable silence followed that Gordon broke finally by putting his arm cautiously about his sister. "Well, El, some day when I am a general, you will look back on all this and laugh."

"I doubt it," she replied. "You have put us both in such a spot, brother, that I may never forgive you. Good night. Come back Friday for the paper."

She left him standing, open-mouthed, by the fireplace.

She finished the paper Friday morning, when the candles had burnt out and the sun was struggling over the barren, winter-swept hills. Her eyes burned and her back was sore. With a sigh, Ellen gathered her night's work and took it to the window. She perched on the window seat and watched the sun rise. She looked down at the closely written pages in her hands. *I could have done better*, she thought, tracing the words with her finger. Flipping to the last page, she read the ending again. "Oh, it is good," she whispered out loud.

In another moment, she was seated at her desk again, writing out a fair copy for Gordon. When she finished, she added a note, admonishing him to read it through first before he sprang it on himself in front of an audience of scholars, and summoned the footman. Her eyes drooping with exhaustion, she gave him Gordon's directions and another shilling.

Back in her room again, she finished the box of chocolates and fell asleep in the middle of a pile of notes.

When she woke, the room was tidy again and Becky was just stacking the last of her notes and first draft in neat piles on the floor. Ellen sat up and rubbed her eyes.

"Best burn them, Becky," she said. "I would only get in trouble if Fanny chanced upon them and put two and two together."

"Very well, Miss," Becky said, "although it seems a shame after all your work."

She attended her classes that day, nodding off over the geography of Cyprus and then struggling in vain to make sense of her embroidery. She could only bow her head in misery over the scathing criticism that Miss Dignam rained down upon her head. With her eyes closed, she even dozed a little, waking up when Miss

Dignam shook her and demanded to know how in the world she expected to find a husband if she knew so little about the domestic arts.

"I . . . I don't know that I have ever given it much thought," she managed finally when the headmistress just stood there, hands on hips, glaring at her. Finally, she raised her own cool blue eyes to Miss Dignam's red face. "I shall have to trust Papa to find someone among his horsey acquaintances who will have me with all my faults. He will probably want to examine my teeth and watch my gait about the paddock. After all, what can a girl expect?"

The other students in the room gasped.

"Miss Grimsley, go to your room," Miss Dignam ordered, her voice perfectly awful.

Ellen went, grateful to collapse in sleep upon her bed again.

She was still sleeping the next day when Becky shook her awake.

"Miss Grimsley! Gordon is below, and I have never seen him so excited!"

She sat up and stuffed her feet into her shoes, looking about for a shawl to hide the wrinkles in the dress she had slept in. "I am amazed that Miss Dignam let him in."

"Oh, she does not know. He is belowstairs in the kitchen." Ellen followed the maid down the servants' stairs and into the kitchen, where Gordon strode about like a caged animal.

When he saw his sister, he ran to her, lifted her off her feet and whirled her around.

"El, I have been declared a Shakespeare prodigy!" he crowed, ignoring her request to set her down.

"How lovely for you, Gordon," she said, when he finally stopped whirling her about like a top.

He smiled modestly. "Of course, I'm not sure what a prodigy is, El, but since everyone was standing on their feet and applauding—the ones who weren't cheering, anyway—I guess it is a good thing."

Ellen sat down and merely regarded her brother in silence until he recalled himself and sat beside her.

"Well, tell me," she said, when he just sat there grinning.

With a laugh, he leaned back in his chair. "I was almost scared spitless when I read your conclusion about Shakespeare being written by a woman."

"Gordon! I told you to read the paper over first!" she scolded.

He ducked his head in embarrassment. "I meant to, really I did, but the men in the next room were holding a mouse race, and when that was done, we went to the Cock and Hen, and there just wasn't time. You understand, El."

"Of course," she replied promptly. "Never let education interfere with the business at hand."

"I knew you would understand. Well, when I finished my paper, you could have heard a pin drop. And then someone started applauding, and others were on their feet cheering me. It's the greatest feeling, El."

She could think of nothing to say except hot words that she would regret later, so she had the wisdom to knot her hands in her lap, grit her teeth, and be silent.

Gordon touched her arm. "The best part, El, the best part of all! Someone had invited the Vice Chancellor of Oxford. Come to think of it, he was sitting beside Lord Chesney." Gordon grinned at the memory. "He told me I was a credit to my family and the whole nation."

Ellen leaned forward. "Did Lord Chesney seem to enjoy it?"

"Oh, El! He's the one who called me a Shakespeare prodigy." He closed his eyes, a dreamy expression on his face. "Gordon Grimsley, boy genius, England's gift to the world. El, everyone should have a sister like you."

She swallowed the tears that threatened. "Did . . . did you see James Gatewood?"

He frowned. "I don't know this Gatewood chap you are always going on about." He shrugged. "Who cares? Lord Chesney was pleased, and so was my warden, and I can't think anything else matters."

"I don't suppose it does. Did you get the copy back?"

He slapped his forehead in contrition. "Would you believe that Lord Chesney insisted upon having this one too?"

Ellen uttered an exclamation of disgust. "Gordon, I particularly told you not to let that happen! I was too tired to write out another copy, and see here, I told Becky to burn my notes and rough copy, so there is nothing left."

He looked at her with an expression that wavered between pity at her shortcomings and brotherly condescension. "I don't see how you can possibly blame me for that, El. Besides, what can it matter? What can he possibly do with those papers?" He put his arm around her. "And what use can you have for them, sis?"

She nodded slowly. "I suppose you are right, although it does make me uneasy that I have no copies of anything."

He laughed and tugged at her curls. "Great Godfrey, El, what were you planning? To publish a book of your collected essays?" He gave her a hug and pulled her toward the door. "Who do you think would ever read a stodgy old Shakespeare collection by the world-renowned Ellen Grimsley?"

It did sound unlikely, put that way. Ellen felt her face grow red. *Was I honestly imagining that I would ever publish those works someday?* she asked herself as Gordon prattled on about inanities and finally took out his watch.

"I'm off, El," he declared finally. "Some of the chaps are hosting a dinner for me." He puffed out his chest. "I've become a credit to University College, don't you know."

"Gordon, what you are is a fool," she said, not mincing her words and softening none of the sting.

He only looked at her fondly and kissed her cheek. "Yes, ain't I?" he agreed, all amiable complacency. "Maybe it will be enough to get me sprung early from this pile."

"Either that, or it will make you so valuable that University College—and Papa—will never let you go."

He stopped and looked at her with an expression close to horror. "I never thought of that, El!" he squeaked, his voice suddenly raised into the upper registers by the prospect of a life of study. "Whatever you do, sister, do not make the next essay so brilliant, will you?"

He opened the door. She put her hand out and closed it again. "What essay, Gordon?" she asked, her voice quiet. "I am writing no more essays for you."

His face lost its usual healthy glow, and he swallowed several times. "See here, El. You must," he managed, when he could speak.

"I don't have to do anything of the sort," she retorted. "And I am thinking of applying to Papa to spring me from this pile."

He gripped her arm. "El, you must help me."

"Oh, must I? I suppose you will tell me that Lord Chesney insists upon another essay," she said, opening the door for him.

He closed it this time. "As a matter of fact, he did, El, and he wants this one to be about . . ." He paused to reflect, rolling his eyes. "Dash it all, something about a storm, and more of them foolish fairies, or sprites. Lord C. went on and on about 'brave new world,' whatever the devil that means."

"*The Tempest*, you block," she said and opened the door again. "Very well, but no more after this one, Gordon. I have done enough for you."

He only smiled, but she did not like that smile.

Chapter 8

*I*F SHE EXPECTED A VISIT FROM JIM Gatewood that afternoon, she was mistaken. For someone who seemed so interested in her progress, for someone so willing to help, he was notable by his absence.

Even Ellen's first official expedition outside the academy in the company of a maid, footman, and other select females failed to rouse her from her disappointment.

What is it that I expect? Ellen thought as she walked along the High Street with the other students. With a blush, she looked away from her own reflection in a shop window. *I want his approbation*, she thought. *I want him to tell me what a fine job I did on this essay.* She looked down the street to the spires of All Souls.

It could be that I just want to see him.

The thought made her pause in the middle of the street. The other Christmas shoppers hurried around her, looking back in irritation.

"Ellen! Hurry up!" called one of the girls. "You are becoming a trial!"

The afternoon was cold, the kind of blue-gray cold that she was familiar with from her own corner of the Cotswolds, the cold that burrowed in between the shoulder blades and never let go until spring. Ellen tugged her woolen scarf tighter about her neck and shoved her hands deep into the pockets of her pelisse. Dutifully, she followed the others from store to store along the High, exclaiming over ribbons and fancies until she was heartily bored.

A reminder from one of the other students about the closeness of Christmas inspired her to find a doll for Martha, a strand of coral beads for Horry, and gray kid gloves for Mama. Papa would content himself with his favorite pipe tobacco. She felt disinclined to buy anything for Gordon and turned her interests to Ralph.

"We must go to the bookstore," she said as the others were starting back. "I think it is not far," she coaxed when the girls groaned and began a litany of complaints about their feet, the weather, and the weight of their packages, at least the ones that the footman, burdened as he was, was unable to carry.

"I have to find something for my brother," Ellen declared. She gave her scarf another yank. "Just . . . go on," she ordered, "and leave Becky Speed with me. Surely that's proper enough."

Grateful not to have to surrender their footman,

the others agreed. In a moment, they were hurrying toward the warmth of Miss Dignam's asylum.

Ellen tucked her arm in Becky's. "I'm sorry," she apologized, "but suppose I am punished next week for some misdeed or another and cannot escape to finish my Christmas obligations? I would hate to disappoint Ralph."

Becky only smiled, even though her nose was red from the cold. "If we cut through the alleys, we will be there quicker."

They hurried through Oxford University's alleys. Soon Ellen saw Fletcher's sign, swaying in the stiffening breeze. They ducked inside, and Ellen sighed with pleasure. The walls from floor to ceiling bulged with books of all types and sizes. Clerks scurried like sailors up and down the ladders that moved on tracks the length of the narrow store.

A clerk appeared at her side.

"I say, can you show me a copy of Shakespeare's complete works?" Ellen asked, when her mouth had thawed sufficiently to permit the formation of words again.

He disappeared, climbed a ladder, and retrieved a duplicate of the copy James Gatewood had sent to Miss Dignam's last week. He quoted her a price that made her eyes open wide.

"Mercy on us," she exclaimed. "I haven't near enough!"

Disappointed, the clerk whisked the book away before she could sully it with one more glance. Ellen whispered to Becky, "Oh, I am so embarrassed! James

Gatewood paid a small fortune for that book he sent me. I had no idea it was so dear. Becky, that was probably all his money in the world!"

The maid eyed her doubtfully. "Surely not, miss. Surely Mr. Gatewood has other resources." She thought a moment. "Well, perhaps he does not, considering the state he is always in when we see him." She giggled behind her well-darned mittens. "He always looks like he came backward through the shrubbery, doesn't he?"

"And I am afraid he has gone to awful expense for me," Ellen said mournfully, thinking of the beautiful book on her desk with "Good luck!" scrawled across both inside pages.

After another moment spent in real discomfort, Ellen settled on a more modest volume of Shakespeare's histories and let the clerk carry it away to be wrapped in brown paper.

"I must remember never to petition James Gatewood for books," she said out loud and then glanced at Becky. "I feel that for my penance I should write that sentence one hundred times. Oh, dear!"

Becky took the package from the clerk. "Well, it can't be helped now, Miss Grimsley."

"I suppose it cannot," Ellen said.

The wind outside Fletcher's staggered them backward. Snow was falling. Ellen linked arms with the maid and they turned, heads down, into the wind.

It fairly carried them along, swooping and dodging through Oxford's warren of alleys and hidden streets. Ellen's dress whirled up around her knees, and she could only be grateful that no one else was abroad on such a chilly afternoon to witness such a brazen display.

Almost no one. She was turning to attempt some remark to Becky as they struggled along, when suddenly James Gatewood separated them and put his arms through theirs.

"What a duo of silly chits you are," he said mildly, as the wind ruffled through his already untidy hair. "I expected that England's next preeminent Shakespeare scholar would have the wit to keep warm."

Ellen giggled despite her misery. "We are on Christmas errands," she shouted above the wind.

"You'll only get a lump of coal from me, if you do not seek shelter soon," he shouted back, still cheerful.

Becky tugged at his other arm. "Please, sir, I live only one street over. We could duck in there for a moment to get warm."

Gatewood smiled at the maid. "Capital notion, my dear!" he declared. "How glad I am to know that one of you has a particle of sense." He laughed out loud when Ellen dug him in the ribs. "My dear, if the shoe fits . . ."

He had to duck his head to get through the low doorway into the Speed house, a narrow set of quarters built along the same lines as the bookstore. A woman who looked very much like Becky Speed was sitting beside a thin, sunken-faced man with no expression who lay on a daybed close to the fire. She blew a kiss to Becky and took in the situation at a glance, rising to her feet.

"Come close to the fire," she said, gesturing toward the small mound of coal that glowed in the grate. After a slight hesitation, she hurried to the cupboard on the dark side of the little room and took out two china cups.

In another moment, Ellen was sipping the weak tea. She smiled her appreciation. The woman beamed back as Becky put her arm around her.

"Mr. Gatewood, Miss Grimsley, this is my mother," Becky said and then tilted her head toward the man on the daybed. "And my father. He was a stone mason and fell from the walls of Magdalen while making repairs last year." Her voice faltered and she tightened her grip on her mother. "We think he can understand us."

Gatewood hesitated not a moment. He walked to the daybed and sat down in the spot Mrs. Speed had vacated. "Then we thank you for your hospitality, Mr. Speed," he said, his voice gentle.

Beyond a slight movement of his head, Mr. Speed lay still.

With increased appreciation, Ellen watched James Gatewood as he sat where he was, addressing pleasantries to the man who could not answer him. She turned away and found herself looking at Mrs. Speed, who was watching Gatewood.

Becky kissed her mother's cheek as Mrs. Speed began to dab at her eyes with her apron. "I think he reminds Mama of Tommy, who went to Spain to war and never came home."

"Becky, I am so sorry," Ellen said. Her throat felt scratchy and her eyelids burned. She sipped her tea-flavored hot water, her heart troubled. *And Spain is where Gordon thinks he must go,* she thought. *I was so unkind to him this afternoon.*

In another moment, Mrs. Speed directed her attention to the fireplace. Carefully, she took out two more lumps of coal from the nearly empty pasteboard box that served as a coal scuttle and arranged them on the little fire with all the skill of a bricklayer. Ellen's eyes clouded over as she remembered the maids at home tumbling coal into the grate, careless of it.

Gatewood remained by Becky's father until the man closed his eyes and relaxed in sleep. He looked at Ellen then, who had removed her pelisse and was sitting close to the fire, her hands extended to it.

"You look so nice in a dress," he whispered so none of the Speeds could hear him. "Much more flattering than a scholar's gown."

She raised her eyes from her contemplation of the struggling little fire, as though she had not heard his small compliment. "James, I think they intend to have us for supper."

He sat close beside her. "We can't put them to that embarrassment," he said softly, "even though I would like to sit with you by the fire a little longer."

"Well, you cannot," she said and then glanced at his face. "You could come to Miss Dignam's parlor some evening."

"No, I could not," he replied enigmatically and then changed the subject by wrapping his scarf about his neck again and pulling on his gloves. "Mrs. Speed, Becky, thank you so much for rescuing us from the storm, but I must return this waif to Miss Dragon's."

Becky giggled. Ellen couldn't help but notice the look of relief on Mrs. Speed's face.

"If you must," Mrs. Speed began.

James held out his hand. "We must. Miss Grimsley is so often in and out of trouble that it would not be wise to tempt the Fates. Good day to you all. Here, Ellen, let me help you."

Becky reached for her cloak again. James shook his head.

"I can see Miss Grimsley home. After all, I am going in that direction too."

Ellen buttoned her pelisse and stood still while James wrapped the muffler about her neck. She held out her hand to Becky. "I am sure I will be fine." She frowned. "Becky, wasn't this your half day, anyway?"

Becky nodded. "I didn't mind the shopping this afternoon. I love to look in shop windows, even if I do not buy."

"Mind you hurry then, Miss Grimsley," Mrs. Speed said as she opened the door. The snow blew in and nearly extinguished the exhausted fire. "I wouldn't want your cold or sore throat laid at my door!"

Ellen smiled and touched the woman's arm. "I am never sick," she declared. "It is a sore trial to my mother, who thinks I would be more interesting if I could languish a bit, like my sister."

They said good-bye and set out, arm in arm, through the alleys. It was too cold to talk. Ellen clutched Ralph's present to her, grateful that the footman had taken the others on ahead.

After walking in silence through the winter twilight, James stopped, pulling Ellen up short. "I, for one, am grateful you are never sick," he said, speaking distinctly to be heard above the wind. He started walking again.

She looked up at him in amusement "Well, thank you, sir!" she declared.

"Seriously, El," he replied, "think how handy that will be when you are slogging through the malarial rain forests of Brazil, or the frozen steppes—Heaven help us—of Siberia. The world was never explored by weak people."

Ellen stopped this time. "You don't think I am foolish, like all my relatives do, and Miss Dignam, and Fanny Bland, and Vicar Snead?"

He tugged her into motion again. "I don't think you are foolish," he said quietly. "Not at all, Ellen Grimsley. You may be a little ahead of your time, but so was Galileo."

"You put me in august company," she shouted over the wind.

"It's where you belong." He stopped at the top of the steps to the female academy and rang the bell. "The only difficulty I foresee is finding a husband obliging enough to let you traipse off around the world."

"It is a problem," she agreed, rubbing her hands together and taking a firmer grip on her package. "He will have to be quite wealthy and excruciatingly patient." She laughed and extended her hand. "Should you ever meet anyone like that, please send him calling to Miss Dignam's! Thank you for your escort, sir."

He only leaned forward and kissed her cheek. "If it were any colder, we would be stuck together right now, and then Miss Dignam would have you writing thousands of sentences," he murmured, his voice close to her ear.

She smiled and touched his face. The door opened, and the footman stood there, grinning at them.

"One moment."

Gatewood took her arm and led her down the steps again.

"We have not even had time to discuss your much-applauded essay."

"Did you like it?" she asked, wishing the footman would close the door again. He just stood there, leaning against the frame, whistling softly to himself.

"Like's not the word, Ellen. It was a masterpiece," he replied. He took her hand again. "Meet me tomorrow afternoon at the bridge at the end of the High. We'll go punting. Wear your scholar's gown, of course."

She stared at him. "But it's snowing! And cold!"

He looked up at the sky. "See the stars peeking through over there? It will be clear tomorrow. And this is a perfect time to punt. No one will bother us while we discuss your next paper."

"But . . ."

Gatewood was already backing away down the street. He waved to her and ran across the street to the All Souls entrance.

Ellen stood there a moment until she heard the footman clearing his throat. She turned back to Miss Dignam's, shaking her head. *James Gatewood is an odd one indeed*, she thought. *He must be almost as eccentric as Lord Chesney. It's no wonder those two are friends.*

Ellen woke in the morning to sunlight streaming

through the curtains. With a sigh of contentment, she snuggled deeper into the pillow and regarded that portion of sky she could see from her bed. It was a beautiful, crackling blue, untroubled by a single cloud.

For a moment, she wished herself home, where the upstairs maid would bring her cinnamon toast and hot chocolate, and she and Horatia would share her bed and plan their lives. Her smile faded. Horatia's life was already planned, and soon she would be married to Edwin Bland, the silly son of a sillier baronet.

And then Horry will be a wife, and likely a mother, and I will be an aunt, she thought. *We will forget we were ever sisters who giggled over life in bed on Sunday mornings.*

Ellen turned over on her stomach and lay there, her face pressed into the pillow. There was an ache somewhere in her body as she thought of Gatewood's words of last night. Would she ever really slog through malarial swamps or conquer frozen steppes? It seemed unlikely.

She rested her chin in her hands. *I wonder if Thomas Cornwell has ever been up to London*, she thought. *He has seen no more of the world than I have, but the difference is, he doesn't care if his horizons extend no farther than the farthest Cotswold hill. His only interest in the horizon would be to own it and sow it. Tom's idea of an excursion would be a trip here to Oxford, and even then, he would only come here because it was a market center, and not because it was the seat of all learning and wisdom.*

Ellen sat up cross-legged in bed, her pillow propped behind her, wondering at the feeling of homesickness that washed over her suddenly. At home they would be rushing around, getting ready for the ride into the village and church, steeling themselves for the prospect of another of Vicar Snead's stupefying sermons.

In the afternoon, Mama would knot lace in the sitting room and carry on about the neighbors, while Papa, his mind and heart on horses as always, would pace the floor from sofa to window and back again, chafing because it was Sunday and Mama would allow little else. As soon as he settled himself in a chair, Martha would climb into his lap, and they would both fall asleep.

They were silly, idle people, but she missed them and loved them in her own way. *And they love me*, Ellen thought suddenly. *Mama thinks that Thomas Cornwell is the best choice for me.*

The pang of homesickness did not go away as she thought of Horatia, sitting close to the fire, deep in loving silence with her ridiculous fiancé. Ralph would find an excuse to steal from the room to the company of his beloved Shakespeare.

Shakespeare. Ellen rolled her eyes and plopped her hands in her lap. "Dear Willie of Avon," she said, "you are rapidly becoming my greatest trial in life."

She looked around, feeling foolish that she had spoken out loud, and in such decisive tones, and then remembered that Fanny Bland was away until tomorrow. She tightened her lips, seeing in her mind's eye Fanny and the other symmetrical bridesmaids, giggling with each other as they received their final fitting of that divine deep green lawn.

Mama and Horry had gone round and round over the tiny puffed sleeves and low-cut neckline. "But my dear, it will be winter!" Mama had protested. "They will have to carry warming pans instead of nosegays!"

"I hope you all come down with galloping consumption and putrid sore throats and chilblains," Ellen declared, looking at Fanny's bed, all tidily made up with not a single wrinkle. "And frostbite," she added for good measure.

But none of those things would likely happen. The tall, elegant bridesmaids would march down the aisle, Horry would be shot off, and Ellen would be left to keep the younger children in line and see that Martha did not eat too many sweets. And when it was all over, Mama would look her over once or twice and ask her how she felt about Thomas Cornwell. "Such a nice young man, and from such a good family," Mama would say.

What a pity that James Gatewood is so ineligible, Ellen thought and then smiled at the idea of the casual Mr. Gatewood, in his shabby collars and wrinkled clothes, bowing over Mama's hand. It would never do. Even if he combed his hair and pressed his clothes, he would still be just a horse trader's son.

A pity, Ellen thought. *We could probably have dealt so well together.* The notion made her blush. What was she thinking? Mama would never understand what she saw in him. Ellen was not sure herself, except that she felt better when he was around.

Ellen wrapped herself tight in her blankets again. *It can not be love, at any rate*, she thought. Horatia had informed her that love was a feeling of total delight. Horry had never mentioned the restlessness that Ellen felt when she was away from James Gatewood, or the feeling of wanting to tidy him, and organize his life, and bully him into eating better than toasted cheese and rather bad tea.

It must be infatuation, she decided as she threw back the covers and pulled on her robe. She headed for the dressing room but got no farther than the window. She sat at her desk and looked out at the lovely spires of Oxford. *I suppose I am also a little bit in love with Oxford too.* She smiled to herself. Like her infatuation with James Gatewood, it would have to pass, and quickly too for her own peace of mind.

Church was a quiet business. Many of the older parishioners from Oxford's center had stayed indoors, kept there by the bracing cold that brought a bloom to Ellen's cheeks. She sniffed the air appreciatively as they walked from church in decorous ranks of two. The fragrance of wood smoke, captured and held in the bowl-shaped valley by the cold, competed with musty smells off the River Isis and cooking odors from every hearth. Ellen knew it was her imagination, but she thought she could smell the delicious aroma of leather bindings on old books.

Ellen thought twice, and then three times, about sneaking out of Miss Dignam's after the noon meal. *I can have no business out of this building with James*

Gatewood, she told herself as she picked up her embroidery basket and gazed at it in dismay. *How was it that those threads seemed to knot and tangle of their own accord? I declare it is perverse*, she thought, *a conspiracy to remind me of my failings.*

She tried not to think about the scholar's gown hanging in the back of the dressing room, hidden from prying eyes. Ellen looked out the window then, and her resolve weakened. The sky was so blue, a dramatic backdrop for the honey-colored stones, mellow with age, that made up many of Oxford's colleges. Resolutely, Ellen turned away from the window and took her embroidery basket onto her lap.

After a futile half hour spent trying to follow each errant thread to its source, she dropped the basket at her feet and kicked it under the desk. She looked in the direction of the dressing room and got slowly to her feet.

No one was about as she crept down the backstairs, the scholar's gown draped over her arm, shirt and breeches underneath her dress.

Becky was the only servant in sight, the rest having taken themselves off for the afternoon, away from Miss Dignam's crotchets. The maid scrubbed the pans in the scullery, looking up with a smile when Ellen stepped out of her dress and fluffed her wilted shirt points.

Becky dried her hands and hurried to shake out Ellen's dress and hide it in the broom closet. "Where are you going today?" she asked as Ellen pulled on the scholar's gown.

"James Gatewood has some harebrained scheme about punting on the River Isis," Ellen said. "I think he is crazy."

"No, Miss Grimsley, he is wonderful," Becky said, her eyes shining.

Ellen stared at her. "Whatever do you mean?"

Becky dabbed at her eyes with her apron. "This morning, the beadle from the parish came tapping on our door. Behind him was a coal wagon. He backed that wagon up to the cellar window and shoveled in a mound of coal that still has the neighbors wondering."

"My word," said Ellen, her voice soft. "And you think it was James Gatewood?"

"Who else?" Becky asked. "When I woke up, Mama was crying and piling coal on the grate until I thought she had taken leave of her senses."

Ellen sat down at the table. "I simply do not understand where he finds the money for his philanthropies. Horse trading must pay beyond my wildest imaginings."

"There's more, Miss Grimsley," Becky said as she plunged her hands back into the dishwater. "The beadle told us that as soon as the coal gets low, we are to notify him. Miss Grimsley, we will be warm all winter!"

Ellen felt tears prickling her eyes. "I will definitely confront him with this evidence of his kindness," she said.

"If you think it won't embarrass him," Becky said.

"It won't hurt to embarrass James Gatewood," Ellen replied as she opened the door and peered out.

"Sometimes I have the distinct impression that he is not giving me straight answers."

The afternoon was clear and cold, the street deserted. Ellen huddled in her scholar's gown and hurried down the High to the bridge. The street was icy, so she took her time, asking herself again what she was doing outdoors tempting fate like this. Only the knowledge that Miss Dignam insisted on quiet Sunday afternoons, spent in meditation of some sin or another, kept her going. No one would miss her.

"Watch your step, Hermia."

She looked down from the bridge. James Gatewood stood halfway up the little steps that led to a small landing on the river's edge. He held out his hand to her, and she gripped it.

"This is insane," was her only comment as he helped her down the ice-covered steps.

"Yes, isn't it?" he agreed cheerfully. "Consider it advance training for an adventure at the North Pole, grim Miss Grimsley. Your sleigh awaits."

He gestured toward a punt that bobbed on the choppy water.

Ellen chewed her lips and looked back at Gatewood doubtfully.

"Trust me, Ellen," he said.

"I should not," she said promptly, wondering at her own wildness. She would never be so brazen at home, where her most forward act had been a stroll unchaperoned in the shrubbery with Thomas Cornwell. Not that her virtue was ever in any danger from Thomas. All he could talk about was the price of grain. "No, I should not," she repeated.

"That is up to you," he replied and held out his hand to help her into the punt.

She hesitated and then took hold of his hand again. He made no comment but regarded her with an expression she had not noticed before. There was none of the casual amusement in his eyes that she had become familiar with in their brief acquaintance. He was serious about something, and she did not entirely understand.

"You'll not regret it," he said as he followed her into the boat and picked up the pole.

She was silent as she settled herself into the little craft. His was not a statement that seemed to require comment. In some inscrutable way that was currently beyond her understanding, she sensed that he meant much more than he actually said.

I should change the subject, she thought as the stillness between them became uncomfortable, and then she blushed. There was no subject to change.

Gatewood poled in silence into the middle of the stream. Gradually, the somber, almost sad expression left his face. He concentrated on punting into the stream and down the river. Soon he was humming to himself.

Ellen leaned back against the cushion and watched him. How odd it was to be on the river in December. She had read in feverish novels about punting on the Isis in warm, romantic summer, with a picnic hamper and champagne, and a hero with burning eyes. She smiled. James Gatewood's eyes looked a bit red, as though he had not slept much recently, and it was so cold that her nose tingled.

He looked back at her and smiled. "Open that basket," he said, indicating the wicker basket midway between them.

She lifted the lid. A dark green bottle nestled in the straw, with two glasses tucked stem to lip beside it. She smiled up at Gatewood.

"You, sir, are a complete hand."

"Champagne is, I believe, a requirement for a punt on the Isis," he replied. "If it is not frozen, we will be in luck."

She popped the cork and poured them each a glass. He accepted it without missing a push against the pole as they glided along. He raised his glass to her.

"And now, Miss Grimsley, shall I tell you what I think of *Measure for Measure*?"

When he finished, the bottle was half empty. The warm glow in her stomach had traveled down to her fingers and toes, leaving her slightly piffled and charitable to the world at large that drifted by.

"Your ending was particularly adroit," he was saying as he accepted a refill. "I own that I felt sorry for Gordon. He is, I regret to say, too dense by half to realize that you wrote the whole thing in jest. I am sure he still thinks that Shakespeare really was a woman."

Ellen joined in his laughter. Gatewood drained his glass and held it out again, but Ellen shook her head and tapped the cork more firmly into the bottle. "You have had enough, sir," she said.

"You are a bit of a tyrant," he replied, tossing the glass over his shoulder. It bobbed on the current and then sank beneath the waves. "But I will tolerate this heavy-handed cruelty if you will tell me: what is your next assignment?"

Ellen made a face. "Gordon has committed me to *The Tempest*."

She regarded her glass of champagne, wrinkling her nose as the bubbles rose. She swirled the liquid around and around. "Tell me what you think, sir. I believe I will write this paper as a travel guide to the New World. You know, something along the lines of Hakluyt's *Navigations, Voyages, Traffiques and Discoveries*." She frowned. "That is, provided I can find a copy of that work among the moldy, unused stacks of the female academy."

"And if you cannot, I . . ."

She held up her hand, sloshing the champagne from the glass. "You will not—repeat not—invest in such a book at Fletcher's, James!"

"But it gives me pleasure," he said simply, as if that was all the argument there was to consider. "And besides, Hakluyt was a Christ Church man."

"Let us see how pleased you will be when you have run through your quarterly stipend and there is no bread and cheese to be had," she retorted.

"My dear Miss Grimsley," he began, his voice filled with dignity that sounded almost ducal to her ears, "I happen to know that Lord Chesney possesses the Hakluyt collection in his library. I will beg the loan of one volume for you. He is a Shakespeare scholar of such renown that he could never resist a plea on behalf of the Bard." He held up his hand this time to ward off her objections. "Not a word, Miss Grimsley. In this, I insist. You will have the book by tomorrow noon."

Ellen did not argue. She drew her cloak tighter about her shoulders. The afternoon sun was beginning to dip behind the hills. She looked up at Gatewood, who was smiling down at her.

"I have an idea for another paper," she began, picking her way among half-formed thoughts. "It is for me alone, I suppose."

"Some topic that Lord Chesney has not poked his long nose into?" he asked.

She looked at him quickly. "Oh, do not think that I am ungrateful for all he has done, and I have truly enjoyed writing those papers. I have learned so much. This is just an idea of my own."

"I would like to hear it."

"Only promise you will not tell Lord Chesney," she insisted.

"I promise," he said. "But why not?"

"Maybe I will surprise him with it. Maybe I will even sign my name to this one."

"Bravo, fair Hermia," said Gatewood. He steadied the punt and turned his full attention to her. "Speak on."

She clasped her hands over her knees. "Let us pretend that Romeo got Friar Lawrence's message in time to rescue Juliet from 'yon Caple's monument.'" She nodded toward James, her eyes merry. "And then . . ."

"Let me guess," he interrupted and laughed out loud, missing a beat with the pole and setting the little craft rocking. "Excuse that! And they both live happily ever after. Only, perhaps they don't?"

Ellen clapped her hands. "Exactly!"

"Oh, ho!" Gatewood chortled. "Imagine the possibilities of domestic discomfort in the palazzo of Mr. and Mrs. Romeo Montague. Now why did I never think of that?"

"You are not the Shakespeare scholar."

"Alas, yes."

Ellen put the bottle back in the wicker basket. "That title belongs to your friend, Lord Chesney. By the way, sir, why do you not bring him along sometime? I owe him so much and would like to thank him in person for smoothing my way here."

"He is a bit shy around women, Ellen," James said.

"Well, I would be shy too I am sure," Ellen said. "Imagine meeting an actual marquess! I am sure that beyond expressing my thanks, I would be quite intimidated and have nothing of significance to say."

"Surely you could think of something," he coaxed.

"No," Ellen said with a shake of her head. "I am sure I could never be comfortable around a peer."

"You could, Ellen, you could," Gatewood said, his voice suddenly serious. "He's not so fearsome."

"Too rare for me!" she said with a wave of her hand. "Still, I would like to tell him good-bye and thank him."

"Good-bye? Are you still intent upon leaving?"

"Yes. When this paper is done, I am writing to Papa to come and get me," she said.

"Giving up?" he asked quietly.

She nodded and met his eyes. "Exactly so. All I

want is Oxford University, and I cannot have it. I write papers, and others get the applause."

"I never thought applause was your motive," Gatewood said.

She shook her head. "It is not. Oh, James, I fear that I would grow bitter if I stayed around Gordon and watched him squander the riches here." She shook her head. "No, it's high time I returned home. Christmas is coming, and then there is a wedding to prepare for. I am needed at home."

Gatewood poled toward the bridge in silence for several moments. "I understand your bitterness," he said at last.

"You couldn't possibly," she burst out. "You have this university education spread before you like a feast, and I never will!"

"I didn't mean it that way," he retorted. "I am saying that I know what it is to feel the weight of family responsibility." He leaned on the pole and gazed across the river. "I am reminded in frequent letters that I should be home too."

Ellen looked away, embarrassed with herself for reminding him of his own meager condition. She imagined the drain of his education on his parents' limited resources, and she was ashamed.

"I am sorry," she said, her voice soft.

The sun was behind the hills now, and she shivered. "I really don't belong here."

"I think you do," was all he said as he poled the boat alongside the landing.

She could think of nothing to say as Gatewood

helped her out of the punt. He held her hand and helped her up the steps, which were now sheathed in shadow. She felt disinclined to let go, even when her footing was sure.

They walked slowly up the High Street in awkward silence.

Finally Gatewood nudged her shoulder. "Tell me something, El." He let go of her hand as others appeared on the street. "It's about your paper on *Romeo and Juliet*. Do your parents have a happy marriage?"

She stared at him, startled at his astounding question. After a moment's thought, she smiled, her good humor restored. "You are wondering where is my authority for a paper on marriage?"

"I suppose I am."

"Yes, they do, I think," she said. "I have never given it much thought until lately. Ah me, perhaps I am homesick."

He stopped and gestured grandly toward Miss Dignam's.

"What? You can have all this and be homesick?"

"Silly!" She clasped his hand again when the people passed and unconsciously slowed her steps as the academy loomed closer and closer. "My parents are pretentious and silly, but they love each other. Mama will humor Papa when the weather is rainy and he cannot ride, and he will listen to her silly stories about the neighbors. But sometimes she is afraid when he storms and stomps about."

"Can that be love?" he asked in amazement, with a twinkle in the eyes that looked so tired.

She smiled. "I think it is. They know each other so well, faults and all, and it does not disgust them. And that is how my Romeo and Juliet will be."

"Ellen, you astound me," Gatewood said finally. "I never suspected you for a cynic, my dear." He touched her under the chin.

"No, sir, I am a realist," she replied quietly. "I hope to be as fortunate as they, some day. It may not seem like much, but perhaps it is. How will I know until I am there myself?"

Gatewood put her arm through his as he helped her down the steps leading to the servants' entrance. "Perhaps you will be more fortunate, Hermia."

She took her arm from his and opened the door, her mind on Thomas Cornwell. "Who can tell? I suspect that one must work at success in marriage, as in any other venture. Good night, Jim. Take care."

He kissed her fingers and hurried up the steps without a backward glance.

She watched him go, listening to his footsteps as he crossed the empty street, and then went into the servants' quarters.

Becky met her at the door of the scullery, her eyes wide.

"Miss Grimsley, do you know what time it is?"

"Why, no," she said, startled.

"Miss Dignam has already summoned all the young ladies for Psalms in the sitting room," Becky said as she hurried Ellen toward the stairs.

Ellen stared at her. "It is that late?"

"Oh, hurry, Miss Grimsley!"

Ellen gathered her robe about her and took the steps two at a time. She opened the door into the main hallway and looked about. Young ladies, armed with needlework, were headed toward the parlor. Ellen closed the door to a crack. When the last girl had passed, she opened the door and ran to the back stairs.

To her relief, the upper hall was deserted. She tiptoed down the corridor to her room and threw open the door. Fanny was seated at her desk. She looked up in surprise at Ellen, who stood before her in shirt, breeches, and scholar's gown. The only sounds in the room were Fanny's sharp intake of breath and Ellen's gasp of dismay.

Her whole body numb, Ellen closed the door. She clasped her hands in front of her.

"Well, say something," she said at last, when Fanny continued to regard her in silence.

Still Fanny said nothing. After a moment's observation, she rose from her chair and walked around Ellen, who followed her with her eyes.

"Charming," she ventured at last.

Ellen felt the tears start in her eyes. "Are you going to tell Miss Dignam?"

"Of course I am," Fanny replied, unable to keep the triumph from her voice.

Ellen closed her eyes and thought of the papers yet to be written, and Lord Chesney's disappointment.

"When?" she croaked.

Fanny laughed, but there was no mirth in the sound. "When I am good and ready, Ellen Grimsley."

Chapter 9

ELLEN UNDRESSED IN MISERABLE SI-
lence while Fanny busied herself at her desk.
Shivering in her chemise and drawers, Ellen
balled up the breeches, shirt, and cloak and threw them
in a corner of the dressing room. Her face set, wooden,
she pulled on a dress and ran her fingers through her
tangled hair. She followed Fanny downstairs to the sitting room, where she bowed her head and waited for
the ax to fall.

It did not. Fanny said nothing to the headmistress
then. Other than peering at them over the top of her
spectacles for being late, Miss Dignam addressed herself to the Psalms and then dismissed the girls to their
rooms.

Ellen got slowly to her feet. She glanced back to
see Fanny and Miss Dignam in earnest conversation.
Her heart plummeted to her shoes and stayed there

between her toes, as her stomach began to ache. She pressed her hand against her middle, wondering what would happen next.

As she slowly mounted the steps, she heard Fanny and Miss Dignam laughing. In another moment, Fanny was beside her.

"You look so pale, Ellen," Fanny observed with a smirk.

"Did . . . did you tell?"

"Not yet," Fanny said. "I will just let you stew and fret this week. Let us see if you choose to make any more cutting remarks about my brother. I advise you to hold your tongue, Ellen, if it isn't too much trouble."

She stopped on the landing and grasped Ellen by the arm. "Do you know, Ellen, I had not thought . . . When my father gets wind of this, I wonder if he will be so happy to see a connection between our two families."

"No, Fanny!" Ellen pleaded, her voice low.

It was as though Fanny had not heard. She released Ellen and gave her a little push. "And, Ellen, Edwin always does what Papa asks."

Ellen held her tongue, silently taking back every spiteful remark she had ever made to Fanny, following Fanny with her eyes. The ache in her stomach did not go away. Soon her head throbbed in sympathy.

Nothing escaped Fanny's sharp eyes during the endless week. She was watching when Ellen, with trembling fingers, opened the package from James Gatewood and took out Chesney's volume of Hakluyt's *Navigations and Voyages*.

"It is for geography," Ellen lied as she tried to make the book disappear on her cluttered desk.

"Silly me," Fanny said calmly. "I had thought we were studying Portugal and Spain this week."

Ellen swallowed her misery in *The Tempest*, working on it by the light of a single candle after Fanny snored in her bed. She could not sleep; the evils of the situation she had placed herself in revolved around and around in her head until sleep was out of the question. She drowned her own uneasiness in the misfortunes of the Duke of Venice, turning his adventures into a travel guide to the New World that was witty, urbane, and written in the middle of her own despair.

Several frantic notes to Gordon, delivered on the sly by Becky or the footman, evoked no response. As she sat, numb, through geography or struggled through embroidery, all she could think was that Gordon, safe in the knowledge that she would do his work for him, had gone to London again. *Wretched brother, more stupid sister*, she thought over and over as she sat at her desk, hand pressed to her forehead, as the words poured from her like nervous perspiration.

She did not know if Fanny had truly made the connection between her writings and Gordon's university triumphs. She shuddered to think of the scandal that would erupt if Gordon were dismissed for cheating. She blamed him for putting her in this delicate situation and blamed herself more for succumbing to her own vanity and writing those clever imaginings that now threatened to choke them both.

Each day dragged past and still Fanny said nothing.

Ellen found herself existing in an unfamiliar world of perpetual fright as she waited for Fanny to take Miss Dignam aside and tattle to the headmistress about the student clothes and gown that were still balled up into a corner of the dressing room. She would be sent home, her reputation in tatters. Ellen knew Fanny Bland well enough to know that, once home, Fanny would continue her malicious work, spreading tales about girls who go away to school and turn into fast pieces who dress in trousers so they can follow men about.

Only one note of brightness illuminated the grim picture: Thomas Cornwell would be so disgusted that Ellen need never fear again that he would offer for her.

It was little consolation. As the hounds of her imagination snapped at her heels, Ellen kept them at bay by plunging into the second paper, on *Romeo and Juliet*. While she kept busy writing, she could almost dismiss her own miseries. Late at night, when her stomach ached and her eyes burned with unshed tears, Ellen wove a fanciful comedy about a young couple, miraculously spared, who are too young and gradually find themselves wondering what they saw in each other in the first place. As the candle guttered out early Saturday morning, she penned the last word, blotted it dry, and then rested her face against the warm wood of the desk.

With a sigh, she put the paper in the desk drawer with the one on *The Tempest* that Gordon wanted. She frowned as she closed the drawer. It was Saturday morning, and Gordon had not made an effort to retrieve his paper.

It will serve you right if you miss the reading, Gordon

Grimsley, she thought as she quietly stood up, rubbed the small of her back, and carried her notes and rough drafts of both papers to the fireplace. Fanny stirred as the paper flamed up and crackled but did not waken. When her scholarship was nothing but ashes, Ellen crawled into bed. Once Gordon's paper was gone from her desk drawer, there was nothing to connect her with the writing of it.

She woke an hour later to the sound of knocking. Fanny opened the door to let in Becky Speed, who carried a brass can of hot water, which she set down at the dressing table.

"It's about time," Fanny said as Becky poured the water into a ceramic basin.

"Sorry, miss," Becky said and bobbed a curtsy.

Fanny turned to the washbasin. The maid came closer to Ellen's bed. "Gordon," she mouthed, so Fanny would not hear, and pointed down toward the lower reaches of the academy.

Ellen rose up on one elbow and looked Becky in the eye. She pointed to the desk and pantomimed opening the drawer. Becky nodded and tiptoed across the floor. Quietly, her eyes on Fanny, the maid opened the drawer and took out its contents.

She had almost reached the door when Fanny, her face soapy, turned around to watch her progress. Fanny's head came up and her eyes narrowed as she stared at the papers in the maid's hand. She looked at Ellen and then back at Becky, a smile spreading slowly across her damp face.

"Wait right there," she commanded.

Becky froze where she was, the papers tight in

her hand. Ellen lay back and closed her eyes as she felt the blood drain from her face. Once she saw the title, there was no way Fanny could mistake the connection between Gordon and the papers.

Fanny held out her hand for the papers as Becky backed up against the door. As Ellen held her breath, Fanny began to rub her eyes.

"Drat!" she exclaimed and turned around for a towel to wipe the soap from her face.

In the moment she turned, Becky threw open the door and ran down the stairs. Fanny, clad only in her chemise and petticoat, could only stare out the door and watch.

Ellen sighed and thanked the Lord who watches out for miserable sinners that Fanny Bland was too much of a lady to go charging half-naked after the maid.

"That was for Gordon, wasn't it?" Fanny exclaimed, whirling on Ellen. "And don't try to weasel out of it, Ellen Grimsley. You've been doing something for your brother, haven't you?"

Ellen made no reply, other than to get out of bed and tug down her nightgown, her mind made up. She ignored Fanny's questions as she crossed to the dressing room and calmly removed the scholar's gown. Deliberately she shook it out and laid it across her bed.

With a smile on her pale face, she touched its folds one last time. Moving fast to take advantage of Fanny's amazement at her brazen behavior after a week of miserable cowardice, Ellen pulled on the frilled shirt and breeches.

"Do you know, Fanny," she commented as she smoothed out the dark hose she had hidden in her bureau drawer, "these garments are so comfortable. I think that men have been keeping such a secret from us. If we knew how wondrously liberating trousers were, we would have worn them years ago. It's such fun to sit with your legs wide apart or propped up on a desk."

Fanny sputtered and wiped the soap from her face. Ellen scuffed her feet into the shoes, touching them up with the corner of the bedspread. "Of course, I don't doubt, Fanny, that when you marry, you'll wear the pants. If you marry."

"You . . . you . . ." was all Fanny could say as Ellen swirled the student's gown around her with a flourish.

"Brilliant repartee," Ellen said as she bowed elaborately to her roommate and closed the door behind her.

She wasted no time in the hall but darted down the back stairs, running past several other students, who shrieked and leaped out of the way. Her face set, her mind working a million miles an hour, she ran to the front door and out into the High.

As she raced across the street, the gown flapping in the stiff breeze, she looked back at her second-floor window where Fanny stood, beating on the frame. She sighed and thanked the Lord again. In another moment she would be protected by Oxford's warren of alleys and safe from immediate discovery.

Once out of sight of Miss Dignam's Select Female Academy, she slowed to a fast walk, breathing hard. To her knowledge, Fanny had no idea which college

Gordon attended. University was only one of many colleges that required Saturday papers of its first-year students. With any luck at all, Fanny and Miss Dignam would take some time finding her.

"And I will hear my paper read," she said out loud, unmindful of the students who stared at her when she spoke so emphatically and grinned at each other.

She knew they would find her. It was only a matter of contacting the Vice Chancellor and searching the student enrollments for each college. Perhaps by then, if Gordon were toward the first readers, she would have heard her paper delivered. There would be the humiliation of discovery and then Papa would be summoned. She would go home in disgrace.

"But I *will* hear my paper first," she whispered as she paused on the steps of University College's lecture hall. It would be something to remember through the dreary winter months at home, and all the months of her life to come, when she was tending Thomas Cornwell's children and running his manor, subordinating all her wishes and dreams to others' needs.

The hall was still empty. Quietly, she sat down in one of the side pews, toward the back. Her stomach pained her. She winced at the pain and shoved her elbow against her middle, looking about at the serenity of the hall, with its stained glass windows and fine-grained wood. The peace of it filled her, and she forgot her own misery.

Her chin went up as she looked about. *I am sitting in the lecture hall at University College*, she thought. *I will hear my paper read.*

Time passed. Even the slightest noise from outside the massive doors made her start in surprise. The unheated hall was frigid, and she could see her breath. She shivered and tucked her hands up under her armpits. The familiar ache began in her forehead.

Soon the students began to file in, laughing and chatting with one another. Some of them carried papers, and others, the ones who looked at ease, carried nothing more than gloves. The sound of their good humor filled the hall and echoed around it.

Tears started in Ellen's eyes. *They don't even know what they have here*, she thought as she dashed the tears away and made herself small in her corner pew.

She saw Gordon in the circle of his friends, his back straight, his eyes triumphant, as he clutched her paper. She peered closer. Just as she had thought. Becky had taken both essays from the drawer, and thank goodness for that. There was nothing left in her room to connect her with the papers. Whatever else there was had gone up the chimney hours before when she burned her notes. With any luck at all, she could get the *Romeo and Juliet* paper back from Gordon and tuck it away, to be hauled out and looked at in years to come.

Not that I will ever need a reminder of this day, she thought, with a slight smile. To her relief, Gordon sat far up front. Her smile broadened. In all her memory, Gordon Grimsley had never sat up front for any event requiring his attention.

The students all rose as the warden, dean, and fellows entered the hall in stately fashion and settled themselves behind the rostrum. Ellen nearly laughed out loud. His hair combed, and his shirt points reasonably starched, James Gatewood sat with them. He crossed his legs in that careless way that she so envied and looked out across the audience.

She wondered why he was there. Sitting next to him was a distinguished gentleman, with deep creases etched in his face like sculpted marble. As she watched, the two men put their heads together and exchanged a pleasantry that set them both laughing.

Ellen looked back at the open door. If there were time, she would get that *Romeo and Juliet* paper from Gordon and share it with James Gatewood. It was the least she could do for him. *Dear James, without your help, I would never have had the books I needed. Someday I will find a way to repay you*, she thought as the chaplain asked them all to kneel for prayer.

The prayer was long and in Latin. When it ended, the students seated themselves, coughed, and shuffled papers until the warden called them all to order.

"Young masters," he began, "you all know why we are here." He looked around and beamed at the faculty seated behind him. "We applaud your eagerness to rise at this disgraceful hour on a Saturday and contribute to the stamping out of ignorance."

The scholars laughed; it was the polite, appreciative mirth for a joke heard often. Some of them sat up straighter in anticipation of their own ordeal to come.

The readings began in no discernible order that Ellen could make out. She jumped in fright as the massive doors were closed behind her. The student sitting closest to her looked at her in surprise and then looked away, bored, as the next student rose to speak.

The hour dragged along. Some of the papers were witty, brilliant even, and Ellen applauded along with the other students in appreciation. Others were pedestrian and stilted—*the kind of paper that Gordon would have written, had he been compelled to do his own work*, she thought. The reminder of her own iniquity in the matter of Gordon's success came back again as she shivered and drew her gown tighter about her slight shoulders.

"Gordon Grimsley."

At the warden's announcement, the students whispered to each and then were silent, expectant, as her brother rose and walked slowly to the podium, papers in hand.

Ellen smiled, forgetting her own discomfort at the sight of her handsome brother mounting the podium, his back so straight, his head upright. *I should be so jealous*, she thought as he arranged the papers in front of him. *He has caused me considerable anxiety and anguish over this.* She shook her head. It was enough to be there.

"'*The Tempest*,'" he announced in carrying tones. "'A Travel Guide to the New World of English Literature.'"

Ellen beamed at the sounds of appreciation from Gordon's audience. It was a good title. She had labored over it when her stomach ached and she was so exhausted she had to lay her head on her books to rest for a few minutes each hour.

His voice carried well in the medieval hall. She listened, tears gleaming on her cheeks, as her useless brother made her happier than she could ever remember. *No*, she thought, *I was this happy once before, and that was in James Gatewood's chambers at All Souls, eating toasted bread and cheese and talking about Great Ideas.*

The thought of Gatewood turned her attention to him. She looked at his face, pleased to see the delight in his animated eyes, even from this distance. She only wished that he did not still look so tired, as though he slept no more than she did. *What can be troubling you, sir?* she thought, her mind miles away from Gordon. *Did you truly give away all your quarterly allowance to buy me books, and now you are hungry?*

She turned her attention to Gordon again. The door opened behind her, but she was caught up all over again in the magic of Shakespeare and did not feel the puff of colder air until it spread over the hall and then diminished as the door closed again.

Out of the corner of her eye, she saw the porter, note in hand, hurrying toward the podium. Ellen watched in mounting uneasiness as the man handed it to the college warden and then stepped back respectfully, his hands behind his back.

She sucked in her breath as the warden rose behind Gordon and put a heavy hand on his shoulder.

Surprised, Gordon stopped in midsentence. "Stand to one side, lad," the warden said.

The students looked at each other and began to whisper among themselves. Ellen swallowed several times and felt the blood drain from her face.

The warden looked down at the paper in his hand

and shook his head over it. He looked out across the audience, his eyes searching as the silence deepened and filled the hall. "Ellen Grimsley, come forward at once."

She did not move.

The warden continued his search of the hall, his lips set in a firmer line. His voice was softer but carried with it command.

"Miss Grimsley, we will find you in this hall, of this you can have no doubt."

The students burst into excited chatter, looking about them. Someone laughed. Gatewood had uncrossed his legs. His hands were on the arms of his chair, as though he were about to rise himself.

You cannot do that, she thought suddenly. *Any connection between us would be worse than my discovery in the Bodleian. It would ruin you.*

She leaped to her feet, propelled there by sheer nerves, and stood clutching the pew in front of her.

"Ellen!" Gordon gasped. "What the devil are you doing here?"

She stood as tall as she could and drew the cloak tighter around her as the hall fell immediately silent. "I wanted to hear the paper, Gordon. That is all."

The voices buzzed again as she forced herself to walk into the center aisle and stand there, her back straight.

The warden was shaking his head. "No, that is not all, Miss Grimsley. I have it on good authority that you are the author of these papers that Master Grimsley has been favoring us with week after week."

The talk rose to a roar that hushed with a wave of the warden's hand.

Ellen clasped her hands in front of her, marveling how cold they felt. She waited for the warden to speak.

"Did you write these papers, Miss Grimsley? Speak up now." The full knowledge of what she had done descended with a thump on her shoulders. As she watched the warden leave the podium and start toward her, she realized that admission of the truth would mean Gordon's immediate dismissal from University College. And no cavalry regiment would ever allow him to buy a pair of colors.

She lowered her eyes to the stone floor as the warden approached. *Isn't that what you want, Ellen Grimsley?* she asked herself calmly. *It's Gordon's fault and blame entirely. He was lazy, and he ought to be made to suffer for his sins.*

She looked up at Gordon, his face as white as hers, his mouth open to speak, his hands tight around the papers. The look in his eyes was naked, pleading.

James Gatewood had not stood up yet, but he was perched on the edge of the chair, his eyes on her face. She managed a smile at him, which the warden misinterpreted as he came closer.

"This is hardly a smiling matter, Miss Grimsley," he thundered. "Did you or did you not write those papers?"

Ellen closed her eyes for an instant and then raised her chin higher.

"Of course I did, sir."

It took the warden several moments to quiet the lecture hall.

Gatewood was on his feet now, starting toward her. She shook her head and he stopped. Gordon clutched the podium and bowed his head.

The warden was directly in front of her. He towered over her like a bird of prey in his long robe with the velvet bands on the sleeves. He waved the note under her nose.

"You wrote them?" he asked again, the incredulity in his voice unmistakable. "Impossible! Females cannot do such work!"

It stung worse than she had imagined it would. How dare this man think that, because she was a woman, she was incapable of scholarship? But so he would have to think, she decided. One last glance at Gordon convinced her. She managed a slight smile.

"Yes, sir, I did. If you knew my brother's wretched handwriting, you would understand why he came to me and begged me to make fair copies of his Saturday talks. I did not think it would hurt. I came only because I wanted to hear him read one."

Several students began to laugh. The scholar closest to her nudged another and remarked how he wished he had a beautiful sister with good handwriting so conveniently at hand.

The warden did not smile. His agate eyes remained unreadable, even as his lips relaxed slightly. He shook his head.

"I have knowledge from Miss Aloysia Dignam of

her Select Female Academy that you are the author of these papers, Miss Grimsley."

Ellen swallowed again and took a step toward the warden.

"Prove it," she said, her voice loud and clear, even as her legs trembled and would scarcely hold her up.

The warden stared at her, his mouth open. He looked over his shoulder at the podium. This time, the tall man next to James Gatewood rose to his feet.

Everyone rose. Ellen blinked in surprise. Who was this man?

Majestically, he strode down the aisle. The warden bowed as he approached and stood in front of Ellen Grimsley, whose knees had begun to shake by now.

He looked at her long and hard, and then turned his attention to the warden.

"She has admitted to no guilt. This ends the matter, sir, as far as the scholarship is concerned." He looked back up at the aisle at Gordon, who had not relaxed his grip on the podium. "An Oxford man would never lie about such a thing. If Gordon Grimsley makes no disclaimer, then we will not question you further. Sir?"

Wordlessly, Gordon shook his head and then bowed it again.

"Then here the matter rests, Warden." The man turned his attention to Ellen again. "Miss Grimsley, I am Vice Chancellor of Oxford University. It is my duty, in very deed it is my heartfelt pleasure, to expel you from these premises. Please go and do not return."

Without a word, or another glance at the podium, Ellen turned and fled the hall. The door was heavy, and she thought she would never get it open, but in another moment, she was in the quadrangle of University College. Miss Dignam, nostrils flaring, eyes blazing, took her by the arm and hurried her across what seemed like acres and acres of wintry stubble. Ellen looked back once at the entrance hall. Some of the students had opened the narrow medieval windows and stared out at her. Someone waved.

She turned away in shame as tears of rage ran down her face. Miss Dignam gave her arm a good shake. "It's very well that you feel humiliated, Ellen Grimsley," she exclaimed. "I don't know what this will do to the reputation of my school!"

Ellen shook herself free, sobbing out loud in frustration and anger. She looked back once more. "I am better than all of you foolish scholars who waste your time," she shouted. "Some day this will change!"

The wind carried her words away over the walls of the quadrangle as though she had not spoken them.

Fanny said nothing to her as Miss Dignam escorted her to her room. She sat at her desk, cool and tidy as usual, looking down her long nose at Ellen's rumpled gown and her tear-streaked face. She met the rebellion in Ellen's eyes for one brief moment, then looked away, her face pale.

Miss Dignam marched Ellen over to her desk and plumped her down. "You will remain in this room until your father comes to get you, Miss Grimsley. I have already sent for him. I do not doubt that he will be here soon." The headmistress rolled her eyes and fanned herself with her hand. "I cannot imagine what possessed you to dress so indecently and parade yourself in front of all those students."

Ellen sighed. Thank heavens Miss Dignam had made no mention of the papers. "I wanted to hear Gordon read," she repeated stubbornly.

Fanny was turning around now and frowning. "But Ellen wrote those papers!" she exclaimed.

"Absurd!" Miss Dignam snapped. She slammed the door behind her.

"You wrote those papers, Ellen Grimsley," Fanny said quietly as Miss Dignam's footsteps retreated down the hall.

"You will have to prove it, Fanny," she replied, her eyes boring into the view of Oxford before her.

Fanny jumped up and crossed the room to Ellen's desk, jerking open the drawer. It was empty. She ran her hands over the books on Ellen's desk, searching for stray papers, going at last in frustration to the fireplace, where she stood, her fists clenched, looking down at the piles of ashes.

"You burned your notes. All of them. Didn't you?" she asked.

"I have nothing to say," Ellen said. After one last look, she tugged at the curtain pull and removed the panorama of Oxford from her sight. She changed clothes and lay down on her bed, her face to the wall. In another moment, she slept.

Chapter 10

SQUIRE GRIMSLEY, EVEN MORE RED-faced and pop-eyed than usual, was there by morning. He was standing over her bed, his riding crop twitching against his leg, when she woke.

White-faced, Ellen sat up. The squire pulled a chair to the bed and sank into it as he unbuttoned his mud-flecked coat. He looked over his shoulder at Fanny Bland, who sat at her desk, studiously ignoring them both.

"Fanny, find someplace else to sit," he said and stared at her until she gathered up her embroidery and swept out of the room, shutting the door with a decisive click that bordered on the insolent.

The squire turned back to his daughter. He said nothing for several minutes, until Ellen wanted to dig her toes into the mattress.

He sighed finally and leaned back in the chair. "I

can be grateful, I suppose, that you did not tease me with one of those 'But Papa, you don't understand,' arguments that Horatia favors."

"I really don't have anything to say, Papa," Ellen managed at last. Her tongue felt too large for her mouth, as though it would impede her very speech and breath.

"Well, I do, Ellen," he replied and glanced around to make sure that the door was shut.

When he finished a half hour later, his face was as white as hers. He was looking out the window at the view she had renounced the day before, and from the way his knuckles were stretched so tight against the draperies, it obviously brought him little pleasure.

"A scandal like this could ruin a family, Ellen," he was saying, almost more to himself than to her. "A man's daughter parades herself around a university in breeches? What does this tell about her parents, her upbringing?"

Ellen could only stare, dry-eyed at last, at his broad back. *Why is it so wrong to want to learn*, she wanted to cry out. *Why must I sneak around to study? Why can I not use the library and the study halls, listen to the lectures and ask questions of dons and fellows?*

"Well, what do you think of that?" Papa was asking her.

"I am sorry, I was not listening," she stammered.

The riding crop crashed on the desk. "Have you even heard a word I have said, daughter?" he raged.

Ellen burst into tears again.

Papa snorted in frustration and dragged his damp handkerchief back out of his pocket.

"Come on, Ellen, perhaps in time Thomas will get over this unfortunate bit of high spirits," he said. "Goodness knows he would still be in the dark, if someone had not send an anonymous letter from Oxford."

"What!" Ellen gasped, clutching the handkerchief. She sank back down in the bed, resisting the urge to pull the blankets over her head and retreat. "Who could have done that?" she asked, only to know the answer already. Fanny must have told him—meddling, jealous Fanny.

But Papa was talking. She forced herself to listen.

". . . and he almost insisted that I let him come along, daughter. I told him it was still a family matter." The squire sat down again, this time not meeting her eyes. "He said, 'All the more reason I should be there.'"

Ellen was silent, digesting this oblique bit of information. "What has Thomas Cornwell to do with our family?" she asked finally, knowing the squire's answer before he spoke and dreading it.

"Well, we have been talking, these past few weeks," was all he said, his voice unsure for the first time since their grueling interview began.

"Did you tell him I would marry him?" she asked quietly.

The squire nodded, taking in the distress on her face that she did not try to hide. "Ah, daughter, we all have to do things in life that we don't relish!" he burst out when she did not speak.

"Not marriage!" she exclaimed, sitting up straight. "You don't need the money, do you, Papa?"

He shook his head and then looked at her. "Think of the land, Ellen! He may not have a title like Horry's future father-in-law, or that Bland prestige, but he has land." He threw up his hands. "We can join the farms for twice the profit, and I'll get that little parcel of land over by Lowerby that I have had my eyes on for years."

"You would do that to me?" was all she said. "Papa, I don't love Thomas Cornwell. I don't even like him."

"What does love have to do with our discussion?" the squire said after several long moments dragged by in silence. "What indeed? Get your clothes on, Ellen. We're going home."

"How could you, Papa?" she whispered.

"Because it is my right!" he raged.

He left the room, but she lay where she was, contemplating the ruin of her life, and all because she had written a few paltry papers.

A moment's reflection convinced her that the papers had nothing to do with it. While she had been away at Oxford, Papa had schemed and meddled with the Cornwells until all she had to do was return home and in a few weeks slide into Horatia's wedding gown, still warm from the Bland wedding. Papa would likely exchange a few acres of his own for those acres of the Cornwells' he had been coveting, and the deed would be done.

It had nothing to do with Oxford, except that her sojourn there, if only for a few weeks, had let Papa wheel and deal to his heart's content.

She thought of the papers, particularly the unread paper on *Romeo and Juliet*, wondering again if Gordon still kept it, or if Lord Chesney has appropriated it in all the excitement yesterday in University College Hall, or if Lord Chesney had even been there. She closed her eyes against the humiliation still so fresh in her mind. Pray that Lord Chesney was not there.

"I did so want you to see that paper, Jim Gatewood," she said softly as she pulled on her clothes and checked the room one last time to see if she had forgotten anything. "I wish I could have said good-bye, and thank you."

The books lay on the desk. She picked up the Hakluyt book, turning its old and mellow pages, breathing deep of the fragrance of worn leather, ink, and rag paper from an earlier century or two. She wrote a hasty note to the footman, asking him to see that this was returned to its owner, and then crammed the complete words of Shakespeare into her little trunk, along with Chesney's *Commentary and Notes on A Midsummer Night's Dream*. She could give Gatewood's gifts to Ralph. Better he should have them than she should see them mock her from her bookshelf.

If Cornwell's house even had a bookshelf.

She was dressed and downstairs in a matter of minutes. No one was in the halls, and she tiptoed along them, but she heard doors open as she passed and knew that the other inmates of the academy were staring at her. The knowledge burned, but she did not turn around to confront their rudeness.

The door to Miss Dignam's office was closed. She regarded it for a moment, then sat in the straight-backed chair against the wall. She gazed across the hall at the art Miss Dignam chose to hang where students awaiting reprimand could see it. The print was an old one of Hogarth's illustrating the course of life open to young ladies who choose to be disobedient, fractious, and disagreeable.

Hogarth had limned his topic well, but as Ellen stared at it, she couldn't help suspecting that A Fate Worse Than Death might be more tolerable than waking up each morning for the rest of her life and seeing Thomas Cornwell snoring beside her.

She listened to the low murmur of voices inside Miss Dignam's sanctum sanctorum and was startled to hear the sound of laughter.

"Sadists," she muttered under her breath and then sighed with weariness. She had slept only after a night of tossing about. All she wanted now was to endure one final scold from Miss Dignam, pull her cloak up about her ears, and go home to her own bed. It couldn't come soon enough.

The door opened. She jumped in spite of herself as Miss Dignam stepped into the hall, her face wreathed in smiles. Ellen blinked in surprise and slowly rose to her feet.

"Good morning, my dear," Miss Dignam said, her smile at its toothiest as she closed the door behind her. "I trust you slept well."

"Quite badly, actually," Ellen said, her eyes wide with wonder at the spectacle before her.

"Very good, my dear, very good. Come along inside, if you will."

This is worse and worse, Ellen thought. Only a case-hardened veteran of the French Revolution could smile that way as the blade dropped. She put up her hand as Miss Dignam started to open the door again. "Miss Dignam, were you in France during the Revolution?"

It was Miss Dignam's turn to stare and then laugh indulgently. "Ellen, what won't you say?"

Ellen shook her head to clear it and followed Miss Dignam into her office. Her father, all rage and animosity vanished, looked back at her. Her jaw dropped in amazement as she glanced at the occupant in the easy chair by the window, who sat so carelessly with his legs crossed.

"Jim!" she exclaimed. "How did you get dragged into this?"

Miss Dignam tittered behind her hand. "It appears you two *have* already met. My lord, you are a naughty, naughty boy! Ellen, let me introduce James Gatewood, Lord Chesney, of Chesney, Hertfordshire, and Chesney Hall, London."

Ellen could only stare in stupefied silence.

Gatewood stirred himself. "I think I am a bit of a surprise to her," he commented to the squire, who nodded and laughed in appreciation, goodwill written all over his florid face.

"Ah, that you are, your worship!" Squire Grimsley said. "One hardly ever finds Ellen at a loss for words." He paused, and then stumbled into the conversation again as Gatewood opened his mouth to speak. "Not that she is a chatterbox, or a gossip monger, my lord. Oh, no! She's the soul of circumspection and the delight of her mother and me."

Ellen stared at her father. Less than fifteen minutes ago, he had given her the scold of her life, and so much as sentenced her to endless matrimony with the worst bore in the county. Now he was all smiles and good cheer.

Miss Dignam was no better. She nodded and bobbed her head until Ellen grew almost dizzy with watching. "My best pupil ever," she declared, even as she dabbed at her eyes. "I will miss her more than I can say, my lord."

"You . . . you never told me," she began and stopped, plopping into the chair by the door because her legs would not hold her up.

"No, I didn't, did I?" Gatewood began. He blushed and stared down at his hands. "I really owe you an explanation but would prefer to reserve it for some more private moment."

"Oh, la, my lord, we can arrange that in a moment," simpered Miss Dignam.

She cleared her throat and then poked the squire, who scrambled to his feet, giving Ellen a broad wink. "Miss Dignam, we can easily retreat to the sitting room, and you can tell me again your theories on education."

Ellen stared at her father, who had never once, in all the years of their acquaintance, come within a ten-foot pole of theories of any kind. Here he was, bowing and scraping and making a perfect cake of himself, where only minutes before he had been hard as nails.

And then she understood and was filled with the

greatest humiliation she had ever known. The misery she had inflicted upon herself yesterday in University College's lecture hall held no candle to this new agony that washed over her and left her drained. It was the humiliation of being ashamed of her family.

As they watched her, Gatewood's eyes hopeful, Miss Dignam and her father eager to please, Ellen felt the bile rise in her throat. All her life she had known the security of being the daughter of a prosperous squire from a prosperous county. There was comfort in knowing that no matter how she personally regarded each family member's silliness and vanities, they were unknown to others. The Grimsleys' name in Oxfordshire was enough.

And now, here was this new squire she had never seen before, twittering about Lord Chesney like a moth to a flame. In one introduction to Lord Chesney, Papa had gone from respected man in his own little sphere to a very small frog in a very large pond. The knowledge caused her unspeakable embarrassment.

She looked at Lord Chesney, who was on his feet by now, running his fingers through his tousled hair. His face was agitated; unlike the others, Gatewood had seen the look in her eyes and understood what it meant.

"See here, Ellen, I am sorry," he began, only to be interrupted by the squire.

"No, lad, no! I mean, your worship. It was only a high-spirited prank on your part!" The squire laughed, showing all his teeth. "Ellen doesn't mind, do you, my dear?"

"I mind greatly," she said, her voice low. "Why

didn't you tell me who you were? Why did you lead me on down a path that you must have known would end as it did yesterday?"

"I . . ."

The squire could see that the tide was not turning in Lord Chesney's favor. He chucked his daughter under the chin, choosing not to notice when she drew back from him and made herself smaller in the chair. "Ellen! It's all right and tight! Lord Chesney has explained that you wrote those silly papers that Gordon read! Miss Dignam and I would never tell a soul, so your secret is safe."

Ellen noted that, to his credit, Lord Chesney winced at her father's artless confession.

"You are wrong, Papa," she said, her voice rising slightly. "Gordon should be expelled from university for what he did, and there is no censure great enough for my part in it. We did a disservice to this great university." She turned her fine eyes on James Gatewood, who by now was at the window again and chewing on his fingernails. "I do not know why you took such an interest in my scholarship, sir . . ."

"He is a lord, Ellen, not a sir!" her father hissed at her.

"Sir," she continued, her voice cool even as her face flamed. "Who are you? A duke? an earl? a marquess? a viscount? The chancellor of the exchequer?"

"Ellen!" the squire groaned. He leaped to his feet. "My lord, she does not mean any of this."

"I am sure she means all of it, sir," he replied, "and I, for one, do not blame her." He crossed the room to stand before Ellen, who rose slowly to her feet. "We share a weakness, Ellen. It is scholarship. It has gotten you in trouble, and I was the author of your humiliation."

"I am sure she can overlook this little fault," the squire said magnanimously.

Ellen said nothing. *Papa, you are such a toady*, she thought. *I am so ashamed.*

But Lord Chesney was speaking. "I am a marquess, Ellen. I am worth a bit more than Edwin Bland's four thousand a year, although I have never had the feeling that such trivia mattered to you. I am also somewhat shy. That was why I created this fiction. I had a feeling that you might not care for a marquess over much. Was I wrong?"

"Nonsense!" the squire brayed. "Ellen knows what's good for her." He laughed out loud, and Miss Dignam joined in.

"Papa, please stop," Ellen begged. She edged toward the door. She held out her hand to James Gatewood. "Good-bye, sir. I . . . I . . . cannot say that I am sorry to have written those papers, but I am embarrassed that you have seen us as we really are."

He took her hand. "I love you, Ellen."

She froze, even as her father clapped a meaty hand on the marquess's shoulder.

"Well said, your worship," he exclaimed. "Do you know, Ellen, he has already talked to me this morning about settlements, and Gordon is even to have a cavalry regiment of Lord Chesney's choosing. I call that magnanimous."

"I call it foolish," Ellen said, withdrawing her hand from Gatewood's. "Good day, my lord. I hope you choke on your scholarship."

"Ellen!" the squire gasped and then turned it aside with a little laugh. "She'll come around, your worship."

"Possibly," Lord Chesney replied. "If you'll excuse us, Squire?"

Before she could protest, Gatewood took her by the hand and dragged her into the hall. He pushed her against the wall and grasped her by both shoulders.

"I didn't mean any of this to happen, Ellen. You must believe that," he said, his voice urgent. Doors were opening all along the hallway. He looked around in annoyance. "I hate this place!" He sighed and released her to run a finger around his shabby collar. "See here, I've never proposed before, and I am sure I have done it all wrong, Ellen. But I love you. Will you marry me?"

She said nothing. He pulled her close and kissed her, his arms tight around her. To her ultimate humiliation, she found herself kissing him back. Her fingers were in his untidy hair, smoothing it, caressing him.

When the buttons on his coat began to dig into her, she came back to herself. With a shock, she leaped back, took a deep breath, made a fist, and struck him on the face.

He reeled back in surprise, his hand to his flaming cheek. They stared at each other, breathing hard. Her humiliation complete, Ellen felt the tears starting behind her eyelids. She stamped her foot.

"I hope I never, ever see you again, Jim Gatewood!" she sobbed.

He said nothing for the longest moment. She watched his face, waiting for some sign of repugnance, some indication of his disgust of her after her shameless kiss and then that dreadful punch that still seemed to echo in the hall. Instead, he reached in his pocket and gave her his handkerchief.

She blew her nose vigorously. "I'll . . . I'll have this laundered and returned to All Souls," she said, her voice stiff.

He smiled then, even as a bruise of impressive proportions began to form on his cheek. "Are your knuckles all right?" he asked, his voice mild. "That was quite a facer from someone of such unsymmetrical proportions."

She looked down at her hand, with the knuckles cracked and bleeding, and dabbed at it with the handkerchief. She was unable to think of a thing to say, except to stammer again that she would return the handkerchief.

Lord Chesney shook his head and then winced and clapped his hand to his cheek again.

Ellen writhed with inward embarrassment.

"No need, my dear," he said as he started backing toward the outside door. "I'll be seeing you in a couple of weeks."

"I doubt that!" she declared and blew her nose again.

"Doubt it not, fair Hermia," he said as he continued down the hall, backing away from her. "Your father has invited me to Horatia's wedding, and I accepted with great alacrity and greater pleasure."

"He didn't!" she wailed.

"He did! See you soon, you dreadful wench." He paused with his hand on the doorknob. "Do you know, I am relieved that you are such a pugilist."

She sobbed harder, whether in rage or humiliation she could not tell.

"I need never fear that harm will come to me while we are mapping the world, fair Hermia!"

Chapter 11

HER KNUCKLES THROBBED ALL the way home, and Ellen welcomed the pain. "Maybe if it hurts bad enough, you will remember not to be so stupid in the future," she told herself as she sucked on the swollen joints.

She could not imagine what had possessed her to deliver such a wallop to James Gatew . . . to Lord Chesney. Even if Mama was a flibbertigibbet of the first stare, Ellen had been raised with great circumspection. She knew better than to flirt with young men, or to even sit down in a chair recently vacated by one, because it would still be warm. That she should cut loose so entirely as to assault a marquess was a continuing astonishment to her as she rode in solitary splendor through magnificent scenery turned sour by her mood.

It was a relief that her Papa had ridden his horse to Oxford and was therefore compelled to arrange a post chaise for his daughter. Ellen curled up in one corner of the vehicle and tucked her chin into her cloak, grateful that there was no need of conversation, except that mighty scold that she dumped upon her own head like hot coals and ashes.

Oh, how could Papa invite Lord Chesney to the wedding! She started to twist her hands together, uttering a yelp of pain when she encountered her knuckles. It was too bad, utterly too bad. *He will see us at our worst: Papa chafing and swearing if the weather is too inclement for at least one canter about the countryside each day; Mama even more unmanageable than usual, with her silly spasms over the tiniest slipup in her plans.*

And Horry, Horatia would be worse than useless, mooning about the house as soon as Edwin—with many a backward glance and thrown kisses—nudged his horse down the lane. Either that, or some of the reality of marriage will have set in and she will be scared spitless and cowering in her dressing room.

Ellen retreated farther into her cloak. *And then Mama will give her improving lectures on the evils of men in general, and reassure us that all will be well, or at least, as good as can be, considering that it is woman's lot in life to suffer.* Ellen shuddered. *It is a wonder to me*, she thought, *that someone would really want to be mauled about in that way. Horry is stupider than even I suspected.*

She reflected on that thought and felt her cheeks grow red.

She hadn't minded a bit when James Gatewood had grabbed her by both shoulders and kissed her so soundly. In fact, she recalled with some personal irritation that the worst part about the whole, regrettable incident was the nagging feeling that she couldn't get close enough to him. *And did I really thrust myself against him? Oh, dear, I hope he did not notice.*

There, she had thought the unthinkable. *Goodness, Ellen, you are a worse ninnyhammer than your sister,* she thought. Nice girls didn't reflect on those rather impish thoughts that had raced through her mind as she clung like a barnacle to James Gatewood.

"Lord Chesney, not Jim Gatewood anymore," she said out loud. "It is Lord Chesney, and he has done you a bit of no good."

So he had. For weeks and weeks he had led her to believe he was someone he was not. He had placed her in several compromising situations that would have sent Mama into terminal spasms, should she ever find out.

Or had he? Ellen drew her knees up and rested her chin on them as the post chaise swayed along. She had been in no danger from Lord Chesney's designs, or so Mama would put it. They had spent an afternoon together in his chambers, and another on the river, discussing Shakespeare and nourishing each other's minds. It was the kind of conversation she envied among the scholars of Oxford, that equal exchange of thoughts and views.

"I wonder if men and women will ever be permitted such freedom of thought," she asked out loud. "I . . . I guess I was lucky."

She smiled at the memory and then sobered as she thought about the rest of her family. Ralph would acquit himself well, this she knew. Lord Chesney—no,

Jim Gatewood—would be captivated by her little brother and his serious approach to scholarship. Should he come for the wedding, she would see that Jim and Ralph saw plenty of each other during the days before the wedding. And Martha? It would be her duty to keep Martha out of the chocolates.

She let her mind rest a moment and then laughed out loud. "Ellen, you are a true idiot," she said. "You will be safely out of this ridiculous infatuation when Jim sees your family as they really are. No need to apologize for them. Just let him see for himself."

She nodded to her reflection in the window glass. In a short space, he will be so disgusted that he will probably beat a hasty retreat even before Horry's nuptials. End of problem.

The thought did not relieve her as she had imagined it would. For no reason that she could discern, she burst into tears.

Her eyes were long since dry by the time she tapped on the glass and stopped the post chaise before they turned off the main road and traveled down the lane. Papa reined in his horse and leaned toward the carriage as she rolled down the window.

"Papa, I forbid you to mention one word of this affair to anyone," she ordered, keeping her knees tight together so they would not quake at this unheard-of insistence by daughter to father.

"Oh, you do?" he asked. To her relief, his voice was mellow.

Obviously, Squire Grimsley was still basking in the idea of an alliance far beyond his wildest dreams.

It was on the tip of her tongue to assure him that such an event would never come to pass, but she let it go and smiled sweetly up at him instead. "Yes, Papa, I insist! It is Horry's big day, and nothing is settled, and it would be the height of rudeness for us to trumpet these imaginings about the countryside."

"I suppose so," he agreed, his voice filled with reluctance. He brightened. "But I shall have to say something to Mama, or she will think only the worst about my sudden trip to Oxford." He frowned and shook his riding crop at her. "And you are still a scamp, Ellen Grimsley."

"Yes, Papa," she said, and there was no subterfuge in her voice. "I was. But I mean to reform."

"Very well, miss. Now, roll up that window before pneumonia carries you off and I can never tell my comrades that I am closely related to the Marchioness of Chesney!"

She sighed and did as he said. *I hope he will not take it too badly when I continue to refuse Jim's offer of marriage*, she thought as they proceeded down the lane. *I suppose I had better consider Thomas Cornwell more seriously.*

Ellen was happier to see them all than she would have thought possible. Horatia was as silly as ever; Mama as nervous. Ralph wanted to discuss Great Ideas, and Martha nosed about for sweets. As she stood in the hallway, still clad in her traveling cloak and hiding her swollen knuckles, Ellen could only regard them with affection.

"I have missed you all," she said simply and wondered why she felt like tears again.

222

Mama's chin trembled. "I hope you were not in terrible trouble in Oxford, my dear, else why would Mr. Grimsley rush off in such a hurry?" She rested her hand against her forehead. "I have been imagining the worst."

"'Tis nothing, my dearest," the squire soothed. "Let us discuss this matter in private."

Mama nodded and watched him retreat down the hall, whistling to himself as he swatted at the potted plants with his riding crop. "He is in rare good humor," she observed, then turned to her daughter again. "Ellen, it is too bad! Your papa refuses to spend one more penny on food for the reception, and I have told him it is not enough."

"And he is being a perfect beast about the music in the church," Horry added, handkerchief to her eyes too. "He insists on all his favorite hymns, and you know how old-fashioned they are!"

Ellen took off her bonnet and tossed it to Ralph, who grinned and beat his own retreat before the Grimsley females began to weep in earnest. Slowly, Ellen unbuttoned her pelisse and smiled upon her sister and mother. *Last week, I would have been so impatient with you both*, she thought.

Tears came to her own eyes as she embraced them, urging them not to fret, telling them that she would make things right with Papa. She hugged her silly mother and sister, deeply cognizant of the fact that even their combined foolishness did not equal the enormity of her own folly.

"There now, Mama, I am certain I can convince

Papa to lay out some more blunt for refreshments. Now, go along and hear what he has to tell you."

"I wish you would not use such dreadful cant," Mama scolded, but she did as Ellen said.

Ellen turned to Horatia. "Horry, dearest, all you have to do is slip in one or two of Papa's own favorite hymns, and he will allow you the rest. You know he will. Don't be a goose."

"Do you think so?" Horatia asked.

"I know so."

Horatia blew her nose. She was silent a moment as they walked arm in arm toward the stairs. She stopped suddenly to more closely observe her sister.

"Ellen, you act as though you had something on Papa."

"It could be that I do, my dear."

"Oh, tell!"

Ellen laughed, even though she did not feel particularly jolly. "It is nothing that cannot wait. Come, dearest, and let me hear your plans."

She lay wide awake in bed late that night, long after Horry had yawned for the last time and taken herself off to her own room, eyes bright with wedding plans. Ellen thought about dinner and turned restlessly onto her side. Mama, bursting with Papa's news but sworn to secrecy, was all smiles and dimples from first course to last.

It is bad of me to encourage her, Ellen thought as she turned to her other side and flipped around the pillow for a cool spot. *I should tell them all flat out that I have no intention in the world of marrying Lord Chesney.*

Or do I? She hugged her pillow to her, thinking of James, head thrown back, laughing at something she had said that afternoon in his chambers. James with his feet propped up so negligently at his carrel in the Bodleian. James poling so expertly on the river rimmed with ice, a glass of champagne in one gloved hand, and good ideas tumbling out of his head. James that first afternoon on the hill overlooking Oxford, letting his shredded letter blow into the wind.

With a shake of her head, she got out of bed and stood by the window. It had always been her favorite view, that long expanse of valley before her, wooded, and with streams flowing.

Now it was merely cold and wind-scoured. The trees had surrendered all their leaves and the streams were clogged with ice. The distant hills that were so invitingly purple in the summer were only dim, dark shapes now. She closed her eyes, wishing with all her heart that she could open them upon the Oxford landscape.

She rested her cheek against the curtain. "I shall write an essay on the permanence of impermanent things," she decided as she allowed the tears stifled since her homecoming to flow. "After all, what are the quads, halls, chapels, and libraries except symbols of ideas that will never die?"

But there would be no time for essays, not in these hectic days before the wedding. She glanced at the large volume of Shakespeare on her desk, a gift from James Gatewood. She had not given it to Ralph yet. Perhaps it could wait another day or two, when the reality of being home, and all that it meant, set in with a vengeance.

If it ever does, she thought as she crawled back into bed. *I have changed. It was only a paltry few weeks, but I have changed.*

Whether it was for the better, she could not tell. As the sound of her fist against James Gatewood's face echoed through her head, she knew that she could not possibly have improved. *How could I have done that?* she asked again. *I have never been that angry at anyone before, and here I thought I liked him.*

Earlier that evening, she had approached Horatia cautiously, when they were both sitting on her bed, asking if she had ever felt angry enough to strike Edwin Bland. Horry's eyes had widened as her hand went to her mouth. "Mercy, Ellen, of course not! He is my true and only love!"

"Don't you ever get angry at him?" Ellen had asked.

"I couldn't possibly. Edwin is everything that is proper and right."

"Oh."

Ellen sighed in the dark. Whatever it was she felt for James Gatewood obviously wasn't true love, then. She blushed. *Dear me*, she thought, *it is much worse.* Last year, Mama had sat them both down one afternoon when they had the house to themselves. With blushes and long pauses, Mama had divulged some of the mystery surrounding the male sex. Mama had warned them about the "animal instincts in men."

Do women have such base instincts? Ellen asked herself. *Dear me, I wish there was someone I could ask.* She scrunched herself into a ball and pulled the blankets over her head, reflecting on this compounding of her sins. She would never marry Lord Chesney, no matter what Mama and Papa thought, so the matter of her base instincts would likely never surface to trouble her. And if she married Thomas Cornwell? Ellen shook her head. She had not the remotest wish to plant either a facer or a kiss upon him, so the matter could be considered safely closed. Cornwell would likely never inspire those tempting thoughts that had filled her head and now left her ashamed.

Still, Jim's lips had been so warm and . . . she cast about for the right words to describe his kiss. She decided after much thought that there was no single adjective. Gatewood's kiss had been a complexity of many feelings. *I felt that he and I were doing something that no one else in the world had ever done before*, she thought. *I didn't give a rap who saw us. The only thing that mattered was Jim.*

Ellen burrowed deeper in her bed. "Miss Grimsley," she began, her voice muffled by the covers, "you will begin by not thinking of him as 'Jim' anymore. He is Lord Chesney, a peer of the realm, who thinks himself in love. A Christmas visit with his own kind will wake him up, I am sure."

That thought was a bucket of cold water on her nervous imaginings. He would never show up for the wedding. A little cool-eyed reflection of his own would show him the wisdom of staying far away from Squire Grimsley's manor. He might feel honor-bound to send a gift, but he would not bring it in person, she convinced herself.

It should have been a reassuring thought, but it wasn't. She dwelt upon it long enough for the monotony of that single idea to send her off to sleep finally.

In the morning, she disappointed Ralph by insisting that her walk into the village be solitary.

"My dear, since I am not returning to Oxford, we have ages and ages to discuss Shakespeare," she told him as she pulled on her gloves. She touched his cheek. "On my desk is an early Christmas present to you. That should distract you sufficiently for me to have a comfortable chat with Aunt Shreve."

She watched her brother hurry up the stairs. Tears welled up suddenly as she thought of the "Good Luck" Jim Gatewood had scrawled across both inside pages. She dabbed furtively at her eyes, looking around to make sure that she was not seen. *I simply must get over this lachrymosity*, she thought, as she let herself out of the house.

With the door carefully closed against the servants, and a comforting fire in the hearth, Ellen told her aunt everything that had happened during her brief Oxford career, leaving out no detail, no matter how gory. When she finished, Aunt Shreve merely sat there, a slight smile on her face, as Ellen stirred up the coals in the fireplace.

"I gather then that I do not need to sacrifice my one remaining bottle of Palais Royal just yet."

"It seems so, Aunt," Ellen replied quietly, her chin on her palm, as she stared into the flames that briefly rose and then died because there was nothing left to feed upon. "It would never have worked. I have been a fool, and I freely admit it."

Aunt Shreve took Ellen by the hand. "But I must know, my dear, did you enjoy writing those papers?"

Ellen laughed out loud, her misery shoved aside for the moment. "I did! It was glorious fun. I only wish I had them to show you, Aunt."

"Perhaps you can ask Lord Chesney about that when he arrives for the wedding," Aunt Shreve suggested.

"He will not come," Ellen said. "I am sure of it."

"You will not think me foolish if I beg to differ with you?" her aunt asked, a twinkle in her eyes.

"He will not come," she said again. "I know it. Let us find another subject to discuss, Aunt."

They did, touching upon the weather, Horry's wedding, the approaching Yuletide, and the visits of Aunt Shreve's own children, one of whom was symmetrical enough to be in Horry's bridal party.

"Tell me, Aunt," she said suddenly, during a lull in trivia. "Do you know anything about the marquesses of Chesney?"

"It hardly matters," Aunt Shreve replied, her dimple much in evidence. "He will not come."

"Aunt! I am merely . . . curious."

"Go to the bookcase. My dear Walter used to enjoy thumbing through *Great Families of England*. I believe our copy is up to date within ten years."

Ellen found the book. Perching herself on the arm of Aunt Shreve's chair, she turned to the section on Hertfordshire. Aunt Shreve peered at the book too. "Hertfordshire, is it? Excellent country. I wonder, does he hunt?"

"Only for mice in the Bodleian," Ellen murmured. She ran her fingers down the page. "Let us see: Casewell, Charterus, Chesmouth, Chesney." She read to herself and then looked up. "It is an old title, Aunt. Dear me, they appear to own half of Hertfordshire!"

"It is a small shire," Aunt Shreve commented, a smile playing about her lips. "Why, in Northumberland, that would be merely a farm."

"Aunt! It would not! And why in heaven's name would anyone want a seat in Northumberland?"

"Why indeed? Dreadful slow place!"

"You are quizzing me," Ellen said mildly. "They have been a distinguished family too. Look here, there have been ministers to the crown, ambassadors, and any number of soldiers."

"But not recently," Aunt Shreve said as she scanned the page along with her niece.

"No. They appear to have done nothing of merit for at least one hundred years." Ellen closed the book and put it back on the shelf. She leaned against the bookcase. "Jim—Lord Chesney—claimed he was descended from a long line of 'window dressers and horse traders.'"

Aunt Shreve nodded. "Perhaps, of late, the Chesneys have been more concerned with cutting a dash at Brooks and Watier's and racing horses at Newmarket. Do you suppose that was what he meant?"

"Likely it was." Ellen made a face. "Even then, Aunt, he is much too exalted for the likes of the Grimsleys."

Aunt Shreve shook her head. "I don't know, my

dear. From what you have told me, James Gatewood is neither exalted nor common. He sounds like a rare gem to me. Do excuse the pun."

Ellen groaned. "How vulgar, Aunt!"

"Yes, indeed." She peered at her niece more closely. "I own I do not precisely understand what your objection is to this paragon."

"He is no paragon," Ellen said quickly. "He is deceitful."

Aunt Shreve considered this. "Perhaps he must protect himself. You mentioned some remarks of yours that were somewhat disparaging of the peerage. Could it be that you are too proud? And do you suppose, my dear niece, that this man has been hounded for his wealth by females with more on their minds than scholarship? Is he handsome?"

"Well, no, but he does have quite a nice smile," Ellen admitted. "In fact, it is a very nice smile. And he has an air about him . . ."

She stopped and then laughed at herself. "Listen to me. You would almost think I cared. But I do not!" she added hastily. "He was so untruthful."

"And you, a little too proud?" Aunt Shreve asked again, more gently this time.

"How odd that I should feel too proud for a marquess," Ellen mused and then took a turn about the room, stopping in front of her aunt. "Actually, Aunt Shreve, I think I just wish to control my own destiny. I see how wrapped up in Edwin Horatia is, as though she had no mind of her own." Her chin went up. "I intend to resist this."

"Well, resist away," said Aunt Shreve. She idly picked at some lint on her sleeve. "As your dear Uncle Walter would say to me, 'This is moot, Jeanie, moot indeed.' For after all, Ellen, he will not come."

"He will not come."

By the time Christmas was little more than a memory of too much eggnog and not enough sleep, Ellen had resigned herself to the fact that Lord Chesney had really changed his mind. There had been no communication with Papa from the Marquess of Chesney, not even to reaffirm the day of the wedding and give assurances of his own arrival. Papa's optimism in the face of his daughter's good fortune dwindled and expressed itself only in an occasional weak smile in Ellen's direction.

Ellen kept her feelings to herself. As the house began to fill up with relatives and close friends come to witness this first Grimsley wedding, she occupied herself with keeping Mama and the cook far away from each other. By judicious council and earnest appeal, Ellen managed to keep Cook's threats to resign down to a minimum of a crisis per day.

Gordon returned from London, where he had spent Christmas with one of Aunt Shreve's sons. Ellen had her own doubts that Giles Shreve had actually invited Gordon, but she did applaud her brother's newly acquired wisdom in staying away from the wrath of the squire. As it was, the squire only frowned at him, threatened vaguely "to have a few words with you, my boy," and soon forgot his Oxford misadventures after Gordon's present of a new riding crop and a spanking dash across the landscape with his eldest son. He returned, charitable and forgiving.

Sensing that the coolness between himself and his sister had not warmed appreciably, Gordon trod a narrow line with Ellen. He tested the waters gradually.

She interrupted him one afternoon in the library, where he had gone to sleep off a massive luncheon. He sat upright when she entered the room to return several books to the shelves.

"Best sofa in the house, Ellen," he ventured.

"It ought to be," she replied crisply. "No one uses this room except me and Ralph."

"I wouldn't, either," he assured her. "It's just that this place is filled with kin, and where there is not a relative sitting, there is a present or two."

Ellen smiled and shelved the books. She prepared to leave the library, but he stopped her.

"El, guess who I saw in London?" he asked.

"Dick Whittington and his cat? King Arthur, or perhaps Sir Gawain?" she asked in turn.

"No, silly! I do not run with a royal crowd! No, it was Lord Chesney."

"Oh?" she replied, raising her eyebrows. "And what makes you think I am interested?"

"Well, I thought you might be." He lay down again. "Sorry I brought it up."

She remained at the door. "Well, he wasn't in trouble or anything, was he?" she asked, keeping her tone casual.

"No! He was in Tattersall's with a bunch of his friends. D'ye know, he looks different when he is not in that old student's gown. I almost did not recognize him in real clothes."

"Did he see you?"

Gordon shook his head. "I thought it best not to announce myself. El, it wasn't auction day at Tat's, but they had pulled out a regular show of the most beautiful bits of bone and blood I ever saw. Lord Chesney must run with a plummy crowd, El. You'd never know it to look at him."

"There is a lot you'd never know about Lord Chesney by looking at him," she replied and turned the door handle. She looked back at her brother. "How . . . how did he appear?"

"Bored! I don't think I ever saw anyone looking so bored. I think if I had that line of thoroughbreds to choose from, I would at least try to appear interested."

"Gordon, it is not given to everyone to be horse-mad," she reminded him.

"Still . . ."

He closed his eyes. Ellen let herself out of the library and ran straight into the arms of Thomas Cornwell.

"Oh! Beg pardon!" she stammered and would have stepped back, but the door was closed.

His face fiery, Cornwell leapt aside. "You . . . your butler said I could come on in, Ellen," he said. He took her by the hand and swallowed several times. "We have been away for Christmas, or I would have been here sooner."

Wordless, she stared up at Thomas Cornwell, noting the way his ears stuck out and the way his chin and his nose seemed to be growing toward each other.

This is my destiny, she thought. *I am safe from my baser instincts.*

She held out her hand. "How do you find yourself, Thomas?" she asked.

"Well, I just look down, and there I am, Ellen," he replied, puzzled.

He still held his hat in his hand, and he turned it around and around, worrying the brim into a shapeless mass. "I want to talk with your father," he managed at last.

Ellen groaned inwardly and took Thomas by the arm, leading him away from the library door and any possible encounter with Gordon, who would only tease. "Thomas, I think this is not a good time, what with Horatia to be married in two days and a houseful of guests."

He thought about that for a long moment, considering the pros, cons, logistics, strategy, and implications until Ellen wanted to tear her hair. "I suppose you are right," he said at last, the words dragged out of him. "I should wait until after the wedding?"

"I think that would be an excellent idea."

She guided him toward the door, and in another minute he found himself on the outside steps, almost without being aware how he got there.

"I missed you, Ellen," he said simply as she started to close the door. He fumbled in his pocket and handed her a folded piece of paper, his face turning scarlet. He jumped back down the steps as though they burned through the soles of his thick boots. "It's just a little something I wrote."

Mystified, she opened the paper as he backed into the yard and stumbled against his horse.

"'Bye, Ellen," he whispered as he vaulted into the saddle and tore off down the lane.

She closed the door and leaned against it, looking at the soggy page before her. Her eyes misted over. Thomas Cornwell, sturdy yeoman, wealthy landowner, son of the soil, had written her a love poem.

She read it through once, twice, noting the misspellings and splotches where he bore down too hard with his pen or repeated himself. She marveled at the variety of ways he found to rhyme "love" but felt no urge to laugh at the bumbling effort she held in her hand.

"Dear me," was all she could say as she refolded the poem. "This will never do."

That afternoon, Papa took her aside and asked if she thought Lord Chesney was really coming. "For if he is not, we can use the best guest room right now."

"I think he is not coming, Papa," she said. Her hand went to the poem in her pocket.

Papa could only shake his head. "And I was so sure he would."

She was spared the necessity of further conversation on the painful subject when Mama called, her voice edged with hysteria.

Papa looked up at the first-floor landing. "Ellen," he began, his eyes on the sewing room door. "I think I should go check and see if that roan of mine has dropped her foal yet."

Ellen couldn't resist. "Papa, you told me the foal wasn't due for another six weeks!"

Mama called out again for Ellen. Papa started down the hall at a gallop. "You can't be too careful!" he shouted over his shoulder.

She found Mama in the sewing room with two bridesmaids, who shivered in their sketchy gowns. Fanny Bland glared at her as she rubbed her arms to tame the goose bumps.

"Hello, Fanny," Ellen said as she hurried to Mama, who was by now sobbing helplessly into her handkerchief. "Mama! Whatever is the matter?"

Mama leaned against her daughter and gestured feebly with her free hand. "Look you there. Maria Edgerly has grown two inches taller since she was measured for her gown." Mama sobbed into Ellen's shoulder. "Can you think of a more beastly trick to play upon me?"

The bridesmaid in question burst into noisy tears and fled the room. Fanny looked on in silence, her eyes ahead, her own expression stony, as Mama followed Maria down the hall, calling after her.

Ellen turned to Fanny, waiting for a cutting remark. She dreaded the sight of that arch look that would signal to her that Fanny had been busy spreading the news of Ellen's Oxford career about the countryside. To her surprise, there was no expression on Fanny's face beyond a vague sadness.

"Fanny, I trust you had a pleasant Christmas," Ellen said cautiously.

"Well enough, thank you," Fanny said, and nothing more. Ellen looked at her in confusion. Her amazement grew as she watched tears well up in Fanny's eyes and spill down her cheeks.

"Why, Fanny Bland, whatever is the matter?" she asked in surprise. She held up her hand to help Fanny down from the chair she stood on.

Fanny sank into the chair and dabbed at her eyes, even as she shivered in her skimpy dress. She sniffed once or twice, not looking at Ellen.

"Did Thomas Cornwell . . . did he bring a poem to you?" she asked.

Ellen nodded. It was on her lips to relieve the tension by joking about the misspellings and primitive rhyme pattern, but something in Fanny's expression prevented her. "He did."

Fanny could not bring herself to look at Ellen. "I have known Thomas Cornwell for years and years, even as you. He brought that poem to my house yesterday morning and made me go over it with him. He wanted every word right. I . . . I couldn't bring myself to correct any of it, because it seemed perfect just the way it was."

Fanny's face crumpled up, and she sobbed into her handkerchief. Ellen watched in bewilderment until the truth came crashing down around her. Boring, vindictive, spiteful Fanny Bland was in love with boring, well-meaning, earnest Thomas Cornwell.

I wonder, does this account for your unkindness to me? Ellen thought as she watched the spectacle before her. *During my miserable stay at Miss Dignam's, you were jealous. Oh, Fanny.* Slowly she sat down next to Fanny and touched her shoulder. Fanny did not pull away, but only sobbed harder.

"And I know he came to propose, be . . . because

he told me he was going to," Fanny blubbered. "He tells me everything!"

Ellen handed her another handkerchief. "Well, he did not," she said. "I sent him away because it really wasn't a good time. Oh, Fanny, don't cry! Surely we can work something out!"

"I don't know what," Fanny sobbed. "It isn't fair, Ellen, that you should be brilliant and beautiful and have Thomas Cornwell too."

Ellen gasped. "I am not beautiful, Fanny!"

"Thomas thinks you are!"

"Thomas Cornwell is all about in his head," Ellen said, only to blink in surprise when Fanny turned on her.

"Take that back, Ellen Grimsley," she snapped. "Thomas Cornwell is the most wonderful man in Oxfordshire."

She retreated into her handkerchief again and Ellen apologized, wondering if everyone within hearing distance had gone lunatic and she was the only sane person. She heard the doorbell jingle.

"You'll have to excuse me, Fanny," she said, eager to flee the sewing room. "Mama is having a fit somewhere, Papa has escaped, Horry is not speaking to any of us, and I don't know where the butler is."

She hurried down the stairs, only to stop and stare at Lord Chesney coming toward her, a certain spring in his step. Squire Grimsley trailed along behind him, smiling and bowing whenever the marquess looked his way. Ellen gulped and searched about for an avenue of retreat, but there was none.

"Look who has arrived," Papa was saying, as though he had gone personally to fetch the marquess. He wagged a playful finger at his daughter. "And you thought he would not come!"

Ellen blushed. *Papa, stop!* she wanted to shout. *Do not play the mushroom to this man. You demean yourself and embarrass me.*

Lord Chesney only smiled. "You thought I would not come? After that fond farewell in Oxford?"

"Silly me," was all she could manage as Lord Chesney took full advantage of her confusion, wrapped his arms about her, and kissed her thoroughly.

He was still cold, but he smelled of woodsmoke and the outdoors, two of her favorite things. She had no intention of kissing him back, but there he stood with his arms around her, his lips upon hers. What was she to do?

"Merry Christmas," he murmured a moment later, his lips in her hair. "I was hoping you had not forgotten me entirely."

"No, no," she stammered, out of sorts with herself again, and recalling with painful clarity the result of their last kiss. She turned her head slightly to stare at the fading bruise of greenish-yellow on his cheekbone. "However did you explain that to your relatives?" she asked.

"I occasionally tell the truth when it suits me," he replied, touching his cheek. "I told them that a young woman I rescued from the Bodleian library slapped me silly for proposing marriage. They laughed for days and dismissed it as one of my more harebrained eccentricities." He bowed. "Your secret is safe. No one believes me."

She laughed in spite of herself, just as the front door slammed open and rapid footsteps pounded toward them. Surprised, she peeked around the marquess's arm in time to see Thomas Cornwell, face white, eyes ablaze, grab Gatewood by the shoulder.

"Oh horrors," she said, freeing herself from the marquess. "Thomas, if you . . ."

He did. Without a word, and to the vast amazement of the squire and the marquess, Thomas Cornwell stripped off his glove, slapped Lord Chesney hard across the face with it, and dropped it in front of him.

Chapter 12

LLEN GASPED AS THE MARQUESS reeled from the force of the blow. The squire staggered to a chair and clutched his head in both hands. His fist clenched, Thomas Cornwell struck a pose.

Gingerly, Lord Chesney put his hand to his eye, which had caught a finger of the glove and was starting to water. He looked down at the glove in front of him. "My dear sir, you have dropped your glove."

Thomas frowned and stared down too, as if seeing the glove for the first time.

"Isn't that how it is done?" he asked, whatever fire raging in him banked by Gatewood's calm.

"I wouldn't know," Gatewood said. His hand still to his face, he bent down to retrieve the glove.

"It is a challenge, my lord, a challenge to a duel to the death for the hand of Ellen!" declared Cornwell as though he had just recalled a phrase read in a bad novel and memorized it over too much brandy.

"Her hand?" Gatewood inquired. He dabbed at his eye. "My intentions go far beyond her hand, sir. Tell me, you must be Thomas Cornwell."

Cornwell nodded and accepted the glove. "Yes, my lord. I have loved Ellen for years and years."

"A tedious business, indeed," the marquess said. "I congratulate you on your stamina."

Cornwell grinned.

"Well, I like that!" Ellen declared.

Her bracing words recalled Cornwell to the matter at hand.

"Sir, I demand satisfaction!"

The marquess pursed his lips as though engaged in deep thought and shook his head. "I've never dueled before, sir. I wouldn't begin to know how to go about it."

It was Cornwell's turn to stare. "But I thought . . . I assumed . . . don't you marquesses and dukes and earls and such know all about that sort of thing?"

Gatewood shook his head with vigor and quickly put his hand to his eye again. "It's not one of the rules for membership in the peerage, Mr. Cornwell. I really haven't a clue, and would rather not fight at a wedding. Bad form, don't you know."

By now, the hall was filled with spectators. Fanny Bland, her eyes red and rabbity from weeping, had heard the commotion and come out on the second-floor landing.

Ellen looked from Thomas Cornwell to Lord

Chesney. She took a deep breath. "Alas, Thomas, you wouldn't want to kill this helpless man who is much more at home in libraries."

"Well, I like that!" exclaimed the marquess in turn, a smile playing around his lips.

She ignored him and stepped between the two men. "It was a lovely thought, Thomas," she said, resting her hand lightly on his coat lapel. Fanny burst into noisy tears. "There are times when I think a duel would greatly improve the marquess."

"Daughter!" the squire exclaimed. "She doesn't mean a word of it, your worship."

Ellen colored with embarrassment. She patted Thomas Cornwell's lapel one last time and stepped in closer to the marquess, crossing her fingers behind her back where he could definitely see them. "Thomas, I have promised myself to Lord Chesney."

Fanny stopped sniffling. The squire sighed with relief.

"I mean, if you have any regard for me, you wouldn't want to kill the object of my affection, now, would you?"

"Not a convincing argument, Ellen," the marquess whispered in her ear. "Think of the temptation."

It was Thomas's turn to frown and purse his lips. "I suppose I do not."

The marquess stuck out his hand. "I like your style, Cornwell, I really do."

Cornwell grinned and shook hands. He turned suddenly serious. "But you had better be good to her, my lord."

"I aim to make her happiness my sole object in life." There was a commotion on the upstairs landing. Fanny Bland, prosaic old Fanny, had fainted and was draped over the railing.

Ellen took Thomas by the arm again. "Thomas, be a dear and see Fanny home," she whispered.

He nodded, his eyes on the second-floor landing. He took the steps two at a time. In another moment, he had picked up Fanny—a substantial handful—as though she were a bag of feathers. He came down the stairs carefully with his burden.

"If you should ever change your mind, Ellen," he said, "I'd be happy to shoot this fribble."

Lord Chesney raised his eyebrows as Thomas stalked away, Fanny lolling in his arms. "I've never been accused of being a fribble," he complained. "Come to think of it, I've never been challenged to a duel before. And I thought the country would be slow. Ellen, you have made me a happy man."

She could tell by the twinkle in his eyes that he was about to burst into sustained and uncontrolled merriment that would be difficult to explain to Papa, who was eyeing them both with an expression bordering on ecstasy. She took the marquess by the arm and marched him into the book room.

He tried to take her in his arms again, but she warded him off. "I didn't mean a word of it, Jim," she protested.

He didn't take the news badly. "Ellen, do you mean to ruin my new year entirely?" he asked.

"I hadn't planned on it."

"You won't mind then, if I propose to you occasionally during the coming year?"

"Well, I . . ."

"Just to keep in practice?"

"Be serious, Jim!"

"I am!"

"You are not!"

"Oh, yes I am!"

Ellen opened her mouth and then closed it again, embarrassed. *Here I am, worrying about the impression my family is going to make on this man, and I sound like Martha brangling with Ralph.* Her chin went up. "Very well, sir, you may do as you choose. As I am not returning to Oxford, I doubt our acquaintance will extend much beyond this wedding."

Lord Chesney only nodded and looked thoughtful. Ellen watched him with suspicion.

"You are scheming something, I know it!" she declared flatly.

He merely bowed and opened the bookroom door. "My dear, let me set the record straight. The Marquess of Chesney never schemes. As a matter of fact, he hardly ever gets angry."

"Thank goodness for that," she retorted, preceding him through the door.

"What he does do is get even."

She couldn't even be sure he had said that.

The house was crammed with relatives, and it was easy to avoid the marquess, especially as her father kept dragging that obliging man from uncle to cousin to aunt, introducing him as "His Worship, Ellen's future husband, even though we are to keep it under the hatches."

She cringed at her Papa's bad manners with one part of her mind and heart, while the other part applauded his vulgarity, convinced that a steady application would soon send the marquess screaming into the night.

But James Gatewood was made of sterner stuff. He bore the toadying and vulgar stares with aplomb. To her amazement, he even seemed to enjoy himself with the younger cousins in a bloody duel to the death with jackstraws, while the older members of the family yawned over cards.

"I like him, Ellen," Horatia ventured to say, when she could tear herself away from Edwin and his slack-jawed devotion.

Ellen set down the bridesmaid's dress she was hemming. "He is an unprincipled rogue, Horry!"

"He could never be that," Horatia declared, "else you never would have fallen in love!"

Ellen picked up the dress again, struck by her sister's words.

"Do you know, Horry, that is quite the nicest compliment from you."

Horry merely patted her arm and rose to return to Edwin, who looked bewildered, sitting by himself. "I know you would never love a rake."

She watched her sister return to Edwin and sit on the low stool at his feet. She observed with some amusement the way Horry looked up at her husband-to-be with such adoration and trust. *I am sure I am not in love*, she thought, attending to her hemming again and wondering why it was coming out so uneven. *Of course, I am not so sure that Jim would find it comfortable to have me crouch at his feet like a spaniel. I know I would not care for it.*

She raised her eyes to the marquess, who was sitting on the floor with her rowdy cousins, Martha in his lap, as she shook the jackstraws. *If our common touch does not disgust you, Lord Chesney, then I suppose you will be harder to dissuade than I thought*, she considered.

As she watched him, he turned and winked at her. To her further disgust, she winked back.

Because the house was full, Lord Chesney was condemned to room with Ralph. He accepted his sentence with a cheeriness that amazed Mama.

"I would have thought that such an exalted personage would be picky about his bedmates," Mama whispered to her as they handed out candles to the relatives and bid them good night.

"Mama, do not call him exalted! You act as though he were a member of the Blessed Trinity!"

"I am sure I do not!" Mama protested. "It wouldn't hurt you to appear a little more lover-like, my dear."

Ellen rubbed at the frown between her eyes. "Mama, this is Horry's big occasion. I will not turn it into a circus, not for anyone."

"Yes, but you have scarcely said more than five words to him all evening."

"No, I have not," she agreed quietly. What she really wanted was a turn about the shrubbery with Lord Chesney, to assure him once again that she had no intention of marrying him. But the shrubbery was cold this time of year. She sighed. And the house was full of relatives.

She caught up with Ralph and Lord Chesney on the stairs, heads together, engaged in earnest conversation. "Jim," she called out. "I mean, Lord Chesney."

"I still prefer Jim," Gatewood replied, stopping and handing Ralph the candle they shared. "Go on, lad. I'll join you in a minute." He turned to Ellen. "I trust you are not planning to apologize for the accommodations, as your father has done, this half hour and more. Ralph and I have been discussing *Hamlet* and the scene in Act V that Shakespeare did not write and should have, in Ralph's opinion."

"Will you have him write a paper?" she asked as he trailed her down the hall to the lesser-used third-floor landing. She sat down on the steps and drew her knees up to her chin.

"I believe I will. If his scholarship is sound, it could be an excellent essay to secure him entrance into Winchester, my old school."

"Papa would never allow it," she said. "He says Ralph is to go to my uncle's counting house in the City."

"We shall see, dear Ellen, light of my life."

"You have got to stop talking like that. I crossed my fingers behind my back when I told that fib to Thomas."

"So you did," he agreed, his good humor intact.

He touched her lips with his fingers before she could draw away. "That mulish look on your face tells me that I had better change the subject. My dear, I do not have to cross my fingers to tell you that your paper on *Romeo and Juliet* has no equal for wit and sarcasm. Even Dean Jonathan Swift—*requiescat in pacem*—would agree with me, I am sure. It is a classic."

"I would like to have it back."

He shook his head. "I did not bring it." He took her by the hand. "And why, may I ask, did you give your complete Shakespeare to Ralph?"

She would not look him in the eye. "I probably will not have any use for it here at home."

"Not even to press flowers?" he asked lightly and then sobered immediately. "That was rude of me. Excuse it. No use?"

She shook her head.

"That remains to be seen," he said. "Come, my dear, and kiss me quick. Tomorrow is going to be an awful day, I assure you. Desserts will burn, flowers in the church will wither, relatives will fall out with one another, and the weather will turn sour." He laughed. "At least I need not fight a duel too. And Horry will probably finally realize that marrying her elegant blockhead means going to bed with him."

"Jim!"

He looked about elaborately. "No one heard me."

When she refused to kiss him, he pecked her on the cheek and strode down the hall to Ralph's room, humming softly under his breath.

The tune sounded like a wedding processional.

The day began precisely as Lord Chesney had predicted on the third-floor landing the night before. The desecration of burned pudding permeated the entire house, and Mama was finally forced to lie down and sob out her misery in the lap of her sister, who had been through a similar ordeal the year before. Horatia stalked about the house, her face pale, her expression wooden. Gordon was quarreling with his cousins in the stables, and Martha sulked in her room because she had to share her toys.

Only Ralph appeared content. Ellen found him in the library, sitting cross-legged on the sofa with her folio open to *Hamlet*, and scribbling notes at a furious rate. He spared her only a grunt of recognition and then turned back to his labors.

With a snort of her own, Ellen pulled on her sturdiest boots and cloak and headed for the shrubbery. Her head throbbed with the odor of burned pudding and the quarrels of fractious relatives. Soon Fanny and the others would be there for a final fitting. She did not think she could bear either Fanny's gloom or her malice. "And I do not know which is worse," she muttered to herself as she set out for a brisk walk.

She was scarcely out of sight of the house when a familiar figure came toward her, wrapped in overcoat and muffler but with his untidy hair blowing in the wind.

"You should wear a hat," she scolded as James

Gatewood approached her, bowed, and linked his arm through hers.

"I only lose them. The warden at All Souls thinks that I should sit on them, and then I would know where they are."

He stopped and looked her in the eye. "I have not yet proposed for the day, madam." He went down on one knee. "My dear, would you make me the happiest man alive and consent to share my bed and board?"

"Never," she replied.

He grinned. "Oh, well. Failing that, will you marry me?"

She gasped and then laughed in spite of herself. She tugged on his arm, looking about to make sure that no one saw them. "Now, get up before the moisture soaks through your buckskins and you come down with a dreadful cold, and I am forced to nurse you long after the wedding is over."

"Very well," he replied, rising and taking her arm again. "Now where was I?"

"I refuse to remind you."

He laughed, and Ellen was forced to smile.

"Do you really intend to propose every day?" she asked.

"Perhaps not every day," he said. "Who knows but that some day the element of surprise might prosper my wooing?" He touched her hand. "But yes, that is my intention."

They walked in silence, arm in arm through the shrubbery.

"This is not good weather for lovemaking," he

commented. "Think how much better it will be in Oxford this spring."

"I am not returning to Oxford," she insisted.

"Oh?" he said in that irritating way of his. "Which reminds me somehow. This would be a good time to puff up my consequence with you a little. Do you know what the Genuine Article Lord Chesney has gone and done? He's such a good fellow."

"What has that eccentric man done now?" she asked in mock seriousness. "Dare you repeat it?"

"I do believe he has established a trust fund at Oxford University covering all the workers injured on college property. The idea has caught on amongst all the colleges, and soon there will be a sizable endowment. I believe Adam Speed's family will be the first to benefit."

Ellen stood still and took hold of Gatewood's other hand too. She could not speak for a moment, and even then, she could not look him in the eye. "What would England be without her eccentrics?"

He raised her gloved hand to his lips. "Merely a stodgy little island with indifferent food." He continued on, kindly overlooking her sniffles. "Who knows what he will do next?"

"I wouldn't even hazard a guess."

They walked in companionable silence through the woods, Ellen lost in thought. Without realizing it, she leaned her head against Lord Chesney's arm as they walked along, wondering how she could face the house again. There was the wedding rehearsal tonight, full of unexplored peril.

She stopped walking. "Why do weddings have to

be such uncomfortable events?" she asked the sky. "Oh, beg pardon," she said. "I didn't mean to hang about you like that."

"I didn't mind."

He led her to a fallen tree and sat her down. "Wedding giving you the blue devils?"

Ellen nodded. "I wonder that anyone does it." She brightened. "Perhaps Papa will pay me to elope some day."

"You wouldn't!" the marquess declared.

"Of course not, silly," she said. "What, would I deprive all my relatives of food and high drama?" She scuffed her boots in the spongy soil. "And now Horry is impossible, just as you predicted. I made some offhand remark about Edwin this morning, and she turned ten shades of pale and bolted to her room like a rabbit. She definitely has cold feet." She blushed. "But this is hardly a subject to discuss with you."

He nudged her shoulder when she appeared disinclined to continue. "There was a time when we could talk about anything."

"And I was pretty foolish in Oxford," she replied. She rose. "I must go back and enter the lists again. Come at your own risk. Oh, I shall be so grateful when this wedding is over and . . ."

". . . and I go away?" he concluded.

She considered him, sitting there on the log. "Yes, Lord Chesney. You don't belong here. I come from a family of toadies, fools, and mushrooms. We really don't improve upon further acquaintance."

She started to walk, leaving him behind. *There*, she

thought as she hurried to the house, *if that doesn't tell James Gatewood the time of day, I do not know what will.*

It was a simple matter to avoid him for the rest of the day. Ralph emerged from the library only long enough to beg Cook for two sandwiches, milk for him and ale for Lord Chesney, and plague Ellen for more paper.

"It is famous, sister," he said, fairly jumping up and down in his excitement. "I am writing another scene for Act V. Lord Chesney has such incredible ideas."

"Yes, he does," she said quietly. As Ralph almost danced away, she wanted to call after him, to tell him not to build up his hopes. *It's the counting house for you, Ralph, and country obscurity for me. And Gordon will squander one last term at Oxford, and then didn't Lord Chesney promise him a cavalry regiment? Heaven knows why. Life is decidedly unfair.*

Icy rain was falling that evening as the wedding party adjourned to the chapel in the village for the rehearsal. Mama had insisted that the bridesmaids wear their gowns so she could take one last look at the hems. The girls shivered in their low-cut dresses with the skimpy sleeves. Martha ran in and out of the door with her basket of flower petals until the back of the chapel was quite damp with icy rain. Horry observed the chaos in perfect misery, staying far away from Edwin, who looked like a puppy without a home.

Sir Reginald Bland was there, splendidly over-dressed as usual, and looking about him with disdain at all the others who did not preface their names with "Sir." Ellen experienced one moment of pleasure when her father introduced the august Sir Reginald to Lord Chesney. She felt mean enough to relish the way he wilted and sat down in the chapel, quiet for the rest of the evening. She sat down too, grateful to be a mere onlooker.

"Ellen, Ellen, we need you right now," Mama was saying. She looked around. Mama was motioning furiously to her from the back of the church.

"See here, Ellen, you must stand in for Horatia," Mama said. "It is a tradition that the bride not participate in the rehearsal." She pushed Ellen closer to Papa, who was gazing wearily at his pocket watch.

There was a commotion from the front of the church. The relatives who had come to watch ceased their chatter and looked up with interest. Mama sank into the nearest pew and began to fan herself, even though she could see her breath when she spoke.

"Edwin has fainted, depend upon it," she said in a toneless voice.

So he had, right among the potted plants. Best man Thomas Cornwell, his ears as red as his face, grasped him under the armpits and draped him across the choir seats closer to the altar. Horry charged down the aisle in tears, waving her smelling salts in one hand.

"Well, thank goodness for that," Ellen said to Papa as Horry passed them. "I was beginning to wonder if she was going to avoid Edwin for the rest of their engagement."

Papa only chuckled. "I seem to recall a scene like this some twenty years ago," he said.

"Papa, not you!" Ellen exclaimed, her eyes bright.

He nodded and tucked her arm closer in his. "Ah, well, Ellen, somehow these things are accomplished. Are you ready for a stroll down the aisle?"

In perfect charity with her father, Ellen watched Martha romp down the aisle in front of them, swinging her empty flower basket like a censer. The bridesmaids, sneezing in earnest now, followed slowly. She started next, minding her steps in time with the music and Papa's dreadful sense of rhythm. They lurched down the aisle together, ignoring the snickers of the cousins in the front pews.

And there by the altar was the Marquess of Chesney, standing in for Edwin, who by now was sitting up in the choir seats, an expression of complete befuddlement on his already vacuous face. Horry chafed his wrists and uttered little cries of concern.

Ellen rolled her eyes, and the marquess winked at her. She turned her attention to Thomas Cornwell, the best man, who gazed with something close to rapture upon Fanny Bland, even though her eyes were red and her nose ran.

With only a minimum of confusion, Papa gave her away to the greatest rascal in the peerage, and they knelt together in front of the altar.

"I only hope I am not wearing the shoes with the holes in the sole," he whispered in her ear.

"You really should take better care of yourself, Jim," she hissed back.

"Ellen, make me the happiest man alive and marry me," he whispered.

"Not on your life," she whispered back. "And don't

you think for one minute that this charade gives you any special privileges. We are mere stand-ins."

"Do you mean I cannot kidnap you in front of all these guests? You can certainly put a damper on a wedding rehearsal, Ellen."

She burst into laughter as the priest glared at her. "Sorry, Father Mackey," she said and choked down her merriment.

"That's better," the marquess said. "Have a little countenance, Ellen, on this serious occasion. Gracious, but my knees ache! Sorry, Father."

The priest stood there with his book, glaring down at the happy couple, while Mama inspected all the bridesmaids and scrutinized Thomas Cornwell, the best man, until his ears turned scarlet again. In a voice that made the priest wince, she ordered Martha to stop her fidgeting and pronounced the tableau before her acceptable.

The organist wheezed into the recessional. Martha bolted down the aisle, followed by the bridesmaids, coughing and sneezing. Ellen Grimsley and James Gatewood turned and started down the aisle. In another moment, they stood in the freezing vestibule.

"Thank heaven that is over," said the marquess to Cornwell.

He snatched up a shawl from the back bench and thrust it at the best man. "Here. Put this around Miss Bland before she freezes solid."

Thomas did as he was bid and then scampered back to Lord Chesney's side. "You don't think it would be monstrous improper if I cuddled her a little?" he asked. "After all, she is so cold."

"I think it an admirable stroke, Thomas."

Cornwell drew himself up to his full height and started back toward the bridesmaids, a man with a mission. Ellen watched his stately progress and tugged Fanny aside. "Fanny, let him take you home in his carriage," she whispered, her eyes on the approaching farmer, who had stopped to straighten his neckcloth and gird his loins. "And if you should happen to lean up against him, or . . . or put your hand on his knee, all the better."

"Ellen! That is so improper!" Fanny declared. "My mother would be mortified!"

"Your mother is not here," Ellen reminded her. "Now blow your nose." She gave Fanny a little shove into Thomas's arms, crossed her fingers, and hoped for the best.

She was still smiling as she buttoned up Martha and led her to the waiting carriage. She handed her up to the Marquess of Chesney, who sat Martha on his lap and made room for Ellen.

The carriage filled up with relatives, and there was no opportunity to talk, much to Ellen's relief. She longed for her bed and the peace and quiet of an empty house in which to think about her own future. But she was to share her bed with one of Mama's interminable nieces, and aunts and uncles fairly hung from the rafters. She leaned against the marquess again.

"Ellen," he began, his voice low, gentle.

She put her finger to her lips. "Don't say anything now." He nodded and stared out the window, his eyes serious. He said nothing to her in the house beyond a formal good night.

She thought of him as she climbed into bed and curled up against her cousin who was already asleep. *This wedding can't be over soon enough*, she thought as her eyelids drooped. *When the house is empty, and Gordon back at Oxford, I should make some plans of my own.*

Aunt Shreve had talked of spending the spring at Royal Tunbridge Wells. *Perhaps if I tease her enough, she will allow me to accompany her*, Ellen thought. Tunbridge Wells was in the opposite direction from Oxford. *I must not think of Oxford again*, she told herself.

The wedding day dawned bitter cold but mercifully clear.

Ellen hopped on bare feet by the icy window, gazing out at the beautiful morning until Mama stuck her head in the door and scolded her to hurry up and dress.

She did as she was told, grateful to pull on her favorite dark blue wool dress. *And to think I wanted to be a bridesmaid*, she recalled. *I think I would rather be warm.*

She sat at the dressing table for a longer minute than usual, staring into her own face. *It is a pretty face*, she decided, after a careful scrutiny. *I have excellent pores and all my teeth. My mouth is a trifle large, but it's the only one I have.* She brushed her blonde hair until it stood in little curls all over her head. *Seriously, what does he see in me?*

Horatia was a ravishingly lovely bride, with her blonde hair, elegant height, and enormous brown eyes. Ellen smiled at her sister as she twirled around in her satin dress with the net overskirt and the bodice studded with seed pearls. So what if she was not over bright, and Edwin Bland equally dense? They loved each other, and that seemed to be enough for them. *I wonder if it would be enough for me*, Ellen thought as she attached Horry's train and gave her a last hug.

The church was no warmer, but it was full of relatives and village friends, all come to see Horatia Grimsley married to Edwin Bland. Even the flowers that only last night had looked so sorely put upon by the cold had taken on new bloom for the occasion.

Aunt Shreve patted the bench beside her as Ellen looked about the chapel. She moved over to make room.

"Should we leave room for Lord Chesney?" Aunt Shreve asked. "I don't see him anywhere."

Ellen scooted over, searching the chapel for the marquess. *Perhaps he has allowed discretion to overtake valor and has fled the scene. Thank goodness for that*, she thought.

Aunt Shreve nudged her and nodded with her head in the direction of the vestibule. Ellen smiled. She could see Martha, her flower basket clutched tight, sitting on the steps next to the marquess, who was whispering in her ear. Martha chewed on her lower lip and threatened tears until the marquess said something magical. She brightened and sat up straight again, allowing him to reposition her little headpiece more firmly. She leaned against him as the organist began to play, the picture of contentment.

I have leaned against him like that myself, Ellen thought. She looked down at her prayer book. *And I must admit that once you have done that, it's easier to stand up on your own. Bless you, Jim Gatewood.*

And then it was almost time for Mama, weeping noisily, to be led to her seat in the front. Ellen sat where she was in the back, watching the scene unfold in the vestibule, where the symmetrical bridesmaids sniffled and blew their noses one last time.

Another word and a pat, and the marquess left Martha standing in front of the line with her chin up and a determined smile on her face. He strode down the aisle, searched her out, genuflected outside the pew and slid in just as the groomsman led Mama toward the front.

There was still a little room on the other side of Aunt Shreve, but she seemed oblivious and would not move any more. The marquess was compelled to put his arm around Ellen to find space in the pew. Ellen found herself tucked in tight next to him and her head against his chest this time.

"Sorry to discommode you, James," she whispered as Mama came down the aisle and was seated.

He merely smiled down at her. "I'm happy as a clam," he replied. He sniffed her hair. "Lavender is my favorite, El. How did you know?"

She tried to think of something witty, but Martha was venturing down the aisle, and her little sister had Lord Chesney's full attention.

Ellen watched him keep time with his head as Martha stepped carefully in rhythm, counting out loud, her eyes straight ahead. When she saw him, he made a sowing motion with his hand. Martha looked down at her full basket, as if remembering it for the first time. In another moment, she had moved past them and was strewing rose petals like a professional.

Gatewood's ear was close to her face. She whispered in it, "However did you get her to move? She looked decidedly stubborn in the vestibule."

He smiled, his eyes still on Martha. "Yes, stubbornness runs in the females of your family, doesn't it? I promised her she wouldn't have to be a flower girl at our wedding unless she really wanted to, because the aisle is twice as long and much more frightening. She said she would think about it. Which reminds me, will you marry me?"

"No," she said forcefully and then stood up as Horatia, a vision of net and satin, floated down the aisle with Papa.

The pew was so crowded that Lord Chesney was forced to put his arm around Ellen's waist and hold her close as the bridal party passed. She should have remonstrated with him, but his hand was warm on her waist, comforting. She told herself that she leaned against him only because she had no choice.

Edwin did not faint. Horatia responded distinctly in the affirmative to each query from Father Mackey. Thomas handed over the wedding ring as though he had been performing such a delicate task with regularity on his farm. Hardly any of the bridesmaids sneezed, and Mama cried enough for everyone. It was a beautiful wedding.

The reception was Mama's crowning glory. Each little biscuit, petit four, macaroon, mint, and marchpane fruit performed to perfection and disappeared in short order.

As Ellen was returning from one of her many trips to the kitchen, Mama accosted her, glowing from the warmth of the hearth and too much rack punch. "My dear, yours will be even grander," she beamed.

"Mama, about that . . ." Ellen attempted, but her mother had turned her attention to another of the guests, full of compliments and good cheer.

Cooler heads will prevail tomorrow, Ellen thought grimly as she waved farewell and Godspeed to cousins, aunts, and uncles with a wary eye on the weather, which was turning blustery.

And here was James Gatewood, overcoat buttoned up, still hatless, descending the staircase with Ralph close by. "Have Ellen take a look at your conclusion," he was saying. "If she makes any suggestions, I can recommend them to you."

"Where shall I send it when it is done?" Ralph asked, waving the papers in his hand.

"Send them with Ellen when she returns to Oxford," he replied and set down his portmanteau long enough to shake Ralph's hand. "It's been a pleasure, Ralph. Not only are you a budding Shakespeare scholar like your sister, but you don't snore." He bent down closer to Ralph and whispered loudly. "Does she snore?"

"I don't think so, my lord."

"Ah, better and better," he replied.

Ellen put her hands on her hips and glared at him. "Are you finally leaving, my lord?" she asked, her voice frosty.

"And not a moment too soon, from the looks of things," he replied, the picture of good cheer. "I'll see you in Oxford inside of a week, Ellen," he said as she opened the front door for him.

"Oh, no, you won't," she replied. "I am going to ask Aunt Shreve if I can accompany her to Tunbridge Wells." She held out her hand. "Good-bye."

"Until next week," he said again as he shook her hand and then kissed her fingers one by one.

She jerked her hand back and stamped her foot. "Don't you understand a word I have been saying?"

But he was gone then, hurrying toward the elegant chaise with the crest on the door that awaited him.

Ellen slammed the front door louder than she intended to and thought she heard laughter in the driveway. "That man is a total distraction," she said out loud to her father, who had came into the hall with more of Mama's brothers and sisters. "Do you know, Papa, he still thinks I am returning to Oxford. Imagine!"

It was Papa's turn to look thoughtful and everywhere but at her. "Well, daughter, we did discuss this, the marquess and I. He has secured a place for you at St. Hilda's Hall."

"What?"

"Exactly so, my dear, " Papa said hastily, watching

the storm about to break on her face. "Says it's much more a challenge than Miss Dignam's."

"You see, El, you can take my paper to him after all," offered Ralph, beaming.

"And keep an eye on Gordon, that rascal," Papa added. "I knew you would be pleased."

Chapter 13

~

HE WAS NOT PLEASED, NOT AT ALL, but as Ellen mutinously tossed her clothes back in her trunk a week later and sat upon it while Ralph strapped down the lid, she was hard-pressed to understand why.

The only girl in the neighborhood who did not envy her good fortune at snaring Lord Chesney was Fanny Bland, who had discovered love of the bucolic sort with Thomas Cornwell. She dropped in, two days after Horry's nuptials, to blush and giggle and entreat Ellen to be her bridesmaid in two months' time.

"For had you not thrown us together, I am sure I would still be correcting those dreadful poems which he now writes to me," Fanny exclaimed, patting her bulging reticule.

While Ellen owned that it was kind of Fanny to change her opinion, she could only wonder at the miracle love had wrought. And with Thomas Cornwell. "Love is indeed blind," she said to the closed door after Fanny had exchanged a few more pleasantries that required little attention in return and floated out the door, intent upon other such visits about the neighborhood.

The news of Lord Chesney's intentions traveled on seven league boots about the district, even though the issue was far from resolved, at least by Ellen. Ladies who never would have come otherwise came to visit Mama to drink tea and exclaim over the Grimsleys' good fortune. Ellen could see no other purpose for their visits than to take a peek at her and wonder what on earth a peer of the realm saw to enamor him to Squire Grimsley's singular daughter.

I am sure they do not go away satisfied, Ellen thought as she watched Mama lead the last gaggle out to their carriages, amid laughter behind gloved hands and heads-together communication, and more backward glances at the house.

"I mean, Aunt Shreve, he is offering me the sun, moon, and stars, a house in London, a manor in Hertfordshire, one more house in Bath, I believe, and the worship of countless modistes and milliners," she said one afternoon as she took another turn around her aunt's parlor. "And I almost think I love him, although it doesn't seem to be the kind of love that Mama and Horry think best."

"Thank goodness for that," Aunt Shreve murmured under her breath. She poured her favorite niece another cup of tea as Ellen paused in her restless circuit. "If you wear a path in my carpet, I shall petition my brother for a new one, and won't that irritate him," she said, smiling a little. "I believe I will do it." She patted the sofa beside her. "Come, sit down. You begin to wear me out."

Ellen could only continue her traverse about the room. "Try and try as I might, I cannot seem to reconcile my objections. No more do I understand them," she admitted, sinking down at the window seat and staring out at the fast-waning afternoon. "Oh, Aunt, what is the matter with me?"

She looked at her aunt, noticing the compassion that rendered her features even more dear. "You do know what is troubling me, don't you?" she asked quietly.

"I think I do, my dear," was all Aunt Shreve said.

"Then tell me!" Ellen demanded, leaping up.

"No, I will not," Aunt Shreve said decisively. "You must discover this for yourself." She rose and went to the window herself. "For I discovered it myself, when I was but a little older than you." She touched her niece's hair. "Every woman's response is different, my dear, and you must find your own way through this particular dilemma."

"That's no help," Ellen declared crossly.

Aunt Shreve only embraced her, kissed her cheek, and offered her a biscuit.

I wish I could solve all my problems with biscuits and tea, Ellen thought as she sat at her desk in St.

Hilda's Hall and gazed out upon another afternoon sky.

She looked down at the sheet of problems before her and sighed with pleasure. Two problems to go, and a glance had already told her that she could do them. There would be geometry to follow the algebra, and then tomorrow, more Shakespeare. They were studying the comedies in all their ribald glory, and a paper was due.

Ellen looked around her room with undiminished pleasure, even after nearly a month in residence. The chamber was much like Gatewood's chamber at All Souls, with its narrow mullioned windows, dark wainscoting, and ample bookcases. The headmistress at St. Hilda's, an intense woman with an air of great competence about her, had said that the school had once formed part of a medieval hall that had risen to the status of college and moved closer to the main cluster on High Street.

"And so, Miss Grimsley, the women have indeed moved into Oxford," Miss Medford had declared the afternoon of Ellen's introduction to St. Hilda's. "And we will not be easily dislodged, no matter what our current status."

She had ushered Ellen into her quarters, hiding a smile when she opened the door upon a veritable flower shop. "I believe you have an admirer," was all she said as she ushered Ellen into her room.

Ellen had looked about her in delight that immediately turned to chagrin. She could only shake her head and ask, "How do people like that have access to flowers in January?"

Miss Medford laughed and clapped her hands. "I suppose in summer he will bring you shaved ice brought from the Andes by Inca runners." She coughed delicately. "Lord Chesney has become one of our most enthusiastic benefactors of late. Perhaps he will endow a chair of horticulture."

Ellen laughed and sat on the bed. "Miss Medford, let me tell you this at once. Lord Chesney is of the opinion that I should marry him, but I have no such intention."

Miss Medford only inclined her head, a smile on her face. "So he told me."

"What?"

"He said that you regarded him with complete indifference and . . ."

"'Complete indifference'?" Ellen interrupted, without even meaning to. "Well, I do not know if I would go that far . . . yes, yes, I would! Complete indifference. Pray excuse the interruption, Miss Medford."

"Certainly. I assured him that we at St. Hilda's Hall would keep you sufficiently challenged so that you would never have the opportunity to repine either lost or unrequited love."

"And what did his lordship say to that?" Ellen asked, a smile playing around her lips.

"He laughed long and hard."

"He would! That is so entirely in character."

"And when he was quite recovered, he offered his services here, should we ever wish an occasional lecture on Shakespeare."

"Which you accepted?"

"Of course! My dear, in scholarly circles, Lord Chesney is renowned." She moved to the door. "We accepted his offer gladly and leave it to you two adults to sort out your own private difficulties." She picked up a nosegay of tea roses by the door. "I expect he will prove difficult to argue with, but that, Miss Grimsley, is your problem."

Ellen dealt with the distraction of Lord Chesney in womanly, time-honored fashion: she avoided him. It was an easy matter at first. Her first morning's work at St. Hilda's quickly showed her that this little hall so modestly situated on one of Oxford's more quiet streets far exceeded the mild scholarship available to the unwary of Miss Dignam's Select Female Academy.

Coming as she did in the middle of the school year meant serious catching up. To the balm of her somewhat bruised and trampled-upon scruples, it was no prevarication to send down the upstairs maid with a note stating that she could not leave her studies when Lord Chesney came to call.

It was more difficult to avoid the summons to his maiden lecture on the nature and study of Shakespeare. She tried in vain to resist when she heard he would be discussing *Much Ado About Nothing*, her favorite comedy. She succumbed during the middle of his lecture, sneaking in and sitting down in the back of the hall.

He took no notice of her capitulation other than to raise his eyebrows and make more sure that his voice carried to the back of the hall where she sat.

Following the lecture, he was remarkably fleet

in walking with rapid dignity to the back of the hall and bowing over her hand, which she had reluctantly extended.

"I trust you are still in harmony with Hero and Beatrice, even though I may have muddled their motives," he commented, strolling with her from the hall.

"You did not muddle them at all," she replied. "And you needn't fish for compliments from me. I know you too well, Lord Chesney."

"Jim to you," he added. "I wish you would marry me."

"It was a masterful lecture," she said, ignoring his little aside. She wished he would not stand so close, which made it difficult to resist the urge to straighten his neckcloth. "I took copious notes."

"To what purpose?" he asked, holding the door for her.

She stopped walking and turned to face him. "To refute every argument," she said, looking directly into his eyes for the first time. "I couldn't have agreed less with your conclusion."

"Then write your own, Ellen, and let me see it when it is done."

"I shall," she replied.

He took her hand before she could leave. "I haven't proposed yet today," he began when she cut him off.

"You just did, Jim! And you also sent a note with the flowers this morning."

"I thought I did that yesterday," he replied. "Love is making me absentminded."

She shook her finger in his face. "It is doing nothing of the kind! You are the most calculating man I ever met! And try to deny that your lecture today was given to incite me to a response."

He held up his hands in a gesture of surrender, laughing. "Am I so base, fair Hermia?"

She couldn't help but smile. "You are! But I will write your silly paper. And send Ralph's with it when I am done."

He tucked his arm in hers and headed with her across St. Hilda's small quad. "Ah! I was wondering when you would hear from that enthusiastic young fellow. Did you make any changes in his addition to *Hamlet*?"

"Only a very few. At times, he sounded more like Fielding than Shakespeare, so I aged his words a bit. That was all." She sighed and tucked her notebook closer to her. "I only wish he could be here."

"He could, you know. You could marry me and we could make a home for him here in Oxford. I think your father would not object."

She stopped again. "He would not object because he is a toady! He will do whatever you say." Tears welled up in her eyes and she angrily brushed them away. "Jim, do stop this proposing! I have not the heart for it."

He only put his arm about her and continued walking. "I couldn't possibly stop proposing, Ellen. I love you." He took her by both shoulders. "Can you look me in the eyes and tell me that you don't harbor some small sentiment in my direction?"

She raised her eyes to his and then lowered them quickly.

"Perhaps some small sentiment, but I am sure that is nothing more than friendship." She tugged at his neckcloth. "I wish that you would take a look in the mirror before you venture out of your room! Hold still a moment."

Her eyes serious, she straightened his neckcloth and gave it a pat. "There now, you are much more presentable. Now, sir, I ask you to leave me in peace to make my own muddles here at St. Hilda's."

He looked down at her, his eyes equally serious. "I can help you through your muddles."

"I know you can," she replied quietly. "But don't, please. I don't need your help."

There, she had said it. *I hope I have not wounded you beyond repair*, she thought as she waved a hand to him and ran the rest of the way across the quadrangle. *Requiring your assistance in all matters will make me a cripple.*

The daily flowers became weekly flowers, accompanied by a note requesting marriage, which she ignored. She applied herself to her studies and watched January slide effortlessly into February. If she slept less well than usual or found herself picking over her food, she put it down to the general melancholy that always struck after Christmas and would abate, she knew, with the arrival of spring.

For I truly do not need you, Lord Chesney, she told herself. *I have you to thank for St. Hilda's, but I have come to apply myself to scholarship.*

She was not alone at St. Hilda's in her search for knowledge, but she soon discovered a difference between her and the other students. Most of them were daughters from good families, but daughters of clergymen and teachers, without much hope of excellent marriages to ease their paths through life. Several had told her that when the term ended, they would apply as governesses in England's greatest houses. Two were planning to follow cleric brothers to mission posts in distant reaches of the realm. One other was engaged to a vicar from Yorkshire and seeking only additional polish before her own wedding.

Ellen took it all in, puzzled over what it meant, and continued her Shakespeare papers. As they accumulated in a small stack on her desk, she debated whether to send them to Lord Chesney, as she had sent on Ralph's paper. She dissected all the comedies with particular care but found herself wishing to bounce them off Gatewood's sounding board.

"But I have said I do not need any help," she told herself as she folded the last comedy paper.

In the morning, Ralph stood before her, looking defiant and smelling faintly of pig.

The headmistress, concern showing in the frown on her face, had wakened Ellen from a sound sleep and ushered her into the sitting room where Ralph waited, muddy and tired. "My dear, the cook found him curled up on the doormat at the servants' entrance. He insists upon seeing you."

"Ralph!" she exclaimed, hugging him and then stepping back from the odor that drifted up, even in the cold room. "How on earth did you get here?"

"In Papa's pig wagon," he said. "He was sending a load to slaughter in Morely. I hid in the back as far as the slaughterhouse and walked the rest of the way."

She hugged him again. "But . . . but why, Ralph?"

He began to cry, rubbing at the tears that coursed down his cheeks and streaking his face with mud. "Papa is sending me to Uncle Breezly's counting house in London! Oh, Ellen, I want to study! If I go there, it will only be a lifetime of columns and figures."

She held him close as he sobbed, flogging herself for not warning him sooner of his fate, so he could wear around to the idea before the shock of Papa's demand sent him running away from home in dead winter.

"Perhaps it will not be so bad, my dear," she soothed. "You know that Mama's brother has no sons. In no time, you could head the whole business."

He only cried harder. "Ellen, I do not want that! I want to study and learn, and maybe teach someday."

"Ralph, Papa has probably intended this for years. It is not a bad plan," she said, feeling traitorous to the brother she held so tight in her arms.

He stopped crying with an effort and wiped his coat sleeve across his eyes. "It is not my idea, Ellen," he said as he turned away. "If you will not help me, I don't know what I will do."

She sat back on her heels, looking at him. "You're so young," she murmured.

"I am old enough to be in school," he replied in that decisive tone that reminded her of Papa. "Vicar Snead and I only meet to argue nowadays. Please, Ellen!" he begged.

"What can I do?" she asked, knowing the answer even before he said it and dreading it.

"You can petition Lord Chesney."

"Ralph, I cannot!" she protested. "Especially not after I told him that I did not want his help."

Ralph only shrugged. "I need his help, Ellen. Isn't that good enough?"

She looked at her brother, tired and dirty. *You don't understand*, she wanted to shout. *How can I prove my independence of him—paltry as it is—if I am forever rushing to him for help the moment a crisis looms?*

"We could send a note round to Gordon," she offered. "Maybe he would have a good idea."

The look that Ralph fixed on her was one full of scorn. "Ellen, you know that Gordon seldom has any ideas, and never any good ones."

She could only agree. It was true. Gordon had come to her only the day before, asking for money. "Gordon, it is still six weeks before the next quarter," she had said and sent him away, his pockets still to let.

And even if they did go to Gordon, what would he do but pat Ralph on the shoulder and tell him to hurry home, and maybe Papa wouldn't even know he was missing.

After another moment's thought and misgivings

of the severest sort, Ellen seated herself at the escritoire. With a firm hand that belied the writhing of her insides, she scrawled a hasty note to Lord Chesney, All Souls College, and directed the footman to deliver it at once.

"I only hope that note finds him in," she said to Ralph as she opened the door.

Ralph blinked. "Where else would he be at this time of the morning? It's only quarter past six, Ellen."

"He will be furious!" Ellen exclaimed. "It will serve us right if he does not come at all."

She had expected some difficulty in getting Miss Medford's permission to take Ralph upstairs, but it was given easily enough. With her hand on his head, but standing well back from his somewhat soiled person, Ellen accepted the headmistress's consent, and the provision of an immediate bath.

"I only hope you left a note for Papa," Ellen said as she led Ralph up the stairs to her room.

"Well, I did not," he replied, his defiance lessened by the great weariness that seemed to settle on him with each step. "If he is so wise, let him figure it out."

"Oh, Ralph!"

He turned on her at the top of the stairs, his face white with exhaustion, and something else. She recognized the desperation in his voice, the sudden flash of his eyes. "Ellen, this is my future we are talking about," he said, his voice low, pleading. "Surely you, of all people, understand this."

She did. Ellen put her arm around him, thinking of the strange charity she had felt for her father the night of the wedding rehearsal as they walked down the aisle together, and her despair the next day when he informed her that she would go to St. Hilda's. *Why do those we love the most put us out so much?* she asked herself as she threw caution downwind and hugged her brother.

"Perhaps Lord Chesney will think of something, Ralph." A few minutes later, she closed the door to her dressing room. The maids, all smiles, had set up the tin tub, pouring in cans and cans of hot water, and left a liberal offering of soap there for Ralph, who was noisily splashing. She sat down at her desk and pulled back the curtains on a still Oxford morning.

Although she missed her intimate view of the High Street, she was growing fonder of the sight outside her windows here at St. Hilda's, overlooking as it did the river and the deer park of Magdalen College. The trees were yet bare, but she was patient with nature. In a few weeks' time, there would be the temptation of lime green cascading from the willows along the river. Even if it snowed again, those vanguards of spring would exhibit their early bravery and be followed by wisteria and then hawthorn hedges in bloom. Flowers would poke up from every window box at Oxford.

But now it was still winter and too early for many to be about except the farmers, bringing produce from nearby farms for the great markets of Oxford. And there, coming toward St. Hilda's, was a student running.

She looked closer and rose to her feet. It was James Gatewood, his student's robe thrown over his shoulders, his shirt open-throated without benefit of neckcloth.

I wonder why he is in such a hurry, she thought as she patted her hair and wished she had found time for more than a robe pulled on over her nightdress.

As she wondered, she heard the front door flung open, hurried voices, and then Gatewood on the stairs. In another moment, her door burst open and he threw himself into the room.

Before she could assure him that there wasn't any real emergency, he had pulled her off her feet and had gathered her close. His heart beat rapidly from his exertions, and he could do little else except hold her tight and try to catch his breath.

When he could speak, all he did was bury his face in her neck and murmur, "Ellen," over and over until she began to wonder what she had written in that hasty note that could have led him to this fevered response.

She thought that when he caught his breath he would set her on her feet again, but he carried her to the armchair and held her close on his lap, his arms tight around her. While her first instinct was to push away, she relaxed in his arms, struck by the same feeling of total absorption that had so preoccupied her when he kissed her at Miss Dignam's. It was a wonderful feeling of complete safety; she did not want it ever to end.

And then, when she felt almost limp with well-being, he took her by the shoulders and held her off from him a little.

"Ellen, are you all right? You appear sound. Was it bad news from home? I came as quickly as I could. Please tell me."

She touched his cheek, moved beyond words. He

must have been in the middle of shaving when the note came, for he had shaved half of his face and merely wiped the lather off the other side. Surely nothing in her note had indicated great trouble, but he had come immediately to her side. In wordless amazement at his love, she could only touch her forehead to his and then pull back a little to regard him seriously.

He smoothed down her hair. "When I receive notes at 6:30 that read, 'Please help me,' I am most attentive," he said at last.

"Now when have you ever received a note like that before?" she quizzed, to cover her own embarrassment.

"This is the first, and I pray the last, at least from you. You gave me a turn, Ellen. Now, what is the matter? You appear sound of wind and limb." He straightened the lace around her robe's collar, which he had rumpled. "I don't know when I have seen flannel show to such advantage before."

She got off his lap and seated herself at the chair to her desk.

"It is Ralph. He arrived on my doorstep this morning."

"Ralph!" he exclaimed and then laughed softly, almost to himself. "I am relieved it is no worse than that. And what, pray tell, precipitated what I assume is a clandestine flight from the home fires?"

"Papa told him that he is to go to Uncle Breezly's counting house in the City." She spread her hands out, palms up, in her lap. "Said he has come to me for help, I who am helpless to give it." She blushed. "He asked most urgently that I petition you."

Gatewood leaned back in the armchair, stretching his long legs out in front of him. "And you didn't want to, did you?"

"You know I did not, Lord Chesney," she said, her voice even.

"Jim."

"Jim then," she said impatiently. "You might recall my recent plea to be left alone to make my own blunders."

"I seem to recall something of the sort," he admitted, a slight smile on his face. "Where is this rascal?"

She pointed toward the dressing room. "He spent the night in Papa's pig wagon and was a bit ripe. I thought him overdue for a bath."

He went to the door of the dressing room and knocked before sticking his head in. He closed the door behind him. In a few minutes, he emerged with Ralph in tow. Ralph was clad in another of her robes, the look of wounded pride on his face daring her to make a single comment. He held a sheaf of papers, creased many times, which he handed to Lord Chesney.

"Sorry it smells like pigs," he said, seating himself on Ellen's bed. "I had no idea that pigs could be such nasty customers in close quarters."

Ellen laughed for the first time. "Ralph! And I suppose you will tell me that you brought no change of clothing."

He shook his head. "I . . . I'm afraid I just bolted."

Lord Chesney looked up from the papers in his hand. "So now you have tackled *Macbeth*," he said, holding a page out at arm's length and wrinkling his nose. "'A drum, a drum, the pigs doth come.'"

Ralph laughed out loud. "No, it doesn't say that! But yes, I have written about *Macbeth*. And I have other papers. Oh, sir, I don't want to go to a counting house! Please say that I will not have to."

Gatewood held up his hands as if to ward off an invasion. "Whoa, lad! How can what I say have any bearing?"

Ralph gave him a pitying look, such as a bright lad would give one whose wits had gone wandering. "My lord, let me tell you plainly. My papa will always dance to your tune, and it happens I need your help."

"Ralph!" Ellen exclaimed, her face fiery.

"You know it, El. I know it," Ralph replied calmly. "I cannot bear a counting house. I would rather study. My lord," he added with a gasp, as if finally amazed at his own temerity.

"Lad, your sister is rather at outs with me. I think my stock is not so high with her."

"It is my father, my lord, and he is the one who matters."

Ellen stared at her little brother and felt a chill ripple down her spine. "How calculating you are, Ralph," she said slowly, as her heart began to break. "And yet I am sure you are right. From father to son and on down through the generations. I wonder that women are not put upon hillsides to die at birth." She stood up. "You two must obviously decide this for yourselves."

"Ellen . . ." Gatewood began.

She cut him off, close to tears. "Ralph is right.

A little blunt, I vow, but his plain speaking is what I need." She stalked into the dressing room and pulled out the student's gown, breeches, and shirt she had cleaned and pressed and saved to look at. "Ralph, you had better change into these. Take him with you, Lord Chesney. He will be welcome where I am not. I am sure you have a lecture to attend, or to deliver."

"In Latin, for a fact," he said with a wry face, as if trying to cover up for a blunder of huge proportions. "Ellen . . ."

She continued, her face wooden. "I am sure that the two of you will think of something. Ralph will be a charge upon you, but then, I could have thought of no solution, could I?" She choked back her tears. "Go on, Ralph. I am sure that Lord Chesney will make all things right and tight with Papa. Good day to both of you."

She held the door open and they left, but not without a long backward glance from James Gatewood.

"Ellen, my dear, it can't rest here," he said, his face more serious than she had ever seen it.

"No, I think it cannot," she replied. She managed a smile. "Thank you for your help, sir. And you, Ralph, I owe you more than I can say, for your plain speaking."

She closed the door on them. There was no sound in the hallway for the longest moment, and then she heard slow footsteps on the stairs, descending.

Chapter 14

ELLEN SAT AT HER DESK, WATCHING them move slowly down the street, Gatewood's hand clapped on her brother's shoulder, their heads together. Miss Medford must have allowed Ralph to change in one of the other rooms, because he wore the student's clothing she had thrust at him so angrily. *Oh, Ralph!* she thought as the tears began to fall. *How could I be so hateful to you for only speaking the truth? What is the matter with me?*

She sobbed, hating herself. All her short life, she had known it was a man's world, and now, suddenly, it mattered. Ralph would get his school, Gordon his cavalry regiment. She would likely be bullocked into a marriage with the marquess. *I think I love him*, she thought through her tears, *but that doesn't matter. I will likely marry him anyway, because I am a woman and my opinion counts for nothing.*

The unfairness of it smote her like a blow from a fist. She rested her head on her desk and cried until she was dry of tears. She ignored the summons to class and then to luncheon and continued at her desk, wondering why she had been so foolish as to object to matriculation at St. Hilda's, or to scold Lord Chesney for pressing so hard. It didn't matter what she thought. He would get what he wanted.

She took out her math book and stared at the equations on the page before her. Soon it would be time for algebra. She could not waste this entire day.

After an hour of staring at the numbers that had no meaning for her, she looked up from the book and rested her chin on her hand. *The dratted fact is that I love him*, she thought. She sighed. *Perhaps I only think I do. I feel none of that deference that Horry feels for Edwin Blockhead, and none of the fear that Mama shows to Papa. If Jim Gatewood were in the wrong, I would never hesitate to tell him so. And I could never hang on his words like Horry. I suppose what I feel is not love after all.*

She paced the room in real dissatisfaction with herself. *All this wretched day wants is a visit from Gordon to make it complete*, she thought. *He will ask for money again, or some little favor to smooth his path here. Perhaps he too will demand that I petition the marquess for something or other.* "'El, you need only ask,'" she said in bitter imitation of her older brother. "'He will dance to your tune.'" It seemed only fitting that Gordon would constitute another of the plagues of Egypt that seemed to be dropping on her doorstep in unwelcome heaps. With that thought as consolation, she was not surprised when Miss Medford stopped her after class and said that she had a visitor in the sitting room.

Gordon rose with an easy smile at her entrance. He looked at her face and frowned. "The bloom off the roses today, Ellen?"

She sat down and faced him. "What is it you want, Gordon?" she asked, her voice controlled.

"Why, nothing," he replied, surprised in his reply. "I merely wanted to tell you that I had a visit this morning from Ralph and Lord Chesney, who thought that as head of the family here in Oxford, I ought to know." He laughed. "I can't imagine what good he thought that would do, but so he came. They've gone home."

Ellen clapped her hands together in exasperation. "I wish Ralph would not have dragged him into this! Don't you find it embarrassing that Lord Chesney has to help us out of muddles?"

Gordon shrugged, as though he had not considered the matter before. "I expect he will be my brother-in-law before too long. Might as well put the man to good use. After all, he loves you."

"How . . . how do you know?" she asked.

"He told me." Gordon smiled and took her hands in his, stopping their agitated motion. "I told him he's crazy to love someone so book-mad and more stubborn than Balaam's ass, but it didn't deter him. Besides, what are you going to do except marry?"

"I . . . I have plans," she said.

He got up and went to the window. "Still going to map the world and write guidebooks and travel the seven seas? Really, El! Maybe you should grow up. You can't do any of those things, because you are a woman."

She opened her mouth to protest and then closed it. Gordon, her foolish, spendthrift, care-for-nobody brother, had hit the mark.

He turned to face her. "I know I'm not as smart as you are, sister, but I think there ought to be a purpose for everything, even all this education. What's your purpose? You know you're not going to be a governess, and we don't have any missionary connections, thank goodness, so you can't go toddling off to India and cholera epidemics. What's the reason for all this? Or maybe you don't know."

She joined him at the window. "I thought perhaps I would start a day school for young girls of the lower classes. If some of them could learn such rudimentary skills as reading, writing, and ciphering, they could find better employment."

It sounded stupid to her ears. To her relief, Gordon did not laugh. "Wonderful, sister, but how will you finance such a venture, for it will never turn a penny on its own. Even I know that. And you know Papa will never lay down any blunt on a scheme like that."

There was so much truth in what Gordon said that Ellen could not look at him. She stared out the window, seeing nothing, thinking suddenly of Aunt Shreve's strange words: "You must find your own way through this particular dilemma, as all women must."

She shivered and rubbed her arms. This was the dilemma that Aunt Shreve meant, this realization that all her plans and ideas meant little in the reality of her female situation. She rested her forehead against the cold windowpane, scarcely feeling Gordon's hand on her arm.

She looked at her brother. "This is not the Middle Ages, is it, Gordon? I mean, I could say no to this marriage scheme that Papa and Lord Chesney have hatched between them, couldn't I?"

He nodded. "You could." And then he had to look away. "But you know that Mama and Papa both have ways of making you want to change your mind."

She leaned against his arm, filled with more charity than she would have thought possible for this author of her misery. "Papa would rant and rave and storm about the house. And Mama . . . Mama would sniff and turn pale and take to her bed, and call me an ungrateful daughter, and prophesy the almshouse for all of us."

He nodded again, his arm about her shoulders now. "Or call me an ungrateful son because I wanted nothing to do with Oxford."

Ellen hugged him. He started in surprise and then embraced her.

"Gordon, I am so wicked to think that you were such a fool for not wanting to be here!" She looked up at her brother, tears glistening on her eyelashes. "It never was your style, even though I thought it should be."

He could only nod his head again in complete agreement. "Poor El! I was the one sentenced to Oxford, when you wanted to go."

"But you, at least, have only to endure the rest of

this term," she reminded him. There was no bitterness in her voice anymore. "And then you will be where you want to be."

"Perhaps," was all he said, his own voice subdued.

She hugged him again and then stepped back to regard him.

"I have neglected you of late, Gordon. How have your studies gone at University College?"

He smiled faintly. "No more standing ovations on Saturday mornings, if that's what you mean. The warden has decided that Shakespeare was a fluke with me and he is willing to suffer my mediocrity on Milton. I have done all right, for all that it's my own work now." He cleared his throat and studied the pattern in the carpet for a long moment. "Ellen, I'm sorry for the trouble I caused you."

She only shrugged. "You'll note that I wasn't really dragged into those confounded papers kicking and screaming. It doesn't matter anymore, if it ever did. I'll never forget those weeks." She stopped, not able to bring herself to say anything to Gordon about that wonderful afternoon spent in Gatewood's chambers, discussing Shakespeare like equals, or the December punt on the half-frozen Isis. She would have those private memories to shore her up for years to come.

"Well, what do you think?"

Gordon was still talking, and she hadn't heard a word.

"What?" she asked. "Excuse my vapor on the brain."

"I was just inquiring politely as to the possibility

of your changing your mind about a small loan until the quarter."

"No! Gordon, you are yet a rascal!"

He grinned and grabbed for his cap as he backed out the door.

He paused. "I thought that since you were mellowing a bit, that I would try. I suppose I will have to come up with my own money-making scheme, won't I?"

"I suppose you will," she agreed, no anger in her voice, but only an emotion she could not quite put her finger on.

Still he stood in the doorway, turning his cap around and around in his hands. "Ellen, you're a right one. If you really can't stomach a proposal from Lord Chesney, I'll stand by you with our parents." He clapped the hat on his head. "But I, for one, would like a warm brother-in-law who has elastic purse strings."

He was gone then, slamming the door behind him. She stood at the window and blew him a kiss. *Gordon, you will always be a rascal*, she thought. She leaned against the window again. *And you, Ralph, are a bit of a Machiavelli where your own interests are paramount. Neither of you have measured up to any of my ideals of what brothers should be, I suppose, but then, no one has measured up lately, not even me.*

She returned to her room and her books. Ellen sat down at her desk and thoughtfully fingered the stack of Shakespeare essays she had written in the last few weeks. She walked with them to the fireplace.

"Ellen, you could toss these on the flames right now and be done with them," she told herself. "Or you could keep them for your own children, or your nieces and nephews to find, yellowing in a trunk someday, or lining mouse nests. Or you could give them to Lord Chesney," she said out loud. "That may have been all he wanted from you in the first place."

She stopped. That was unfair. Her face red again, and not from the nearness of the flames, she remembered the look in his eyes when he threw open the door and grabbed her. There was nothing of a calculating scholar in that instant. He was a man desperate with worry for his love.

She wavered in front of the flames, holding out the pages until her fingernails started to hurt. She could not bring herself to drop them.

"No," she said decisively. "These are mine, at least for the moment." She put the pages back on her desk and went to the dressing room for her warmest cloak.

A walk will do me good, she decided as she joined the other students who were setting out for their weekly expedition to Fletcher's Book Shop. On the way downstairs, she stuffed her essays into a box, scrawled "Lord Chesney, All Souls College," on top and thrust it at the porter, with instructions.

Ellen breathed deep in the brisk air and listened with half an ear to the talk of the others as they hurried along. Soon she did not listen at all, because the talk centered on end-of-term plans. Susan was cajoled into stripping off her glove to give them a glimpse of the ring her missionary-fiancé had sent from India. Millicent and Augusta compared notes on the great houses they had already contracted to teach in and speculated on the probability of finding eligible vicars in the district.

"What about you, Ellen?" one of them was saying as they walked along companionably, arm in arm. "We hear rumors . . ."

There was a pause, and smiles all around. Ellen could only shake her head. *Have we no conversation that does not revolve around men?* she wanted to ask. *Is everything we do dependent upon their goodwill?*

The questions remained unasked because she already knew the answers.

It was an easy matter to see the other girls inside Fletcher's and then duck over to the next block and knock on a low door. As she waited for it to open, she noted a new window box and earth freshly turned, as if lying in wait for a long-promised spring.

The door opened; Becky Speed stood there, dish-cloth in hand, her mouth open in surprise.

"Miss Grimsley!" she managed at last and took hold of Ellen's arm. "Do come in! How glad I am this is my half-day! Mama, you cannot guess who has come to visit us."

In a few minutes, Ellen was seated before a respectable fire, with a cup of strong tea in her hand.

"None of that hot water now, miss," Mrs. Speed was saying. "It's real tea, and I even have sugar, should you want it."

Ellen shook her head. Her eyes took in the new coat of whitewash in the room and two sagging, comfortable armchairs close to Mr. Speed's daybed.

Becky followed Ellen's gaze with her own eyes and

raised her chin. "We were able to redeem them from the moneylender's," she said. "Papa loves to have us close by. I think he even knows we are there," she added and took her mother's hand in her own. "And there is tea."

Ellen sipped her tea, her eyes on Mrs. Speed, who had lost that pinched look.

Becky brought her mother's hand to her cheek. "And doesn't my mum look fine as fivepence?" she asked, her eyes sparkling. "Since Papa now has that pension from the university, Mama has given herself permission to eat something besides bread and hot water."

"Is he better?" Ellen asked quietly.

Becky sat down beside her father. "Nay, Miss Grimsley, and he will likely not improve. But think on this: we have had a doctor in to tell us that himself, so now at least we don't have to wonder if there was something else we could have done."

Mrs. Speed touched Ellen's arm. "Cheer up, miss. There's some comfort in knowing that."

"I suppose there is," Ellen replied. *I refuse to embarrass these good women by tears*, she told herself. *They don't pity themselves, and I should not.*

She sat back in the chair and watched Becky hovering about the inert form of her father, wiping his face, arranging his hands more comfortably on the blanket. *Without a complaint, they have taken their lot in life and made it something whole and dignified. I think there is a lesson in this for me.*

She leaned forward suddenly, nearly spilling her tea. "Tell me, Becky. If you could, would you attend a school—let us say an evening school—where you could learn to read, write, and cipher?"

"I am sure I could not afford such a wonder," Becky replied.

"But if you could, Becky, would you?"

Becky straightened the blankets around her father slowly, carefully. "I . . . I suppose I would."

"And what would you do with your education?"

Becky sat down in the chair across from her. "It's all wild speculation, miss," she protested.

"Perhaps now it is, but tell me, what would you do?"

Becky closed her eyes, a dreamy smile on her face. "I would get a position in a little shop, someplace where the master wants a bit of clerking and tidying up and bookkeeping." She opened her eyes and shook out the dishcloth. "And I'd never darken Miss Dignam's door again!"

"What an admirable course," Ellen agreed.

But Becky wasn't through. "And with a position like that, I could probably find myself a fellow, maybe a tradesman or journeyman who could use a little of the money I saved to help himself into his own business." She blushed. "Stranger things have happened, miss, stranger things."

Ellen set her cup down with a decisive click. "How right you are, Becky." She rose and held out her hand to Mrs. Speed. "Thank you for your hospitality."

Mrs. Speed clung to her hand. "If I'm not too brash and all, will you be seeing Lord Chesney?" she asked, her eyes anxious.

Here it comes, thought Ellen, *here is the petition*

that everyone, me and my brother included, wants. "Yes, I probably will," she replied.

Mrs. Speed kissed her cheek. "Don't mean to be forward, but that's for Lord Chesney, miss. Tell him 'thank you from the Speeds.'"

"Anything more?" she asked, her heart lifting.

Mrs. Speed shook her head. "We can't think of anything we need. Lord Chesney has thought of it all. Just tell him 'thank you.'"

"And I shall," Ellen whispered as she quietly let herself out of the house and hurried around the corner to the bookshop. *Oh, I shall,* she thought as she joined the others. *And when he proposes, I will say yes this time, and Becky will have her school.*

And what will I have? she asked herself as she hurried to keep up with the others. *A husband who loves me.* She stopped, and the others bumped into her. *But do I love him?*

She shook her head and hurried on, ignoring the questioning looks of the others. *I wish I knew what love really was.*

Ellen did not expect to see James Gatewood the next day, not if he had truly been cadged into escorting Ralph home to plead his case for Winchester with her father. She steeled herself against the knowledge that the days would seem infinitely long until she heard from Gatewood again. *I shall take the Speeds as my example and learn to wait and hope with a little dignity,* she resolved.

But it was not enough. Her studies in Shakespeare and mathematics that only the day before had meant the earth to her, she merely endured now. She waited to see Gatewood's familiar figure striding down the street toward St. Hilda's, straightening his neckcloth as he came, pausing to look in a shop window to see if there was any use in running his fingers through his hair again.

My dear James Gatewood, you are a true Genuine Article, she thought. *We will spend our days together here at Oxford, and I will hope to keep you tidier than you are at present, and you will be free to devote yourself entirely to Shakespeare. And I shall run an evening school for girls like Becky.*

Her impatience grew as the week crawled by and Gatewood did not appear. When the flowers he sent every Wednesday arrived, she hurried downstairs, looking among the hot house roses for the note he always sent each Wednesday that read simply, "Marry me."

There was no note this time. Perhaps it fell off, she told herself, as she carried the flowers to her room and searched through the roses again. No note. And no word on Ralph's success.

And then on Friday, when classes were over and she was harrowing up a furrow in the carpet, pacing back and forth in front of the window, she saw James Gatewood strolling down the street toward St. Hilda's.

Only the greatest force of will prevented her from throwing open the window and shouting a greeting to him. Instead, she took a long look at herself in the mirror, wishing that her color were not so high.

Her heart beating at twice its normal speed and threatening to leap out of her throat, Ellen answered the maid's knock and walked slowly down the stairs.

He waited for her at the bottom, extending his arm to her.

"Come, my dear Miss Grimsley," he said. "At the cost of a wall of books, and probably a new wing on this fine, old hall, I have extracted permission from Miss Medford to take you walking in the Physic Garden." He smiled at her, that slow, lazy smile, and her heart slid down into her shoes. "Ostensibly, it is in pursuit of knowledge. We are to admire and exclaim over the gateway, which was designed by Mr. Inigo Jones himself."

She tucked her arm in his. "And so we shall, my lord, Jim."

"Much better." He was silent as they walked toward the garden. They had traveled a block when Ellen stopped. "You must tell me about Ralph. I cannot wait for the Physic Garden!"

"Postponement of gratification is a sign of maturity, Ellen," he said mildly. "It is high time we all grew up."

She ignored him. "What about Ralph?"

He stopped and faced her, his hands on her shoulders, unmindful of the tradesmen and students who passed and looked back, smiling.

"He is to go to Uncle Breezly's counting house."

She stared at him, her mouth open.

"A good thing it is still winter, else there would be a fly down your throat."

Her eyes filled with tears. "He had his heart so set on Winchester," she managed and then hurried to keep up with Jim as he lengthened his stride.

"So he did. It won't do Ralph any harm to be incarcerated in a counting house for this spring and summer." He gave her a little nudge with his shoulder. "Your father—Ellen, he does improve upon further acquaintance—your father and I both agree that he should have ample time to think about his future while totting up Uncle B's columns."

He paused before the entrance to the Physic Garden and pointed to the gate. "Magnificent example of Inigo Jones's art. Memorize it for Miss Medford, and follow me, my dear."

"But I don't understand," she said, out of breath, as she hurried after him.

"Oh, beg pardon," he said, slowing down and taking her by the hand this time. "Neither did Ralph. He cut up a bit ugly, in fact. Your father and I agree, especially after that display of temper, that a counting house right now is just the thing for Ralph. If he is still of the opinion that it must be Shakespeare and nothing else, he will be granted admission to Winchester this fall."

"Oh, my," was all Ellen could say.

"The two papers he wrote were excellent," the marquess continued. "With that, and the fact that I am a trustee of that fine old institution, I foresee no difficulties for your brother."

She squeezed his hand, and he smiled but said nothing more as they strolled about the garden, which contained nothing of interest in early March beyond a few bare stalks of one mysterious plant or another and the ragged remnants of apothecary herbs.

She waited for him to protest his love again and declare himself as he had done on a regular basis any number of times these past few weeks. When he did not, the flutter of anticipation in Ellen's stomach turned into a gnawing pain.

He led her finally to a bench and sat her down. He did not sit but paced the ground in front of her. "We discussed you too, my dear. Squire Grimsley enumerated your numerous virtues and undeniably beautiful parts." He chuckled and sat down beside her. "I had to remind him that you are stubborn and willful and tenacious when it comes to scholarship."

She turned her face away from the quizzical look in his eyes.

"Then you don't love me after all," she said slowly, wishing that the bench were closer to the gate and she could leap up and disappear in a crowd of shoppers on the street.

"I didn't say that, Ellen," he exclaimed, his hand on her arm. "And don't bolt, please. I'm not done by half."

She winced at his words but sat where she was.

"I merely state that I am well-acquainted with your faults, as well as your virtues." He leaned forward and rested his elbows on his knees, looking straight ahead. "And it happens that I share some of them." He glanced at her. "Don't look so stricken! What do you think love is?"

"I have been asking myself that for some time now," she replied finally, when the silence threatened to overwhelm her. She turned to face him. "Horry is Edwin's lapdog, and Mama is so afraid of Papa's bad humor that she does not give him sound advice when he needs it. They are my only examples, and it is not too satisfactory."

The tears spilled onto her cheeks, and the marquess made no comment about them as he handed her his handkerchief. "No, it is not too satisfactory, if this is your glimpse of married love."

She blushed. "I suppose we should not be having this discussion, Jim," she said quietly.

"On the contrary, I contend that more couples should have this conversation before they do something rash and irrevocable."

His words chilled her to the bone. She could not look at him.

He has changed his mind, she thought, and the idea filled her head almost to bursting. She forced herself to listen to him.

"Do you know what my example has been, Ellen? A father who married for convenience and thought nothing of keeping his light skirts on the family premises." He stood up then, and walked to the edge of the garden path. "By all the saints, how humiliating it was for my mother!"

"I . . . I had no idea," Ellen said.

He shrugged. "She is a silly, vain woman, with no ideas beyond the latest fashions and the arrangements of furniture. But I contend that no one, no matter how frivolous, deserves to be hurt like that. I vowed I would never do it, and I shall not."

He sat down again. "So here we are, with your silly notions, and mine." He took her hand. "How cold your fingers are! Where are your gloves?"

She shook her head, unable to speak. He kissed her fingers. "And we must add another ingredient to this witch's brew, Ellen. I can't tell you how I have been hounded and chased by delicate females of impeccable background who would love to partake of the Gatewood monetary benevolence. And all their family members."

Ellen closed her eyes. "Go ahead, Jim, add Ralph and Gordon to your list. Gordon has probably petitioned you, has he not?" she said, her voice scarcely a whisper.

Gatewood smiled. "Oh, my, yes. But since that first time a couple of weeks ago, we have enjoyed several illuminating conversations. Do you know, my dear, he wears well with repeated conversations."

"Gordon?" she asked, her eyes wide with amazement. "My brother Gordon?"

"Yes, Gordon," he said. "Possibly you have not given him his due. Ah, well. I even heard from Horatia this week, who expects me to make Edwin a peer of the realm or something. Oh, Ellen, come back!"

She had bolted from the bench, her whole goal in life to reach Inigo Jones's gateway. Propriety would keep them from continuing this conversation, once they were in the street. *And I thought to petition him for myself,* she said to herself as she hurried along the path. *Love has made me a fool.*

He had her by the arm then, pulling her around to face him.

"I'm not finished, Ellen," he said, his voice low, pleading, nothing in it of disgust. "Ellen! People are always going to be asking me for things! It is my lot in life." He gave her a little shake. "When this term is over, I am finished at All Souls."

"What?" she asked, hardly believing her ears.

"There won't be another year here, or two more years, or a lifetime of sweet scholarship. I am the head of a large, silly, demanding family. I am the Gatewood freak of nature because I do not enjoy their idle pastimes."

He watched her closely to make sure she would not run and then pulled her down onto a bench near the gate. "You're going to hear all of this, my dear Ellen."

She only nodded.

"Now, lean against me like a good girl," he said. "That's much better. My relatives all laugh at me and wring their hands over me and wonder when I will have the good sense to become like them. They are distraught because I do not gamble and race horses, and dip snuff to perfection, and moon about because my tailor doesn't put enough buckram wadding in my coats."

"It's hard to believe," she murmured.

"Believe it," he said, his arm tight around her shoulders. "If you were to marry me, you would be marrying into a sillier family than the one you belong to. They would wear you out with their demands and petitions. You might even extend that disgust to me. That is what I greatly fear."

She leaned away from him just to straighten her

skirt, and he quickly took his arm from around her shoulders. "I thought I had hoped too much," he said, his voice low. He got to his feet. "My dear, let me walk you back to St. Hilda's." He kissed her hand and held it for a lingering moment. "And now the term is almost up. My property manager has done yeoman's duty this year, overseeing the estates, but he has assured me in numerous correspondences that he is retiring in June. I have to go back to Hertfordshire and learn how to manage land, crops, tenants, sheep, and cattle."

"Country life is not so onerous," Ellen said. She tried to take his arm again, but he had moved away.

He looked back at her and stuffed his hands in his pockets. "You see, there wouldn't be any trips to explore and map the world, Ellen. There won't be much leisure to study, either." He chuckled without any mirth. "I am destined to become a gentleman farmer who falls asleep over his soup at dinner because he is so tired. And when I am in London, I will be expected to spend my time in frivolity, or endure the constant remarks of my stupid relatives."

"Sticks and stones, my lord . . ."

He nodded. "I know. I know. But, you know, El, the constant niggling and wrangling wears away at me, until it becomes easier to forget I ever had any dreams of my own."

Ellen joined him then and walked along in silence beside him.

How stupid I have been about men, she thought. She hesitated and then linked her arm through his. He looked at her in surprise.

"Forgive me," she said suddenly.

"For what?" Gatewood asked.

"For feeling sorry for myself because I am a woman. Forgive me for thinking you were so lucky and independent and could do whatever you wanted because you are a man."

He was silent for the length of the block. "Forgiven," he said finally, his voice unsure. "Forgiven time and time again, my dear."

The streets were almost empty of shoppers now as people hurried home to dinner. She slowed her steps, willing him to propose to her again.

He walked with her in silence up the shallow steps of St. Hilda's, worn smooth by centuries of scholars. He took her hand at the top, and she held her breath.

"Ellen, thank you for hearing me out." He kissed her hand and pressed it briefly against his chest. "And thank you for being such a welcome addition to my life this year at Oxford."

He cleared his throat, and she slowly let out her breath. *Oh, please*, she thought.

"Well, let us part as friends, my very dear Ellen Grimsley, who has such plans to take the world apart and reassemble it. I wish I could help you, but my time will never be my own."

He turned to go, stepping down until his face was hidden by the lengthening shadows of early evening. "April will be a busy month at All Souls. Let us do meet again in May before the term ends."

"But . . ."

"Good-bye."

Chapter 15

◈

*I*F THERE WAS EVER A WORSE APRIL on record in the British Isles, Ellen Grimsley didn't know of it. Usually it was her favorite month. She did not even mind drinking the horrible black brew that Mama inflicted on all her children in April to flush the miseries of winter out of their systems. She tolerated the rain because it was not a freezing rain anymore, and it would inevitably lead to a flowering of the English countryside, an event of such heartbreaking sweetness that Ellen knew she could never live anywhere else, even if she did travel the world.

But this April was different, preoccupied as she was by the greatest misery she had ever known. The rain was only rain, colder and more pelting this year, filling the gutters, drizzling down the windows, contributing to a general dampness in the air that did nothing to relieve the ache in her heart.

He still sent her flowers every Wednesday, but there was never a note anymore. She could only wonder if James Gatewood harbored some affection still or had merely neglected to tell the florist to discontinue the standing order in his rush to put her out of his mind and heart.

Her studies were sawdust and dry toast. She stared at her books for hours, deriving no information from the pages. Once, during geometry, she looked up from the meaningless page to see Miss Medford regarding her, a worried frown on her face. Ellen wanted to throw herself on her knees in front of the headmistress and sob out her misery, but she merely turned the page and attempted to apply the wisdom of Pythagoras.

Walks were little help. The favorite route from St. Hilda's took them by a small house with a sign in the window, "To let." Blowing trash from a long winter had accumulated on the front steps, in perfect harmony with a shutter that banged back and forth, and the windows bereft of curtains that stared back like hollow eyes.

She felt like that empty house, abandoned, neglected, dark. She would always turn away from it when they passed and then would be drawn to look back, and suffer all over again. And then she would return to her room, only to stare at the flowers and ask herself over and over, "Why didn't I say yes when he asked me?"

It became the last question she asked herself each night before she blew out her candle, and the first thing she thought of each morning. And from the way her head ached and her stomach hurt, it must have bothered her in her sleep too.

Letters from home were no balm to her wounds. Ralph mailed back the student's gown and breeches she had sent him off in. "It's not safe for me to keep them here, especially since I will soon be with Uncle Breezly," he had written. "And I think I know what they mean to you."

Horry wrote too, all misspellings and enthusiasm for the married state. She dropped a hint about a blessed event far in the future and hoped that Ellen would stroll the aisle soon enough with Lord Chesney so that she could participate without embarrassment.

Ellen sent no reply to either letter. What could she say? She dreaded her return home, and the disappointment that her unwelcome news would cause. Mama would give her no peace, compelling her to go over and over again all that she had said and done to disgust Lord Chesney. Papa would storm and rage and call her ungrateful.

When the pain was too great to bear, Ellen tried the other tack, convincing herself that she never loved him anyway, and they never would have suited. "I would surely have been a disappointment to Lord Chesney," she told herself each night as part of her consoling catechism. "Even if his family is silly, they are still peers. I would be so out of place. It is better this way. And besides, I'm still not so sure that I loved him."

Then why don't you feel any better? she asked herself one afternoon when the sky was bluer than blue and the willows along the river had finally burst into bloom.

She could see the Isis from her window. With a pang, she observed that students were already out punting.

I wonder if he even thinks of me, Ellen thought as she leaned her elbows on the open window and watched the little boats drift past. He is probably too busy.

When the maid knocked on the door, she jumped. "Someone to see you below, miss," the maid said and giggled behind her hand.

Ellen leaped to her feet, patting at her hair and cramming her feet into her slippers. She straightened her dress on the way down the stairs, regretting that it was her least attractive kerseymere.

Gordon waited below. "Oh," she said from the doorway. "It's you."

He smiled. "Who did you expect, the chancellor of the exchequer?"

She shook her head.

"Speaking of which, dear El, are you sure you won't make me a small loan?"

"Gordon! The quarter has only begun!" she exclaimed, irritated out of her lethargy. "How can you possibly be under the hatches?"

"It's an easy matter when your chambermate is practically a faro dealer," he grumbled. "I shall never turn a card with him again. Ellen, it is a matter of a gambling debt. Surely you will help."

He named the sum, and she paled. "I have not half that amount, Gordon. Whatever were you thinking?" she said.

"I was thinking that I would eventually get lucky," he said.

"Oh, Gordon."

He regarded her low state. "Really, El, can't you do any better than that? I expected at least a resounding scold, and all you can do is look hangdog and tell me 'Oh, Gordon.'"

When she said nothing, he took her by the arm. "Come on, El, let's escape from the halls of academe." He overrode the excuse already forming on her lips. "I saw Miss Medford when I came in, and she suggested that I do this very thing. Said you were blue-deviled about something."

The afternoon was warm, and she did not shiver, even though Gordon wouldn't give her a moment to grab up a pelisse, or even a bonnet. He held her hand, content to stroll along.

"What do you say we turn into the Physic Garden?" he asked. Tears came to her eyes and she pulled back on his hand. "I couldn't possibly go there," she said.

"Very well, then, Ellen," he said, his voice less certain. "My word, you remind me of Lord Chesney. I've never seen anyone so down in the dumps."

Her eyes flew to his face. "Have you seen him lately?"

"Only this morning."

"I had no idea you visited him."

He smiled at her confusion. "Oh, I've been doing that off and on for some weeks now." He laughed. "And now you're going to ask me whose idea that was! Well, it was his at first, but now I go because I like his company. Do you know, El, he's quite an engaging sort, when one looks beyond all that blasted scholarship."

311

"I know," she whispered and then humiliated herself by bursting into tears.

If she had done that six months ago, Gordon would have turned and fled, or laughed in her face. Instead, he pulled her into the shelter of an alley and held her close, patting her back until her tears stopped.

"Poor dear," he said. "I suppose you will tell me now that Lord Chesney has changed his mind."

She nodded and blew her nose vigorously on the handkerchief he gave her. "He teased and teased all term," she wailed, "proposing over and over, and then when I finally thought it would be a good idea, he didn't."

"Scurvy rascal," Gordon said mildly, kissing her cheek. "No wonder he hasn't been much fun lately. I go to his chamber for good conversation and better ale, and he stares into the fire and doesn't hear half of what I say."

"I think I love him," she said, sniffing back her tears, "but how will I ever know for sure now?"

"Well, you could propose to him," Gordon suggested.

"I could never!" she gasped.

They stared back toward St. Hilda's. "I'm fresh out of ideas, El," Gordon said finally. "You know ideas aren't my strong suit. Now, if you want me to call him out or something . . ."

Ellen put her hand on his arm. "No, don't do anything, Gordon," she said hastily. "And I'm sorry I cannot help you with that gambling debt. I'll give you what I have."

He shook his head. "No, not necessary. I think I have a better idea." He grinned and kissed her cheek again. "Maybe if I hang around with you or Lord Mope-in-the-Muck, I'll have good ideas on a regular basis!"

"Better you should apply to Papa," she suggested.

He shook his head vigorously. "That is the last thing I want to do, El. He might change his mind and make me stay here another year. I mean, the war in Spain could be over before I am sprung from this place!"

"What a pity," she said, her mind other places than Gordon's troubles. As she stood in the doorway and watched him saunter down the street, she thought she should have questioned him more closely about his brilliant idea. "I must be in my dotage to think that Gordon Grimsley would hatch a real scheme," she muttered as she climbed the stairs.

The Wednesday flowers were waiting for her on the table outside her door. She sniffed the roses, vowing that she would not look for a note, even as her eyes searched the bouquet.

She dropped the flowers on her desk. "Maybe I should propose to him," she said, looking at the roses. But even as she said it, she knew she would never do it.

"If I just had the nerve," she whispered. "Aunt Shreve was right. I am too proud."

She dismissed Gordon from her mind and only wished it were as easy to dismiss James Gatewood, who traveled lightly through her dreams and occupied her waking hours. She chided herself for her foolishness, knowing that it was well within her power to make his life easier. "If only I had accepted him when I had the opportunity," became the sentence that she wrote over and over in her mind, in atonement for a misdeed greater than any she ever committed at Miss Dignam's.

But as the days passed and no word came from All Souls, she knew it was time to gather what dignity remained and consider what she would say to her parents in less than a month.

The thought of facing them caused her heart to leap about in her throat. *If I were a man, I would take the king's shilling and beat Gordon to Spain*, she thought. *Or failing that, it is too bad I am not missionary-minded. I would rather preach to a thousand Hindus than to look Mama in the eye and tell her that I said "no" once too often to the marquess.*

She was considering the merits of Australia over Canada one evening long after lights-out, when someone pounded up the stairs and banged on her door. Ellen sat up in bed when Becky Speed, breathing hard, threw open the door.

Becky grabbed her by the shoulders. "Oh, Ellen, the worst thing has happened!" she said and then sank down in a chair to catch her breath.

Ellen was out of bed and on her knees in an instant beside the maid. "Is it your father? Oh, please say it is not so."

Her hands clutching her sides, Becky shook her head. "It's Gordon," she managed to say finally. "He's going to fight a duel!"

Ellen sat down on the floor. "You can't be serious," she said. "Even he is not that foolish."

"Oh, yes he is, Miss Grimsley, begging your pardon," Becky said.

Ellen clutched Becky's hands. "Tell me everything you know," she demanded. "I can only hope we are not too late."

Becky leaned forward, tears in her eyes. "It was something I overheard from one of the students at Miss Dignam's. She was telling the other girls that her brother was dueling with pistols tomorrow morning along the river with his chambermate, someone named Grimsley who owed him money."

Ellen felt her whole body go numb. She nodded. "Go on." Becky shook her head. "That's all I heard. The duel is to be somewhere along the river tomorrow morning. Probably it will be at sunrise, don't you think?"

Ellen nodded again as she let go of the maid's hand. "I wish I knew what to do," she said slowly. "There's not time to contact my father." She shuddered. "I wouldn't dare anyway."

Becky cleared her throat. "Perhaps if you got word to Lord Chesney he could . . ."

"No!" Ellen said. "I won't do that! I cannot plague that man with one more problem."

Becky only looked at her. "But you must, Miss Grimsley. He can find out what is going on and stop Gordon, you know he can."

Ellen looked at Becky in silence. Jim would find Gordon and settle the problem. "I don't have any choice, do I?" she asked, more to herself than to Becky, who was already heading for the dressing room.

"If you put on that student gown again and hurry, you might be able to get into All Souls before the porter closes the gate for the night," Becky said as she rummaged through Ellen's clothing. "Here, miss, and don't waste a minute!"

Ellen stripped off her nightgown and dressed herself in shirt and breeches, painfully aware that these were the clothes that Gordon had lifted originally from his chambermate, the same student who was out to avenge a debt of honor with a duel now. She threw the gown around her shoulders and tiptoed down the back stairs, Becky on her heels.

They walked swiftly away from St. Hilda's, mindful of the night watchman who strolled the quiet streets. "How did you get away from Miss Dignam's?" she whispered as they hurried along.

"I hope they still think I am in the kitchen washing dishes," she whispered back. Her voice faltered. "If they do not, then I am out of a job."

"Oh, Becky!"

Rapid walking, and a pause in a darkened alley as the night watchman passed, brought them to All Souls' door. Holding her breath, Ellen turned the handle. Locked. She looked back at Becky in dismay. They ran around to the side door. Locked.

Ellen looked up at the wall surrounding the quad. The ivy that climbed it was only beginning to flourish again, but maybe with a little help . . . She turned to Becky.

"Help me up on your shoulders," she commanded. Becky crouched, and Ellen climbed onto her back, clutching the ivy on the wall as she stood upright on the maid's shoulders. She grasped the ivy more firmly and pulled herself up and over, dropping down into a muddy patch of daffodils.

"Gordon, you had better appreciate what I am doing for you," she muttered as she scraped off the worst of the mud and crept around the perimeter of the quad, careful to stay out of the moonlight.

She tried the handle to the hall door, sighing in audible relief when it creaked and turned. She peeked in. The porter still sat at his tall desk, his eyes closed, his head drooping. She opened the door an inch at a time, holding her breath, and then crept on her hands and knees across the stone floor to the stairway, which was shrouded in welcome darkness.

The upstairs hall was dark. Ellen removed her shoes and padded quietly along the floor, pausing at each door to squint at the nameplate.

There it was, third door from the stairwell. Taking a deep breath, and wishing herself anywhere but at James Gatewood's door, she knocked.

No one answered. She knocked louder. To her ears, the sound seemed to reverberate like a bass drum across the fellows hall, over the quad, and down to the High Street itself. "Gordon, the things I must do for you," she muttered through clenched teeth as she knocked again.

She was about to consider the possibility of going outside and trying to climb in a window when she heard slow steps on the other side of the door.

"This better be really good, Lambeth," she heard as she pressed her ear to the door.

The door swung open. James Gatewood, clad in a nightshirt, stared at her.

"You're definitely not Lord Lambeth," he murmured finally and grabbed her by the arm, pulling her inside and then looking up and down the hall before he quietly closed the door. "Ellen, what on earth . . ."

He looked down and rolled his eyes. "One moment," he said and disappeared into the next room.

Ellen looked around the chamber, lit as it was by the remnants of a fire in the grate. Her heart sank as she took in the crates of books already packed and the half-empty shelves.

Gatewood returned wearing a robe and carrying a lamp, which he held in front of her face. "Just wanted to make sure I wasn't dreaming," he explained.

"I wish you were," she said, grateful that the shadowy room covered her own embarrassment. "I swore I would never plague you again, and I know you are busy . . ." she began. "Oh, Jim, it's the worst thing!"

He sighed and scratched his head. "Can't be, my dear. We've already been through the worst thing."

She looked up at his words, her eyes hopeful, but he was making himself comfortable in his armchair. He motioned to the other one.

"How bad can it be?" he asked, a slight smile on his face as she seated herself on the edge of the chair.

"Gordon is involved in a duel tomorrow morning, Jim," she said, keeping her voice low to mask her own agitation. "You've got to find out where and stop him, please."

"What?" he shouted, leaping to his feet. He pulled her up by the shoulders until her feet were off the ground. "He couldn't possibly do anything that hare-brained at Oxford, not even Gordon!"

She opened her mouth to insist that he set her down, when there was a banging on the wall. A faint voice, "Go to blazes, Gatewood," came through the wall.

He set her down and pounded the wall with his fist. "Eat rocks, Lambeth," Gatewood yelled back. "That should stop him. Now, what is this?"

"It's Gordon," she repeated. "Becky heard one of Miss Dignam's students say that her brother was going to fight a duel tomorrow—oh, my, this morning—with someone named Grimsley who owed him a gambling debt." She burst into tears. "And I would not let him have any money when he came to me."

Without a word, he picked her up more gently this time and sat her on his lap. "Neither would I," he muttered into her hair as he kissed the top of her head. "Now, dry your tears, my dear. I'll go find your dratted brother." He rubbed her arm. "With any luck at all, this will not get to the ears of the warden or, heaven help us, the Vice Chancellor."

She sat up in his lap. *I could propose now*, she thought as she put her hands against his chest. *Oh, but this is decidedly the wrong time. Drat Gordon, anyway.*

"Yes, by all means, please do what you can."

He put her off his lap and stood up. "You stay here

while I get dressed." He hurried to the other room and then looked back. "How did you get in here in the first place?"

"I climbed the wall, Jim," she said.

He burst into laughter, which precipitated another bang on the wall. "Ellen, you need someone to take care of you," he said as he ran across the room and banged back. "For someone who can't matriculate at good old Ox U, you certainly have performed a time-honored custom." He ruffled her hair as he hurried past to his bedroom. "Did you land in the daffodils or the shrubbery?"

She laughed and then put her hand over her mouth and waited for Lambeth to object. When he did not, she came closer to the bedchamber. "I should be going, Jim," she whispered.

In a moment, Gatewood stood before her in his buckskins and a half-buttoned shirt. "Indeed you should, but unless you are a prodigious climber, you will need some help getting back over the wall." He tucked in his shirt, ran his fingers through his hair, and grabbed up his student's cloak.

"Surely you could just open the gate from the inside?" she asked.

"And how are we to convince the porter to hand over his keys?" He grinned. "Ellen, you really don't look like a man. By the way, how did you get past the porter in the first place, or dare I ask?"

Ellen's chin went up. "I crawled on my hands and knees. Oh, the things I have done for Gordon this night!"

Gatewood reached for her hand and blew out the lamp. "Come, my dear, and let us save your witless brother."

The hall was still deserted. They crept down the stairs and peered into the main hall. The porter, very much awake, was reading his paper.

"This will be a bit tricky," Gatewood said, his arm tight around Ellen. "Let me go first. I will engage him in some idle chatter while you creep out the way you came in, right up against the desk where he cannot see you."

"I hope you have a brilliant explanation if he sees me," she said, getting down on all fours again.

Gatewood flashed his lazy smile. "Oh, I will let you think of something. You're a creative person."

As unconcerned as if it were midday, Gatewood sauntered up to the desk and leaned his elbow on the high counter. "Can't sleep, Wilson," he said. "I do believe I'll take a turn about the quad."

"Certainly, my lord. Would you wish me to unlock the gate?"

The picture of casual unconcern, Gatewood shrugged and shuffled his feet as Ellen crawled past him. "I think not. If a walk about the quad doesn't wear me out, then I'll reconsider. Good evening to you, Wilson." He chuckled. "Or should I say, 'Good morning?'"

"Aye, my lord."

He strolled through the doorway into the dark and grabbed up Ellen by the back of her cloak as she crouched in the shadows. "Now let us stay in the shadows and casually stroll toward the daffodils. Ellen, did you do all this damage?"

She looked in dismay at the flower bed. "Surely not!" she declared. "I expect that others have sneaked in after me."

He shook his head. "Nay, my love, most of us go over the back, where there are no flowers." He nudged her shoulder. "You can store that bit of All Souls wisdom for future reference."

"I doubt I'll ever come this way again," she replied, her voice crisp.

He laughed, cutting it short as he glanced back at the porter's light. He cupped his hands and knelt down in the flowerbed. "Up you get, Ellen."

In another moment, she had scrambled to the top of the wall.

Becky, her face upturned and anxious, watched from the other side. Ellen looked down at Lord Chesney. "Thank you, Jim. Do please find Gordon."

"It will be my total duty tonight," he replied, his tone affable, as though he had all the time in the world. "Now I will stroll back to the porter and ask him to let me out the main gate. Scram now, before someone sees you."

Still she balanced on top of the wall. "You will let me know the outcome?"

"I'll let you know." He chuckled. "I don't think that even the long-suffering and vastly tolerant Miss Medford would applaud this excursion of yours."

He blew a kiss to her and started back to the porter's hall. "Jim, wait!" she whispered.

He turned around.

I love you, she wanted to shout, but Becky was calling to her from the other side of the wall. "Just . . . thank you."

He bowed. Ellen let herself down until she was dangling by her hands and then dropped quietly to the pavement.

Becky grabbed her hand and they started at a fast trot for St. Hilda's. Quietly they crept into the servant's entrance again, where the door still hung slightly ajar. Becky released her hand.

"I have to hurry back to Miss Dignam's." She hesitated, then leaned closer. "Did he propose tonight, Miss Grimsley?"

Ellen stared at her in surprise. "Why, no, he did not, Becky," she said slowly. "And I don't think he's going to."

"I just wondered. What a pity," the maid said as she let herself out the door.

Wearily, Ellen climbed the stairs. She stuffed the student's cloak under her bed and pulled on her nightgown again. *No, he did not propose, nor would he ever. Drat you, James Gatewood,* she thought as she tied on her sleeping cap again. *You're going to be noble and spare me from a lifetime of inanity at the hands of your ignorant relatives.* She sighed and threw herself back on the pillow, pulling the blankets up to her chin. *And I am so practiced in dealing with inane relatives!*

She rooted about for a comfortable spot and tucked her hand under her cheek. *You'll choose some brainless wonder who will fit right into your family, like Horry did. What a dreadful waste of you and me.*

She was beyond tears. She thought about Jim, and then about Gordon, and still was wondering which of them was more irritating when her eyes closed.

She was awake just after dawn and standing at the open window, listening with her whole heart for the sound of gunfire. All she heard were the bells of Oxford, reminding scholars of another day. Likely Jim had found Gordon and talked him out of this infantile silliness. They were probably eating breakfast together right now in one of the old inns that flanked the Isis.

Ellen dressed slowly, wondering how long it would be before her thoughtless brother remembered to send a message that all was well. Probably Gatewood would relieve his financial difficulties and sent Gordon Grimsley on his way rejoicing. *What my brother really wants is one of Papa's canings*, she thought, her lips set in a mutinous pout that lasted all the way to the breakfast table.

Ellen had scarcely filled her plate and seated herself at the table when the footman approached her chair. "There is a young person outside to see you," he announced, his face impassive.

Her mind alive with sudden worry, she nodded her apologies to Miss Medford and forced herself to walk slowly into the hall.

Becky pounced on her as soon as the door was shut. The maid grabbed Ellen's hand, tugging her toward the outside door.

"Miss Grimsley, you must come quick. Gordon has shot Lord Chesney!"

Chapter 16

⌒

ITHOUT A WORD, ELLEN GATHERED up her skirts and ran out the door, close on Becky's heels. Her mind was a blank as they raced toward the river, where the morning mist was just beginning to clear.

She ran until her sides began to ache and then she saw them down by the river, Gordon seated on the grass with Jim Gatewood's head in his lap. There was blood everywhere.

"My word, Becky," she breathed as they approached the scene. "Do you know what happened?"

Becky stopped to catch her breath. "Only that Lord Chesney got in the way to prevent them from firing upon each other. There was a scuffle, and the other dueler fled." She averted her eyes from the bloody ground. "I don't see how it could have happened, but it did."

Ellen threw herself down beside Gordon, who looked up, his face ashen. "El, please believe I had no idea . . ." He looked down at the unconscious marquess sprawled across his lap. "Perhaps you should take my place. I will see about a surgeon."

Gordon moved aside, and Ellen cradled Lord Chesney's head in her lap. She rested her hand on his chest and was rewarded with a steady heartbeat. *That's something*, she thought as she gingerly touched the blood-soaked sleeve. Working carefully, her lips tight together, she widened the tear in the fabric and laid bare his arm.

The wound bled, but as she dabbed at it with the remnants of the sleeve, the bleeding stopped. She gathered Gatewood close in her arms and pressed the cloth to the wound. "Jim," she whispered, "I do not suppose you thought your Oxford year would end like this."

His eyes fluttered open and slowly focused on her face. He studied it and managed a lopsided grin. "I know I have not died," he said finally, "because I know better than anyone that you are not an angel, Ellen."

"No, I am not," she agreed, grateful that he had command of his faculties, even though he did seem to be rubbing his cheek against her in rather an unseemly fashion as she held him close. The feeling was not unpleasant; quite the contrary.

He winced as he reached up to touch her cheek and continue his perusal of her face. "You know, Ellen, as care-for-nobody as my relatives are, not one of them has ever used me for target practice."

"I am sure it was a mistake," she murmured,

overcome with shame. "Gordon would never . . ."

She looked up. Gordon and the proprietor of the nearby inn were hurrying toward them, arguing loud and long.

The marquess winced again. "Do tell them to quiet down," he pleaded. "And not to pound so hard on the grass. Godfrey, but I am uncomfortable."

He turned his cheek against her again. "Perhaps not too uncomfortable," he amended.

She put her finger to her lips and the landlord was silent. Gatewood motioned him closer with a nod of his head. "Bend down, my good man."

"Yes, my lord."

With a grunt and a creak of stays the landlord moved close. "I can have the constable here in a shake."

Gatewood shook his head. "That is precisely what I do not wish," he said, his voice scarcely more than a whisper. "And if word of this should get out, I will never lift another tankard in your inn. I will also tell everyone at All Souls, Balliol, and Oriel to avoid your place as they would the plague."

"Yes, your worshipful sir," the landlord gasped as he worked his way to his feet again. "But someone ought to make an example of young chubs what duel."

"I will deal with him," the marquess said. He closed his eyes. "Now if you would send for Mr. Charris, the surgeon at the corner of New and St. Giles, you will make me a happy man."

"Done already," the landlord assured him. He glared at Gordon. "You are sure you do not wish the constable?"

327

"Positive," Gatewood said. "Leave us alone for a moment, will you?"

The landlord took his ponderous way toward the inn while Gordon climbed the bank and sat there, head in his hands.

Ellen looked down at the marquess. "There is never going to be a right time for this," she said, tracing her finger along his cheek.

"For what?" Gatewood asked. He opened his eyes and then closed them again, as though the sunlight were too bright.

"I will simply have to jettison my pride and get it over with, won't I?"

"Ellen, you are making no sense at all," he protested, "or else I am in such a shape that I do not know good sense when I hear it."

"That is likely the case," she said and took a deep breath. "Will you marry me, please, sir, so I can protect you from my family?"

The marquess smiled but did not open his eyes. "Novel idea," he said, and his words slurred together. "Discuss it later. Not at my best . . ." He relaxed in her arms as his head lolled to one side.

She touched his pale lips with her finger. "Now was that a yes or a no, my lord?" she asked him. She glanced over at Gordon, who was watching her with a slight smile on his face. Her eyes grew thoughtful. *I wonder. Oh, surely not.*

Gordon convinced her to return to St. Hilda's. "The landlord and I will see him to a bed here, El," he assured her. "It will be bad enough if Papa gets wind of this, but if he finds out that you were involved, I am sure it will be quite twenty years before he allows me out of my room for excursions farther than the necessary."

"It would serve you right," she said, careful not to disturb the marquess as she kissed his forehead and gently lowered him to the ground. "Gordon, you are the greatest menace to world peace and the future of western civilization that I ever heard of."

He grinned. "El, I didn't know you cared!"

She sighed in exasperation. "Oh, for goodness' sake! Loan me your cloak. I daren't face Miss Medford with blood all over my dress. And wherever did you get such a cape?"

He swirled it about her shoulders. "Thought it would be just the thing for a duel."

"Gordon, you try me!" Ellen declared, her voice unsteady. She knelt beside the marquess again, who still slumbered among the dandelions, a peaceful expression on his face. "James, you certainly need me," she said and touched his cheek.

Becky did not feel inclined to chatter, so they walked in silence away from the river. The mist had cleared. "What a perfect spot for a duel," Ellen ventured at last, her eyes on Becky's face. "I don't know how Gordon could have planned it better."

"Beg pardon, miss?" Becky asked, her eyes innocent.

Ellen shook her head. "Perhaps I am entirely too suspicious." She looked back at the riverbank. A man carrying a black satchel hurried down the slope, accompanied by two boys with a litter. She waited until they had picked up the marquess and laid him on the litter before she continued down the street.

Gordon, looking contrite beyond relief, stood before her that evening as the students took the air in St. Hilda's quadrangle. "He is resting in testy discomfort at All Souls," he reported and then cleared his throat. "He begs me to invite you to 'one more intrigue.'"

She regarded her brother with vast suspicion. "Gordon, you are a rogue, and I will do no such thing."

He held up his hands. "Those were his very words; so help me! Heavens, but you are suspicious! I am to collect you from St. Hilda's before dawn in two days and meet him at Magdalen College."

"And I suppose he will line us up against the wall there and shoot us!"

"Nothing of the sort," Gordon protested. "See here, El, he's much more of a gentleman, even if he looks like a ragbag half the time. Which reminds me. You are to wear your breeches and student robe."

"This will be the last time," she warned.

He nodded. "Funny, but those were Lord Chesney's words too. And dashed if he didn't wag his finger at me, just as you are doing now." He grinned and hugged her about the waist. "You two will be the death of me."

"Don't you ever use that expression again, Gordon," she said. "It makes me shudder."

To say the next two days crawled by would have

been a gross understatement. Ellen finally turned the clock in her room to the wall because the hands refused to move, no matter how hard she watched them. The nights were much too long, the days even longer. She sleepwalked through her assignments like Lady Macbeth, wondering that she had ever thought scholarship so important.

All the flowers in the room suffered at her hands as she strewed petals about, wondering, "Love me, love me not."

He couldn't possibly love her, not after that fiasco at the riverbank. James Gatewood had suffered nothing but aggravation, irritation, and now blood loss at the hands of her family. He couldn't possibly love her.

And yet, even if his eyes were slightly out of focus at the riverbank, there had been such a light in them. Ellen tugged another handful of petals from a rose, groaned, and tossed the whole vase away.

She would like to have slept the night of April 30, but it wasn't even a consideration. She tossed about on her bed, alternating between tears and laughter, certain that she was in love. She blew her nose and wiped her eyes, thinking of Horatia and her lapdog love for Edwin.

Horry, you have it all wrong, she thought. *Love is aggravation and worry, complete contentment, and the worst sort of discomfort. I wonder that anyone falls in love.*

She thought of James Gatewood with his head in her lap, nuzzling her. *I wonder how anyone can help but fall in love.*

She was dressed and waiting for Gordon on the

steps before dawn. Miss Medford was going to cut up stiff when she knocked on her door for breakfast and found the room empty, but it didn't matter; she was going home soon. Ellen gazed out across the spires of Oxford, still silhouetted in black, timeless monuments to the best efforts of spirit and soul. She did not feel sad. Oxford might be a dream unattainable now, but perhaps one of her granddaughters or great-granddaughters would enter those halls and seat herself without fear or disguise in the lecture rooms.

"Stranger things have happened," she said as she watched Gordon come toward her.

The streets were full of students, all heading toward Magdalen College. Ellen looked at her brother, a question in her eyes.

"It is May Day," he reminded her. "I think even I am glad to be here for this moment." He took her hand. "And especially with you."

"Why, Gordon," she said. "One would think you almost cared."

"Don't let it swell your brainbox, sister," he replied, his voice light. He grew serious then. "I never did really thank you for standing by me during that dreadful Saturday reading. You could so easily have betrayed me. And I would have deserved it."

She smiled, remembering less of the misery and more of the pleasure at actually being there—if only for a brief time—listening to the exchange of ideas, some of them her own. "It was nothing, Gordon. Maybe we have both learned a few home truths this year that you cannot find in books."

Still serious, he linked his arm through hers.

Lord Chesney, looking unusually dashing with his arm in a sling, was waiting for them on the chapel steps. He looked up at Magdalen Tower and held out his good hand for Ellen.

"Let us carol in the May, my darling Hermia," he said and kissed her fingers. "You may come too, Gordon, if you are not afraid that I will do you injury. 'Tis a long way to the ground from the top."

Gordon took his sister's other hand. "I will stand on this side of her." He looked more closely at the marquess. "Are you sure that you are equal to this climb, my lord?" he asked.

"I think I can put one doddering foot in front of the other," the marquess replied. "Come, my love. You too, Gordon."

Almost afraid to speak, Ellen followed her marquess up the narrow staircase, the wood worn smooth by the progress of centuries. They paused for breath part way up.

She put her hand to his chest. "Are you able to continue, Jim?" she asked. "You lost a lot of blood, I think."

He shrugged. "Less than you would suppose. It looked worse than it was, so your brother assures me. One could almost suspect he shot me for maximum effect and little damage." Gordon coughed and looked away.

"And note how romantic I look with this sling. I have given out so many explanations of how I came by it that it would require your calculating mind to keep them all straight."

She laughed and let him lead her up the tower with the other pilgrims to spring.

Near the top, they paused again on the crowded landing. The marquess held her close, his good arm about her waist. He didn't look at her but instead stared upward where they could glimpse the white-ruffed Magdalen students and choirboys waiting.

"Tell me, Ellen," he asked, his voice casual. "Did you mean what you said the other morning, or was I delirious?"

"I meant what I said," she told him, her voice firm. "I love you, and I want to marry you above all things. And I only propose once, my lord."

"Then I accept, with all deliberate speed," he said.

Gordon let out a crack of laughter. "Thank goodness for that," he exclaimed. "I was beginning to fear that I would have to shoot you again."

"What!" roared the marquess, his voice rising several octaves.

Ellen only looked at her brother. "I wondered, Gordon," she murmured. "And Becky was in on this, wasn't she? I did wonder."

He grinned. "I cannot tell a lie, at least not right now. So was my chambermate, who is still suffering from the ill effects of seeing all that blood. I did assure him that I would not shoot anything that Ellen would miss."

"My blushes, Gordon! Give him my condolences," the marquess said drily as he tightened his hold on Ellen.

"That was the best scheme I could devise on short notice."

The marquess could only stare. "But, Gordon, you shot me!"

Gordon nodded. "I am an excellent marksman, my lord, so it wasn't as tricky as you might think. You were really quite safe."

The marquess groaned, and Gordon threw up his hands in exasperation.

"How else was I to get Ellen's attention? And yours too, I might add. I never saw such a gaggle of slow-tops as you two! One would think I had to do everything," he added virtuously.

"Yes. Well," was all the erudite and articulate Lord Chesney could manage as he sank down on the landing, his face a shade less sanguine. He pulled Ellen down with him. "My darling Ellen, do you realize that your brother is certifiable?"

Ellen considered the question for a moment and kissed the marquess. "He is rather a good shot, Jim."

The marquess could only pull Ellen closer to him. "Gordon . . ." he began.

But Gordon had gone farther up the tower. When he was safely out of reach, he looked back down. "You two would probably rather be alone," he said generously, shouting above the sweet soprano of the boys' choir that suddenly burst forth in full harmony as the sun cleared the tops of the hills.

Ellen snuggled closer to her marquess, unmindful of the strange looks she was getting from the students crowded around them on the landing. She kissed his cheek and whispered in his ear, "These students think we are queer stirrups, indeed."

"Oh, we don't care. Listen, Ellen. It is the most beautiful sound."

Her head pressed to his chest, she smiled at the wonderful rhythm of Lord Chesney's generous heart. There would never be any opportunity to explore the world beyond Hertfordshire, most likely. She and Lord Chesney would be too busy managing the silliness of his family or hers, or finding creative ways to help others. There would be that night school, and Becky would find a better future, even as she had done. It was enough; it was more than enough.

Arms around each other, they listened as the choir caroled in the May from the top of Magdalen. "'Like to the lark at break of day arising from sullen earth, sings hymns at heaven's gate,'" he said softly, his lips to her ear. "You'll not object if I occasionally quote the man who brought us together?"

"You know I won't."

When the last crystal notes faded into the morning light, Ellen sighed in complete contentment but did not stir from the marquess's side. Gordon started down from the tower and blew a kiss to them in passing.

"I am so glad you are sending him off to Spain," she said as the other students stepped around them on the way down the rickety stairs.

Gatewood pulled away from her a little, the better to see her face. "Who said anything about Spain, my love? You are apparently laboring under the same misconception as your brother." He chuckled wickedly.

"Jim, what have you done?"

"I told you once that I seldom get angry, but I

invariably get even," he replied, his voice serene. "I believe what I actually said was that he would go into an excellent regiment of my choosing."

"Yes, yes, the Ninth Hussars. You said so," she interrupted.

"They are not all in Spain. Part of the regiment is reluctantly posted in Canada, keeping peace among polar bears and French voyageurs, I don't doubt. *That* is where your rascal brother is going."

She burst into laughter. "You are a sly dog!"

"I have been trained by masters this year," he replied. "He will suffer a boring but relatively safe incarceration in Canada."

He turned serious as he took her hand again. "I have discovered that I have too much regard for your scapegrace brother to willingly send him to the slaughter in Europe. Better he should stay alive and have many, many years to improve his faulty character."

Tears came to her eyes. "And Ralph will have Winchester."

"If he wants it."

She kissed his hand. "You are a wonder."

He shook his head in mock seriousness. "I do not know what I can do about Edwin Bland, though. I am afraid he will always remain a blockhead, and there are entirely too many of them in the peerage already to warrant the inclusion of another, even if it was in my power. Edwin will have to blunder on by himself. Perhaps he can purchase a title like his father."

The stairs were clear, but they did not move. "Why did you change your mind?" Ellen asked. "I know too well that you had decided against marrying me. You were going to be noble and spare me from your ridiculous family."

He rested his chin on her head. "Oh, I was honor bound. You see, I have just received the most amazing proposal . . ."

"Be serious!"

"It's strange. I have a letter in my pocket from Lady Susan Hinchcliffe. You will meet her soon, I fear. Anyway, it was full of misspellings and vapidity, expressing her delight that I was soon to be sprung from the halls of academe. She is as beautiful as she is brainless, and probably even now considers herself just the fitting ornament for the Gatewood family tree."

He kissed her head and was silent a moment. "I just couldn't do it, fair Hermia. I want a wife who will argue with me and challenge my mind and chide me when I get lazy or discouraged. Oh, and someone to make me glad I am a husband at last."

She blushed. "I have base instincts, my lord. You really ought to know."

He kissed her again. "Thank goodness for that."

"You don't mind?" she asked, her eyes wide.

"Why would *any* red-blooded man?" He grinned. "My instincts are pretty base too. We'll just not tell the world."

"I would never!"

He laughed. "There is something else. I am relying on my father-in-law to help me find a new bailiff and perhaps an estate manager."

"That is one thing he is very good at, Jim," she said.

She touched his face. "It will not be so bad in the country. And if you feel that you will miss Lady Susan, I give you leave now to change your mind." She clung to his good arm and leaned against him shamelessly.

"I wouldn't dare!" he insisted. "Gordon would blow my head off!"

He kissed her, leaving her breathless and agitated, and without a doubt that he had already forgotten Lady Susan Hinchcliffe.

Gordon started up the stairwell again. "Really, you two! What would Mama say?"

"Mama would be beside herself with joy," Ellen murmured. She unwrapped herself from the marquess and helped him to his feet. He put his arm around her.

"Let me lean on you, if you don't mind. That kiss made me dizzy."

"You may lean all you choose, sir."

They started slowly down the stairs. "I thought you would enjoy listening to the choir from here," he said.

"What choir?" she asked innocently.

"Witcracker! I should kiss you soundly for that, but I fear we would tumble down the stairs."

They descended carefully. She stopped halfway down. "Of course, you know why I am marrying you."

"Hmm?"

"How else am I ever to get my Shakespeare papers back? Do you know, I have been wondering what became of them."

He pulled her down again on the stairs. "In the grip of my base instincts, I almost forgot. Ah, yes, the book."

"Book?" she asked, not daring to say more.

"In a wild flight of optimism, I gathered your essays and some of my own together, plus those ones of Gordon's—they must bear his name, I fear—and Ralph's. My publisher went wild with joy."

Ellen clapped her hands.

"Only yesterday, still clutched in the grip of fancy, I had them print 'Lord and Lady Chesney,' and 'Gordon and Ralph Grimsley' on the cover and spine. And you know how printers hate to change type, once it is set."

"Oh, Jim!" She kissed him, holding his face between her hands. They kissed until Gordon called up the stairwell again.

"Come on," the marquess grumbled. "Such a lot of stairs. I think that next May we will come here, but we will listen to the choir from the ground." He smiled at her. "Something tells me that you might not feel up to all these stairs by this time next year."

"James!"

"Yes, James! My dear, in all your wondering what good your education is, you overlooked a most important reality; one that is not exalted or lofty, perhaps, but which will likely bring us both joy in years to come. When you educate a woman, you educate a family."

He kissed her hand and tucked it against his chest. "I could wish you the acclaim you deserve in the world of scholarship, but the time isn't here yet. I do promise to stand up every year in the House of Lords and rail on and on about the need for equal education for women. They will declare me a nuisance, but dash it all, who cares?"

"Who, indeed?" she agreed.

"And I suspect you have some ideas of your own on how—outside of general marital conviviality—I can best be put to use. I rest assured that you will correct me if I am wrong."

"I will think of something, my dear."

In 1878, the first women's college was established as part of Oxford University. Not until 1920 were women granted degrees.

About the Author

Photo by Marie Bryner-Bowles, Bryner Photography

CARLA KELLY IS A VETERAN OF THE NEW York and international publishing world. The author of more than thirty novels and novellas for Donald I. Fine Co., Signet, and Harlequin, Carla is the recipient of two RITA Awards (think Oscars for romance writing) from Romance Writers of America and two Spur Awards (think Oscars for western fiction) from Western Writers of America. She is also a recipient of a Whitney Award for Borrowed Light.

Recently, she's been writing Regency romances (think Pride and Prejudice) set in the Royal Navy's Channel Fleet during the Napoleonic Wars between

England and France. She comes by her love of the ocean from her childhood as a Navy brat.

Carla's history background makes her no stranger to footnote work, either. During her National Park Service days at the Fort Union Trading Post National Historic Site, Carla edited Friedrich Kurz's fur trade journal. She recently completed a short history of Fort Buford, where Sitting Bull surrendered in 1881.

Following the "dumb luck" principle that has guided their lives, the Kellys recently moved to Wellington, Utah, from North Dakota and couldn't be happier in their new location. In her spare time, Carla volunteers at the Railroad and Mining Museum in Helper, Utah. She likes to visit her five children, who live here and there around the United States. Her favorite place in Utah is Manti, located after a drive on the scenic byway through Huntington Canyon.

And why is she so happy these days? Carla doesn't have to write in laundry rooms and furnace rooms now, because she has an actual office.